Daring
the Moon

Daring the Moon

SHERRILL QUINN

BRAVA

KENSINGTON PUBLISHING CORP.
http://www.kensingtonbooks.com

BRAVA BOOKS are published by

Kensington Publishing Corp.
850 Third Avenue
New York, NY 10022

All Kensington titles, imprints and distributed lines are available at special quantity discounts for bulk purchases for sales promotion, premiums, fund-raising, educational or institutional use.

Special book excerpts or customized printings can also be created to fit specific needs. For details, write or phone the office of the Kensington Special Sales Manager: Attn. Special Sales Department. Kensington Publishing Corp., 850 Third Avenue, New York, NY 10022. Phone: 1-800-221-2647.

Brava and the B logo Reg. U.S. Pat. & TM Off.

ISBN-13: 978-0-7582-3187-1
ISBN-10: 0-7582-3187-3

First Kensington Trade Paperback Printing: January 2009
10 9 8 7 6 5 4 3 2 1

Printed in the United States of America

Chapter 1

Staring down the end of a shotgun barrel was not the way Taite Gibson had planned to end her day. She bit the inside of her lip and, with two fingers, carefully moved the barrel so it no longer pointed directly at her.

"Listen, Mr. Wheeler, I'm not asking you to testify in court." She left the *yet* unspoken. "I'm just starting the investigation for the Pima County Attorney's Office, okay? I need to talk to you about what happened."

The man's face went dark with outrage. "What happened? I'll tell you what happened! A bunch of punk-ass hooligans came in here and robbed me at gunpoint, that's what happened." Wheeler made a threatening gesture with the shotgun. His ruddy face darkened even more. "I dare 'em to try it again."

Taite held up one hand and tried to inject as much authority into her voice as possible. This wasn't the first time she'd been on the wrong end of a gun, and it probably wouldn't be the last. "Mr. Wheeler, put that away."

He grinned. "Don't worry, Ms. Gibson. It's legal. I've got a permit." He held the gun in one hand and ran the other one down the wooden stock in a slow caress. "Ain't she a beaut? Remington Wingmaster five-shot with walnut stock, twin bead sight, and would you look at the finish on that barrel." He sighed like a man in love.

"I wasn't concerned about the legality," she replied steadily. "Just put it away. Please."

With a mumbled comment and a last, loving caress he complied, stowing the gun under the counter. He walked back around and leaned against the glass case and fussed with a display of cowboy hats.

"Thank you." Taite drew in a breath. She loved the smell of leather. Wheeler carried leather coats, chaps, boots. . . . You name it, if it was made of leather, he had it. She also caught a faint smell of something similar to sage as she walked forward again and pulled out a small notebook from her oversized purse. "Now, as I said, I'm here on behalf of the Pima County Attorney's Office. I'm investigating the robbery in preparation for the trial."

Over the next two hours, Taite got Wheeler's account of events, drilling down to the smallest of details. "And you're willing to testify against them in court? Point them out to the jury as the ones who robbed you?" she asked as she flipped the cover closed on the notebook.

"Yep. Those punks' faces are burned in my memory." He tapped a beefy finger against his temple. Big teeth flashed in a wide grin. "You get 'em in court, and I'll nail their asses to the wall."

She couldn't resist returning his smile. "It's a deal." After tucking the notebook back into her purse, she flipped her wrist to check her watch. Almost six P.M. She had time to stop back at the office to debrief her boss—he rarely quit work before seven. She told Wheeler good-bye and left the store. Making sure she had her keys firmly in hand, two keys poking out between her fingers, she walked toward her car with quick steps.

A spot between her shoulder blades heated. She glanced around, but there was no one behind her. Just the same, she tucked one hand into her purse and curled her fingers around her can of pepper spray. There was no doubt in her mind someone was watching her.

She was so tired of this . . . this *uncertainty*. The phone calls had started a couple of weeks ago, then gifts had begun to arrive at the office—a box of candy, one red rose, then a dozen. Why some nut had fixated on her was beyond her comprehension—she wasn't anything extraordinary. Medium height, medium build, medium brown hair.

Except she was damned good at her job and knew a lot of cops. Maybe the guy just had a death wish.

Another tingle between her shoulders. If it was her stalker, she didn't want to give him the satisfaction of seeing he was getting to her. Still, when she reached her car half a block down from Wheeler's store, she couldn't help herself from turning to glance behind her again.

There was no one there.

No one she could see, anyway.

Taite pressed the button on the remote and unlocked her car. Just as she reached for the handle, she heard a low growl. She whirled, thinking there was a large dog behind her about ready to chomp down. But there was nothing.

Keeping her gaze on the street, she opened the car door and tossed her purse onto the passenger seat. Another growl, off to her right, drew her gaze to a small alley. A pair of eyes glinted in the darkness, reflecting the light from the nearby streetlamp.

Holding her breath, she watched an enormous wolf pad slowly from between the two buildings. She stared at it from across the expanse of the roof of her car. The animal's hackles were raised, lips drawn back from its teeth in a ferocious snarl. Its ears, one white-tipped with a chunk missing from its outer edge, were flat against its head. Growling deep in its throat, it stalked forward.

To Taite everything seemed to move in slow motion. She fumbled, trying to get into the car. The wolf kept its gaze fixed on her, the intensity of which made the hair on her arms stand up. With a small cry, she jumped in the car and slammed the door closed, flipping the locks for good measure.

The wolf leaped against the car, claws scrabbling against the door and window. The animal snapped and snarled, the force of its lunges shaking the vehicle.

Taite screamed and thrust the key into the ignition. Once the car revved to life, she shoved the shift lever into drive and tromped on the accelerator. A few seconds later she glanced into the rearview mirror to see the wolf standing on the sidewalk beneath the streetlamp, watching her. She swallowed and put her gaze back on the road ahead.

A stalker and now a wolf attack. What was going on? By the time she reached her office, she had managed to push the incident to the back of her mind, though it had taken the entire twenty-minute drive to do so. Sitting in her boss's office, she gave him the rundown on her interview with Wheeler.

"Great job, Taite." Luis Valdez stood and pulled her to her feet, enclosing her in a big hug. "God, that's great stuff. We'll nail those degenerates for sure."

She grinned and patted him on the back. When he released her, she picked up her purse and slung the strap over her shoulder.

"You're coming to our party tomorrow night, right?" He went back around his desk and sat down, pulling his laptop toward him. Already his attention had drifted from her and an intense look of concentration covered his face.

She shook her head, used to him by now. "Yes," she said, grinning when he gave a grunt in response. She could have told him she couldn't make it because she'd be shopping on Mars, and he would have given the same reply. "See you tomorrow." Taite adjusted her purse strap on her shoulder and closed the office door behind her.

She was glad he was pleased with her report on the interview with Wheeler. Helping Luis do his job well was what *her* job was all about. She started to turn and bumped into someone, a startled "oomph" leaving her. Twisting around, she saw it was her friend John Sumner. His usually neat hair was in disarray, damp around the edge of his face, the white-blond streak at his part flopping onto his sweaty forehead IIis pale blue eyes were slightly red-rimmed.

He put out his hands to steady her. "Whoa there, sweet thing."

"Sorry." Her purse slipped, and she adjusted the strap again. "You all right?" she asked. "You seem a bit . . . harried."

"Just too much to do and not enough time to do it in," he responded in a gruff tone. Pulling a handkerchief from his front pocket, he pressed it against his forehead for a moment. He balled the linen in his fist and shoved his hand into his pocket. "Not sure why I left a government job. I could be the County Attorney by now."

She shook her head with a smirk. "You're not enough of a political animal, John, and you know it. Well, animal enough, I suppose. Just not political," she joked. She reached out and ruffled the hair that covered the top of his left ear. "You're beginning to look a little shaggy there, Counselor. Methinks you're overdue for a haircut."

John jerked his head away and laughed. He put his finger-tips under his chin and flipped them out toward her with an accompanying grin. "Being a defense attorney is better, any-way. You get to meet all sorts of interesting people. And no one cares if your hair is a little on the long side." He moved closer and leaned one shoulder against the wall. "Hey, you going to the party tomorrow night?"

"Luis's?" she asked, nodding toward her boss's office.

"Yeah."

Taite hesitated. She and John had dated for a few months and, while she liked him well enough, once she'd realized there was no romantic spark between them she'd called things off. That had been six months ago.

Thankfully, he'd been a good sport about it, even though she knew she'd hurt his feelings. But he hadn't seemed to let that stand in his way, not giving up on the idea that they

6 *Sherrill Quinn*

could be an "item." Afraid he was about to ask her to go to the party with him, she finally said, "Yes," with some caution.

His smile was quick and confident. "Why don't we go together? We can save on gas."

She pursed her lips. Even just riding in the same car with him would constitute a date as far as he was concerned. Damn. "I, uh, I'm already going with someone." As she told the lie she gave a quick smile, hoping he'd leave it at that.

He straightened away from the wall. A muscle beneath his right eye twitched and a tic started up in his jaw, but his voice, when he spoke, was congenial enough. "Oh, okay. That's . . . good. Who?"

She should've known he wouldn't let it go. He was like a dog with a bone. A bit panicked, she gave the first name that popped into her head. "Declan. You remember; I've talked about him before."

He nodded. "You'd have a better time with me." He flashed a grin and she relaxed, seeing he wasn't going to flare into anger like he sometimes did. He gave a shrug. "That's all right. I was going to ask Sheila, anyway." He sniffed, then leaned toward her and sniffed again. Wrinkling his nose, he backed away.

"Hey!" Taite frowned. "I'm sorry if my smell offends you. I've had a long day." Not to mention a near heart attack from that wolf.

"Sorry," he muttered. "It's just . . . I have a better than average sense of smell." He squeezed her shoulder. "Well, I have to go. See you at the party tomorrow."

She watched him walk away. Already dreading the party, she turned and headed toward the south exit and the parking deck.

The next evening, Declan O'Connell helped Taite out of his low-slung black Mustang and walked with her up the road toward Luis's house. Cars of other partygoers lined the street, so that Declan had ended up parking about a quarter of a mile from the house.

"And just what will your friend John say about me bein' your date?" Declan grinned at her grimace. When he continued, his rich Irish brogue rolled over her ears and tickled her senses. "It's about time I get to meet him, anyway. See what a wanker he is."

"Declan! Behave." Taite elbowed him in the ribs, shaking her head at his laughter. "I can promise John will *not* get your warped sense of humor."

"Sounds to me like he doesn't have a sense of humor at all, from what you've said." Declan shrugged. When she scowled at him, he grinned. "I'll try to be on my best behavior, darlin'." He crossed his heart with one finger. His smile faded. "But seriously. You know I'm happy to help."

"I know." Taite's heel came down on a rock and her ankle turned. As she pitched forward she grabbed Declan's arm to keep from going all the way down.

He stopped, turning to grab her elbows to support her. "You all right?"

She rotated her ankle, feeling a slight twinge but nothing too bad. "Yeah. Just being my usual graceful self. I don't know why I even bother wearing heels."

"Because they make your legs look sexy. Especially in that skirt."

"Down, boy." She tapped him on the shoulder. "This is a pretend date, remember? Besides, you don't like me that way."

"Doesn't mean I can't appreciate a lovely view." He took her hand and started walking again, keeping his strides short so she wouldn't have as much trouble in her heels. They reached the edge of Luis's driveway and stepped up onto the pavement. "You know, goin' back to what you said in the car," Declan said in response to the story about the wolf attack she'd shared with him earlier, "I'd see it bein' a rabid coyote, maybe. But Tucson doesn't have wolves."

"I know the difference between a scrawny coyote and a wolf, Declan." She glanced at him. "It was a wolf."

"And it attacked your car." His look was as skeptical as his tone. "Wolves just don't attack vehicles, darlin'. If they can't eat it, they don't want it." He shook his head. "I don't mean to upset you, Taite, but maybe your lack of sleep is playin' tricks with your mind. Or . . ."

"Or?" she prompted when he trailed off.

"Or your subconscious is directin' your fear of your stalker in another more primal direction."

"Well, listen to you, Doctor Freud," she muttered. "I would think I'd know the difference between a real wolf and a figment of my imagination."

"Maybe." He gave her hand a squeeze. "It's done now, anyway. Try to forget about it and enjoy yourself tonight."

She wished she could. But at the oddest moments she'd remember the way the wolf's ruff bristled; the way its lips pulled back from sharp, white teeth; the way its eyes seemed to see right through her. . . .

Declan was correct from the standpoint that she had other things to worry about. A stray encounter with a wolf was nothing compared to the almost daily harassment she received at the hands of the stalker. The phone calls that were getting more and more threatening, the continuous gifts that, as ordinary and even romantic as they were, served to make her skin crawl.

Declan let go of her hand and wrapped an arm around her shoulders, pulling her closer in a hug. "Let's enjoy the party, okay? Forget about wolves and stalkers for a few hours." He gave her another squeeze and then, with a hand at the small of her back, let her precede him into the house.

Luis greeted them right away, pulling Taite into his arms for a quick hug and a kiss on the cheek. He and Declan shook hands, Luis with one hand on Declan's shoulder. "Come in, come in. *Mi casa es su casa.*" He motioned to a server, who brought over a tray of champagne.

They each took a glass, and Luis toasted, "To friends."

"To friends." Taite smiled at Declan, grateful to have *him* for a friend, especially during this time in her life. He was a former special forces commando with the Royal Marines who had gotten involved in one of her cases five years ago. They'd immediately clicked. He was like the older brother she'd never had, though she usually told him he was the older brother she'd never *wanted*. Still, their relationship was more that of siblings, and she wouldn't trade it for anything.

He put up with her crap and watched out for her like family. Which sometimes got a little tiring, especially since he tended to drive off her dates. Not that he wanted her that way. Nor she him. She suppressed a shudder at the thought. Declan was a sexy, virile man, but it would feel like incest.

Luis patted her on the shoulder and went off to greet another arrival. Over the next several hours, she talked with friends and coworkers, Declan never leaving her side, seeming the ever-attentive date. And of course he charmed the socks off the men and the panties off the women. He was the kind of man many of the men there wanted to be, and the kind of man most of the women just plain wanted.

At midnight, she linked her arm through Declan's. Going up on tiptoe, she whispered in his ear, "I'm beat. Are you ready to go?" He wasn't much of a party hound, so she figured he was past ready.

He nodded. "Aye, lass, that I am."

"Let's go say good-bye to Luis, then." She wound her way through the crowd, Declan at her heels. When they approached Luis, she saw John standing off to the side on the other side of the room, his date on his arm, his gaze steady as he tracked Declan's progress behind her.

"Luis, we're going to go." Taite pressed a kiss against her boss's swarthy cheek. "Thanks so much—we had a great time."

"I'm glad you came, *chica*. And you, too, Declan." He shook hands with her fake date and looked back at Taite. "See you on Monday?"

"You bet." Seeing that John still watched them, she waved at him, then she and Declan walked toward the front door.

"You leaving without saying good-bye?" John's voice came from behind them.

Taite stopped. Taking a deep breath, she turned with a smile. "John. You looked tied up."

He lifted his chin. His gaze cut to Declan. John held out his hand in greeting and Declan took it.

Taite raised her eyebrows at seeing the men's hands turning red, their knuckles shining white, each refusing to release his grip first. She put her hands on her hips. "Shall I get out a ruler, boys?"

John gave a self-deprecating laugh and let go of Declan's hand. "Sorry. Just wanted to see what your date's made of."

"Flesh and blood, just like you." Declan flexed his fingers and tucked his hand into his pants pocket.

"Well, I wouldn't go so far as to say *that*." John's grin widened. He wore affability like a politician, but a spiteful smirk lurked beneath his placid expression. "After all, you are Irish."

Declan stiffened.

Taite tensed, too. She didn't think Declan would do anything, but he did have the ability to kill a man with his bare hands. If John was his usual snide self, he might just tempt Declan's control.

"Hey, just kidding, man. Lighten up—it's a party." John clapped him on the shoulder and shot a grin at Taite. "I hope you're treating my girl here all right. She deserves the best."

"Aye. She does." Declan put his arm around her waist and pulled her close for a one-armed hug. "An' I don't think she has any cause for complaint with me." His brogue was stronger now, either through irritation or, knowing Declan, on purpose to exaggerate his Irish heritage.

John's lips thinned and anger flared in his eyes for a moment. Then he gave a rueful laugh and shook his head. "Well, you obviously have something I don't. Good for you." He looked at Taite and shrugged. "Can't blame a guy for know-ing what he's missing and being a little pissed off because of it. Can you, sweet thing?"

She wasn't quite sure how to respond. She muttered a lame, "I suppose not," and glanced at Declan, who gave a small shrug. Taite decided to get while the getting was good. "Come on, Declan. Let's go."

He tilted his elbow up, inviting her to put her hand in the crook of his arm, which she did. She said good-bye to John and left the house with her "date."

Taite curled her fingers around Declan's arm, giving him a light squeeze. After walking in companionable silence for a few minutes, she said, "I'm so sorry. I thought he might be a little clingy, but that 'you're Irish' potshot was below the belt. I had no idea he'd be so obnoxious."

"Aye, he is at that. I can see why you stopped seein' him. He's a prick."

She couldn't disagree. "Now you know why I asked you to be my date tonight." She started to say more, but something from the corner of her eye caught her attention.

A blur of movement, a brief shifting of shadows.

Taite gasped and turned her head to look deeper into the blackness of the desert night.

"What is it?" Declan leaned forward, peering around her.

She held her breath, her gaze searching the dark. Another movement, a hulking dark shape moving within the deeper shadows . . . *God, it couldn't be.*

Not another wolf.

"Let's just get in the car." She hurried the last few feet and waited impatiently for him to unlock the Mustang. As soon as she heard the lock click up, she yanked open the door and climbed in.

Declan got in the driver's side and slowly pulled the door closed. "What's wrong with you? You're jumpier than a spooked cat."

"I thought I saw something."

He started the car. When he flipped on the headlights, the beam shone onto a large wolf standing in front of the vehicle.

"Oh, my God." Taite clutched his shoulder. "Look!"

The wolf lifted its lips in a snarl and laid its ears flat against its head. One ear was white-tipped. With a chunk missing from its outer edge.

Her skin went cold. "That's the same wolf."

"Oh, come on, darlin'. How could it be?"

"I'm telling you, it's the same one." As she stared at it, her mind told her it couldn't possibly be the same wolf—yet what were the odds of two wolves having that same ear?

The animal stretched, its rump in the air. Shadows playing tricks, it seemed to elongate and grow larger. It stood upright, as tall as a man yet with the head and body of a wolf.

Taite cried out. "We need to go. Now." As the last word left her mouth, the wolf-man charged the car, his furry form lit by the headlights. She screamed and smacked Declan in the shoulder. "Go. Gogogogogo!"

"Son of a bitch." Declan jammed the gearshift in reverse and punched the gas, pealing backward down the road. He increased their speed until they'd put some distance between the car and the wolf creature. Then Declan pressed down on the clutch, hit the brakes, and twisted the wheel, turning them neatly in a 180-degree turn.

She bit back another scream and grabbed the grip bar at the top of the door with one hand, the edge of the bucket seat with the other, and held on.

Letting up on the brake, Declan downshifted and pressed the accelerator. The powerful V-8 engine roared, and the car shot forward, easily outdistancing the creature.

He kept checking his rearview mirror, his eyes narrowed, his mouth held in a grim line. "Wanna tell me just what the fuck that was?"

"What do *you* think it was?" Taite slowly loosened her fingers from around the grip and wrestled with the seatbelt, finally getting it hooked in place. She crossed her arms over her chest and tried to rein in her scattered thoughts. That thing hadn't been natural. It was more than a wolf.

She didn't even want to say it out loud.

Declan glanced at her then ran his hand through his dark hair. "What I think it was, darlin', was somethin' it couldn't be." He slowed the car and made the turn to put them on Arizona Highway 77 heading north. Accelerating again, he took the car back up to cruising speed.

Taite drew in a deep breath through her nose and let it puff out from between pursed lips. "It was. You know it was. We didn't have *that* much to drink."

He didn't respond right away. She glanced at him, met his gaze, then looked out the passenger window.

"You're sayin' it was a werewolf." He apparently had no problems naming the thing aloud, though disbelief colored his tone.

She couldn't blame him. She had a hard time with it, too. "I'm saying it was a werewolf. God, I feel silly saying it out loud." She sighed. "But you saw it. It was a werewolf."

To her surprise, Declan didn't try to rationalize what they'd seen. He glanced at her again, his gaze considering. He looked back onto the winding road. She studied him, blinking tiredly at the fierce look of concentration he wore. Several minutes later, she rested her head against the headrest and closed her eyes, letting the quietness of the car lull her.

After several miles, he broke the comfortable silence between them. "I may know someone who can help."

"Help with what?" Taite twisted in her seat to face him more fully.

He frowned at her. "With your werewolf problem."

She blinked. "I have a werewolf problem?"

His sigh was loud in the confines of the car. "You said the wolf in town had a white-tipped ear with a piece missin'.

This wolf had a white-tipped ear with a piece missin'." He glanced at her. "Seems to me it's the same wolf, and he's trackin' you."

She hadn't wanted to think past the fact that she'd seen a wolf twice in as many days and that the second time it had turned into something more than a wolf. But something told her that Declan was probably right. "So now I have a stalker *and* a werewolf after me? Great. That's just great."

"Ryder might be able to help."

"Ryder?"

"Ryder Merrick. He's an old friend of mine from university. He's a writer—"

"A writer?" Taite snorted. "How the hell can a writer help me?"

He shot a dark look her way. "If you'll let me finish, darlin', I'll tell you." When she shrugged, he went on. "He's quite a successful horror novelist. I believe the amount of research he's done for his books can give us the information we need to fight this monster."

"We? Who's *we, Kemo Sabe?*" She arched a brow at him, the comfort she felt in his presence alleviating her fear somewhat. For the moment, anyway.

He grinned, a flash of white teeth in the darkened interior of the car. "Listen, Ryder is way out off the coast of Cornwall, lass."

"Cornwall? You want me to go to *Cornwall?*"

"Well, hell, Taite. It's not like I'm askin' you to go to the middle of the Amazon jungle where civilization hasn't yet encroached." He threw her a quick glance. "He has a small island—Phelan's Keep—that's part of the Isles of Scilly. It's an isolated place northwest of St. Mary's."

"Well, if in my new Twilight Zone world were I to go anywhere, it would be someplace silly," she muttered, deliberately mispronouncing the name.

Declan heaved a long-suffering sigh. "Besides, this will get you away from the stalker, too. Kill two birds with one stone."

When she didn't respond, he shook his head and added, "Ryder's a bit of a loner. Too much of one, I'm afraid." He adjusted the speed of the car as they approached the small town of Oracle.

"But . . . Cornwall?"

"It'll be fine, lass. As long as I'm with you."

"No. I don't want you involved after this. It's too dangerous." She frowned. "Besides, what the hell does that mean? You don't trust him?"

"I'd trust him with my life." His answer came without hesitation. "It's just . . . He probably won't let you in. *If* you're alone."

She sighed. She noticed he had ignored her comment about not being involved any longer. He was so damned stubborn; she knew she'd never get him to agree to let her go alone, and she was too tired to fight about it right now. Maybe once she'd gotten some sleep and something to eat, she'd feel more up to a battle with her mule-headed macho friend.

"But if you're with me?" she asked.

"Then we might not make a wasted trip."

Chapter 2

From outside Taite's bedroom window, the admirer watched while she packed a suitcase. She'd already put in a few pairs of jeans and brightly colored shirts. Then came silky underwear and other things—curling iron, makeup bag, feminine deodorant spray . . .

As he thought about where she would use that particular anti-odor product, his eyes went half-mast and his dick jerked to life. Wanting—*needing*—a better look, he moved closer to the window, careful to remain in the shadows.

He put one hand on his burgeoning erection and softly stroked his growing length through the material of his trousers. Already he could feel the material dampening as his flesh prepared itself.

From the moment he'd seen her, he'd wanted her. And she hadn't even been the person he'd initially been interested in. Well, not him per se, but the man for whom he was doing this . . . favor. In return for something infinitely more valuable than mere money, he'd promised to eliminate someone his benefactor deemed expendable.

But the admirer had seen Taite and had gotten sidetracked by her beauty, her vitality, her strength. So while his mission was still on track, albeit taking longer than expected, he had made some modifications to the original plan.

Drawing in a deep breath, he held in the scent of potpourri

she had in various little dishes and decorative bowls through-out the bedroom. Lavender was the predominant aroma. It fit her—he always felt at peace around her. Glancing down at his groin, he grinned and amended his thought. Emotionally, mentally, he felt at peace. Physically was something alto-gether different. She always stirred his body to action.

She had the window cracked about an inch or so, letting the cool air into the room through the screen. The curtain was pushed back only enough so it wouldn't block the breeze. She sat on the bed facing the window, legs splayed, and he imag-ined her sitting there without any clothes on. His gaze focused on her pussy. One day he'd plow that sweet-smelling field. But not now. Not for a while. He wasn't ready to reveal him-self yet. The anticipation, the hunt, was too much fun.

With her cell phone tucked between her ear and shoulder, she chatted away with someone. "Yes, I'll be ready. But I really don't want you . . ." She paused, a frown flitting between her fine brows. "Fine. But don't blame me if your friend won't see us." She waited, obviously listening to that bastard O'Connell on the other end of the phone. With a slight sigh, she shifted on the bed, one leg bent, and leaned her elbow on her knee. "I've already told Luis I need a leave of absence effective im-mediately, which he okayed without question. He's such a good guy."

He leaned closer, a frown on his face. Even though he knew she spoke of her boss, it irritated him to hear her speak of another man with so much affection in her voice. And if she didn't go, he'd have to rethink some plans. But he was versatile. Thought well on his feet.

His gaze traveled around the room. Frowning, he saw she had thrown the flowers he'd left on her stoop in the trash. He narrowed his eyes. Naughty Taite, throwing away his token of affection. She'd learn, in time, to appreciate the things he gave her, the things only he could do for her.

She raised one hand to her face. Realizing she brushed away a tear, he stiffened. He didn't like to see her unhappy. It was such a rare thing. Even after a less-than-ideal childhood and the stress of a sometimes dangerous job, she still managed to find joy in life, which made her sadness even more difficult to observe. He wanted to see her with a smile on her face again. That was his ultimate goal, after all—to make sure she was happy and cared for.

No one would be able to do it better than him. And if he had to cause her pain in the interim, well, so be it. He was a firm believer in the ends justifying the means. Plus it would make her appreciate him all the more once he revealed himself to her.

"Okay, okay, Declan. You win." Taite gave a watery laugh. "Just . . ." She took a deep breath and straightened, shoulders back, spine rigid.

There was the woman he loved. Stiff-backed, determined, and so lovely he was hard-pressed to keep his distance.

He grinned and glanced down at the erection straining against his zipper. Hard-pressed, indeed.

"Just pick me up in the morning and we can go to the airport together." She rang off and tossed the phone into her purse at the end of the bed. Then she resumed her packing. She still looked sad and a little spooked, but was relaxing by the minute. Probably was starting to feel safe, thinking about going away.

Did she think leaving town would take her away from him?

Not likely.

Or, at least, not for long.

Chapter 3

Alexander Merrick's Journal
21 November 1988

Catherine is my life, my reason for being, the only bright thing in this dark world. I love my wife. I love her dearly. Yet I do not see an alternative. If I am to end my wretched existence, how can I in all good conscience ask her to continue on, knowing she will go through this vile misery again with our son?

No, it is better by far to take her with me. Ryder is strong—he'll survive this. And if he's listened to my advice over the years, he'll discover a way to coexist with the demons that ride us. If not . . .

My main concern is for young Miles. He so wants to be part of the Merrick legacy, yet he doesn't carry the bloodline and so it is impossible. He continues to berate me for my lack of cooperation in making it so. Yet I cannot.

One day I hope he will come to realize what a dreadful existence I have saved him from and thank me for it. As for my son . . . One day I hope he, too, comes to comprehend my reasons for doing what I'm about to do. And I hope he will never find himself in the same dark despair as I.

Ryder Merrick tossed his father's journal on top of his grandfather's diary. Dammit. It had been twenty years since his parents' deaths, and he still didn't understand it. How had no one seen how desperate and delusional his father had become?

Ryder had been away at Queen's College when news of the murder-suicide had reached him. He'd cut short his education and come back to Phelan's Keep immediately—only to be greeted by the horrendous reality and his cousin Miles's near hysterics. The police had quickly ruled Miles out as a suspect. Forensic evidence substantiated the report that Alexander Merrick had first shot and killed his wife and then turned the gun on himself, lodging a bullet—one he'd made from melted silver—in his brain.

Everyone was in consensus that Miles had been lucky there wasn't a bullet fired his way. And while Ryder had never really believed his cousin had anything to do with his parents' deaths, there was that nagging little voice that whispered *maybe.* . . .

And for two decades Ryder had never understood it. Sure, there were things the males of his family had to deal with that affected very few other people in the world, relatively speaking. But it could be dealt with in ways other than death.

Isolation was Ryder's solution.

He pushed his chair away from the desk and stood, turning to gaze out the open veranda doors. Huffing a sigh, he leaned one shoulder against the doorframe and looked out over the ocean.

Sea birds flew across the surface, their raucous cries floating upward. They reminded him it would only be a few more months before the puffins returned to their nesting grounds on the south of Phelan's Keep, which was much rockier than this side of the island. He'd always enjoyed the little black-and-white birds' return each season—somehow they made his life a bit more bearable, a little lighter.

The morning sun capped the waves with orange and gold topped with reflective silver. A light breeze brought the smell of salty air to him. He inhaled, wishing the air could somehow make him feel renewed. But, as always, he just felt . . . old.

He glanced over the immaculate lawn that led to the short stone wall at the edge of the bluff. His only live-in employee, Will Cobb, refused to have someone from one of the main islands come over to keep the grounds, insisting that he was more than capable of performing landscaping work. And he was. The house and grounds looked as good as they did when his parents were alive and had half-a-dozen employees caring for things.

Ryder scanned the horizon. As far as he could see there was only blue sky and white clouds, though he knew they were due for rain soon. And this time of year storms could be gale-strength.

Tilting his head to one side, he tried to work out the kinks in his neck. He was on deadline—if he didn't get these last few changes in to his editor on time, she'd have his balls for breakfast. And while the big house operated off an industrial-sized generator, he'd prefer to get as much done as possible before they were hit by the next storm.

He grimaced and turned back to his desk. Flexing his fingers, he settled them on the keyboard and got to work. It wasn't until he heard a knock on the study door that he became aware of the passage of time. He glanced at his watch, surprised to see it was nearly one o'clock in the afternoon. "Come," he called out.

His hardworking Guy Friday pushed open the door and walked in carrying a silver tray. His thinning hair brushed just so and dressed in his normal attire—crisp dark suit, starched white shirt, black tie, and shiny shoes—Cobb took his job quite seriously. He set the tray on the desk and proceeded to pour strong black coffee into one of the two large mugs that sat on one side of the tray.

The aroma wafted to Ryder and his nostrils flared with his deep inhalation. He enjoyed the smell of coffee as much as the flavor. He pushed his laptop to one side and peered at the tray. Next to the mugs were two plates, each holding a meat sandwich. Reaching out, Ryder lifted up one corner of the homemade sourdough bread of the nearest one to inspect the contents.

"It's rare roast beef with lettuce, tomato, sweet onion, and brown mustard," Cobb offered. He lifted a small plate that held homemade chips and placed it in front of Ryder, then did the same with the plate holding the sandwich. "I thought I might be pushing my luck to serve salad for your midday meal two days in a row. You tend to get . . . overly irritable if you don't eat red meat on a regular basis." Moving around to the side of the desk, he picked up a linen napkin and laid the deep burgundy material across Ryder's thigh.

Ryder glanced at Cobb and saw the slight smile that kicked up one corner of his employee's mouth. Ryder grinned in response, shaking his head. "I didn't realize it was as late as it was." He grabbed the sandwich and took a large bite. The mustard hit the back of his tongue and burned a pleasant trail into his sinuses. Swallowing, he took another bite. As he chewed, he studied Cobb.

The other man's dark hair had thinned on top, leaving him almost bald. His nose seemed larger than it used to be—a part of the aging process, Ryder supposed. While Ryder carried his age well and still looked as if he were on the underside of forty when in reality he was two years past it, Cobb looked every minute of his sixty years.

"How are the rewrites coming?" Cobb poured himself a cup of coffee. He sat down in one of the leather wingback chairs facing the desk.

"Slowly. More so than normal." Ryder leaned back, rocking slightly. "I'm bored with the story. Hell, I'm bored with myself."

"You should go on holiday." Cobb brought his cup to his lips and took a careful sip. "Somewhere with white sandy beaches and nubile young women in bikinis."

"We have that here. Well, on the other islands." Ryder sent him a frown. "But you know I can't leave Phelan's Keep."

"No, sir, I don't know that." Cobb leaned forward and set his cup on the tray. He braced himself with elbows on knees and laced his fingers together. "You are not your father. His madness is not yours." He shook his head. "Your father was only a few years older than you are now when the . . . incident occurred."

"Don't remind me," Ryder muttered. He put his half-eaten sandwich down on the plate and snagged a chip.

"I've seen no indications that you're becoming unbalanced." Cobb met his gaze. "You're a good man, sir. An honorable man. One with the notion that what you're doing is the only course of action. I disagree. However," he went on, leaning back in his chair, "it's clearly not my place to tell you what to do."

"I value your opinion." Ryder scrubbed his hand along the back of his neck. "It's just not that simple. It isn't simple now and it wasn't simple then."

"It certainly didn't help matters having Miles underfoot all the time." Cobb picked up his own sandwich. "Always nattering at your father about one thing or another."

"Yes, well, Miles had his own set of challenges, that's certain."

Cobb rolled his eyes, making Ryder grin. "You and your father were both too lenient with the boy," the older man said. "I understand the trauma he suffered, losing his parents at such a young age, but there comes a time—or at least there should—when we grow up and take responsibility for our lives." Cobb picked up his cup and leaned back in his chair again. "When the two of you were teenagers with barely three years separating you in age, there was still a world of difference in your level of maturity."

Ryder snorted. "I'll say one thing for my cousin—he was more than happy to take credit for anything that made him look good. But when things went wrong, it was always someone else's fault. Usually mine." He shook his head. "I wonder on whom he blames things now?"

"I wonder what's become of him. It's been twenty years since he left the island."

"Twenty years since I kicked him out, you mean." Ryder popped the last bite of sandwich into his mouth.

"It was necessary," Cobb said in loyal support. "Always following you around, demanding to be just like you." He scowled and dabbed at his lips with his own piece of burgundy linen. "He's from your mother's side of the family, not the Merrick side, so of course he couldn't emulate you. He should have counted himself lucky your father left him the inheritance he did."

Ryder swiveled in his chair and stared out at glittering ocean waves he could see beyond the edge of the bluff. "Miles was only four when he came to live with us. Mother and Father treated him like their own son from day one, which I didn't have a problem with. It was nice not being the only child." His throat tightened with sorrow over things lost, regret over things that would never be. He closed his eyes briefly and then turned back toward his employee. "And Mother was glad to have a piece of her sister still with us. So it was only natural for Father to remember him in his will."

"But it wasn't enough, was it?" Cobb stood and began clearing the lunch items. "Miles wanted it all."

Cobb wasn't wrong. Miles had alternated between begging and demanding to be given his due, given what he felt should be *his* birthright, too. Ryder had never understood that. Being a Merrick was what had made his father take the drastic steps he had. Why would anyone willingly take that on?

Finally exasperated to the point of almost losing control, Ryder had told the nineteen-year-old to get out. Now, thinking back on it, he still didn't see any other course of action. The inheritance Miles had received had been close to seventy-five thousand pounds. Twenty years ago, that was a good amount of money. Ryder knew that letting his cousin stay could have proven to be too dangerous. To both of them. "I lost track of him after he moved to the States. He stayed in New York for a while, I know, but I don't think he's still there."

"Good riddance to bad rubbish, I say. Nothing but trouble was that young man." Cobb picked up the tray and turned toward the door. "Is there anything else you need, sir?" At Ryder's negative gesture, he murmured, "I shall be in the kitchen if you need me." He closed the door softly behind him.

Ryder heaved a sigh and moved his laptop back to the middle of the desk. He cracked his knuckles. "Just type something," he muttered. "You can always go back and fix it." Fingers back on the keyboard, he began to type.

Drivel. It was all pure drivel.

Damn. What was wrong with him today? He felt on edge, disturbed on an elemental level. He wasn't an inordinately superstitious man, but this restlessness suggested something was going on. Perhaps the change in atmosphere in front of the upcoming storm was responsible.

Perhaps it was something else.

Whatever it was, it was obvious he was done with work for the moment. He wouldn't waste any more time putting such dismally written words on the screen. He saved the document and then turned off the laptop. Pushing back from the desk, he stood and stretched. The bones along his spine popped, and the pressure from sitting hunched over the keyboard lessened immediately.

Ryder left the study and went in search of Cobb. He found the older man in the immaculate kitchen, wiping down the counters. Ryder grabbed his rain slicker from a peg by the back door. "I'm heading out for a walk," he told Cobb. "Hopefully it'll clear my head."

"Be careful." Cobb gave his usual response.

When Ryder opened the door and the wind blew leaves into the room, Cobb turned without a word and headed into the hallway. Ryder knew he was going after a broom. "Sorry," he called out.

"Not to worry, sir," said Cobb cheerily as he walked back into the kitchen, push broom in hand. "Devil's playground and all that."

Ryder grinned. He walked outside and made his way through the small side garden, now mostly dormant except for a few late blooms. He followed the meandering cobbled path until he reached the woods. There the cobblestones ended, and the path was a hard-packed trail forged over time.

As he made his way across the island, heading down toward the water on a natural incline, insects chirped and various small creatures rustled in the undergrowth. Part of him longed to break into a run to try to chase away the demons that continually plagued him, but he knew it wouldn't work. It never did. He'd content himself with listening to the rush of the sea against the rocks as a way to calmness.

Within ten minutes he'd reached the caves. He slowed, then stopped. His heart rate increased and sweat popped up on his skin. The old fear resurfaced. He clenched his jaw and took a step forward. Then another. And another.

He froze. He couldn't do it.

It didn't matter that he was no longer that eight-year-old boy who'd been trapped for two days in the cold, damp darkness. It didn't matter that, three and a half decades later, he knew his phobia was irrational.

He could not make himself go into that cave.

Unlike when he'd been a boy and compelled by curiosity and the hope of finding long-forgotten pirate treasure, he was a man now and able to control his tendency to snoop. He

didn't need to put himself in danger to satisfy his natural in-
quisitiveness.

His writing was his outlet.

Ryder swallowed, staring into the darkness of the mouth
of the cave. His pulse hammered in his throat. "This is completely asinine," he muttered. It was just a fucking cave. After
taking a deep breath and holding it a moment, he exhaled
and strode forward to meet his fear.

About four meters inside the cave he faltered. Irrational
fear chilled his skin, but he kept going. After two more meters, with the darkness closing in on him, he stopped. Sweat
made his shirt stick to his chest and back, and dripped down
the side of his face.

Memories slammed into him, of rocks and dirt crashing
down on him, of Miles crying out that it wasn't his fault.
Ryder remembered the total, absolute pitch blackness. Legs
pinned by rocks, knowing he was bleeding, terrified he would
die. Wondering if Miles had gone for help or had simply run
off.

The recollections still much too intense, within seconds
Ryder was outside once more, bent over, bracing his palms
on his knees as he fought to control his erratic breathing. He
muttered a curse at his own cowardice. Straightening, he stared
toward the pile of hewn rock and vowed, "One day I'll conquer you, you bastard."

That whole ordeal as a youngster was what had started his
misgivings about cousin Miles. But he'd dismissed it as his
imagination. Even now he had a hard time believing that a
five-year-old boy could be so wicked as to try to murder his
playmate, his own cousin.

Unless he was twisted enough to have wanted Ryder's parents all to himself . . .

No. Ryder refused to believe it. Miles had had adjustments
to make, to be sure, but he'd been such an effervescent boy—
there was no way he could have hidden such a dark soul.

Ryder went on, stopping for a few moments in his favorite cove. Hands in his pockets, he sat on a fallen tree and listened to the waves crash against the rocks. He inhaled, slow and deep, dragging the refreshing salty air into his lungs. It was at times like these, when he was alone—just him and nature—that he could almost block out the troubles that were associated with his family.

Almost.

His gaze went upward, where the sun stood sentinel. A few more hours and it would be dark. In another few days there'd be a full moon suspended in the night sky. He didn't want to think about that and made his mind go blank.

After several minutes, an idea on how to reveal the killer's true identity in his latest book hit him. Wanting to get it on paper while it was still fresh in his mind, he jumped up and started back to the house, breaking into a jog about halfway there. When he made it to the kitchen door, he knocked dirt off his shoes on the rough-woven rug, then went inside.

As he went down the hallway and through the foyer, he saw Cobb sitting in the old-fashioned parlor, one of Ryder's earlier books in his hands. Ryder made a detour and went into the small room. Already his breathing had evened out. One positive aspect to his enhanced metabolism.

Cobb looked up. "This one still gives me the shivers." He put his finger between the pages to mark his place. And started to stand.

"Stay put," Ryder said. "I only wanted to let you know I'm going to try to get some more work done." He glanced at his wristwatch. "It's only two thirty—if that walk and the sea air did their job, I should be able to get quite a bit done yet before nightfall."

"Well, there's nothing wrong with working after dark. You do some of your best work at night."

"Ha." Ryder turned and walked to the study. From across the foyer he instructed, "Unless the house is on fire, I don't want to be disturbed."

"Are Mr. O'Connell and his friend still coming?"

"As far as I know they'll be here day after tomorrow or the next day, although I told him not to come." Ryder frowned. "Now is not the best time."

"Yes, I know." Cobb raised his eyebrows. "I could always refuse them entrance, sir. Especially since you expressly told him not to come."

Ryder shook his head. "I haven't seen Declan in a few years, Cobb. As much as I don't want visitors now, I can't turn him away without seeing him. I'll tell him I'm on a tight deadline and convince him they have to leave after one night. We'll just need to keep them out of the basement."

"Yes, sir."

Ryder sighed. "Let's make sure we've a nice dinner for them, Cobb. Put Declan in my old room upstairs. His friend can stay in the adjoining room. Once they arrive, when I get a chance to talk to Declan alone, I'll let him know he's got to turn around and leave straight away the next morning."

"Yes, sir." Cobb's face clearly expressed his misgivings.

"You have a problem with that?" Ryder asked, raising an eyebrow.

Cobb shook his head. "Not with the idea, sir. I am, however, not convinced Mr. O'Connell will merely turn around and go all the way back to America after having just arrived. Feeling unwelcome won't guarantee he'll leave. You know how stubborn he can be. He's much like you in that respect."

Ryder grimaced. "Just . . . have the rooms ready, all right?"

Cobb nodded and put his nose back in his book.

Ryder closed the door to his study and settled in at his desk. The cooling air from the veranda blew across his nape. He twisted and closed the doors that led outside until only an inch-wide opening remained, then drew the curtains. He was so close to completing this—he wanted no distractions. Once the laptop booted up, he went to the area in the manuscript where he'd left off and began typing.

He wasn't sure how much time had passed when he became aware of a scent unfamiliar to him. It smelled like . . . He inhaled. It smelled like honeysuckle and vanilla, but with an underlying hint of musk. All in all, it was an aroma both sweet and spicy at the same time and utterly feminine.

He shook his head and tried to immerse himself in his work once more. A heightened sense of smell was another trait he'd gotten from his father, and it could be damned inconvenient at times.

It was apparent he'd gone without sex for too long. If he was starting to smell something feminine without the woman to go along with it, it was time to get back over to the mainland and renew some of his female acquaintances.

But not now, not with Declan and his friend arriving in the next few days. Ryder heaved a sigh and pushed his chair away from his desk. Standing, he put one hand in his pocket and with the other pushed the curtain aside.

Cobb was right. Declan would demand to know why they couldn't stay. Especially if the situation was as serious as Declan had made it sound.

Dammit. Declan had been fairly cryptic over the phone, merely telling him he was bringing a friend named Taite who was having werewolf trouble. He thought Ryder could shed some light based on years of research for his books.

Of course, coming here to this isolated island wasn't much safer. But they had no way of knowing that, and, if Ryder was successful in keeping his own lycanthropy hidden, they would never find out just how much danger they were in.

He turned back to his laptop and within moments was immersed once more in the story he created. It wasn't until shadows had crept further into the room that he realized his buttocks were numb from sitting in one position for so long.

Glancing at the clock on his desk, he saw another two hours had passed. He stood and stretched, rotating his head to work the kinks out of his stiff neck. He started to turn back toward his desk, then stopped, caught by that same musky-sweet scent, stronger now.

Nostrils flaring, he pushed open the French doors and took a step outside. Vanilla and honeysuckle assailed him and a low growl left his throat before he could stop it. It was a woman, somehow familiar, and she was on his island.

Voices carried to him on the wind. "What do you mean, he doesn't know?" The husky feminine voice with a distinct note of exasperation curled around his senses like wispy smoke, tantalizing him, enticing him.

"Well, when we caught sight of the wolf again in Atlanta, I reckoned we should just get on out here. It's only a few days early, lass." Declan's deep voice was calm, the way Ryder remembered him.

"Okay, but that would mean he's expecting us. Why did you just tell me he isn't?"

He heard the huff of Declan's sigh, then the other man mumbled something that Ryder was too far away to clearly catch, even with his exceptional hearing.

"What?" The woman's voice rose in pitch.

"I said he told me not to come."

"And yet, here we are." Although her tone was rich with sarcasm, she still managed to sound as smooth as honey. Her voice slid over Ryder like silk on skin, tightening his entire body with need. When she added, "What's the plan now, Sherlock?" Ryder almost felt sorry for Declan.

Almost.

His two visitors rounded a curve in the path that became cobblestoned at the edge of the lawn and followed a straight line to the front door. Before they could spot him, Ryder drew back into the study, staring at Declan's companion as she stopped and rounded on his friend.

"I cannot believe you brought me all the way out here. You . . . You . . ." Dropping her two small suitcases, she threw up her hands. "Oh, I don't even have the words!"

Ryder's jaw clenched against the brutal arousal that slammed into him at his first good look at her. The open flaps of the lightweight jacket she wore revealed full breasts above a narrow rib cage and small waist. Hips curved out, inviting a man's hands. Long legs encased in worn blue jeans led down to slender, booted feet, one of which tapped against the ground.

His gaze swept back up and lingered on her face. Even from here he could see the tilt at the end of her pert nose and full lips made for kissing. He had a sudden vision of those sensuous lips wrapped around his cock, her hot, wet mouth sliding up and down his shaft, taking him deep. A growl crept from his chest and he trapped it in his throat.

"That'd make a nice change, darlin'," Declan responded, his grin widening when she made a low, rumbling noise deep in her throat. Setting down one of the suitcases he carried, he laughed and threw an arm around her shoulders, drawing her to his side with a quick squeeze, making Ryder stiffen.

He was outraged Declan had disregarded his wishes, that was it. It wasn't that he was jealous over a woman he didn't even know, no matter how much her scent seemed to meld with his until he had a hard time separating one from the other.

A woman he'd thought was a man, which he knew was what Declan had intended. His *former* good friend had known Ryder—who lived like a monk, and Declan couldn't understand why—would never have agreed to have a woman on the island.

Not that he'd agreed that Declan could be here, either.

With a stealthy movement, Ryder pulled the French doors closed and leaned against the wall, out of sight, and continued to listen to their conversation.

"Well, just tell me what we're going to do when he leaves us standing on his doorstep, Einstein." Footsteps crunched up the walk. "In the dark." Her voice wavered a bit, and she cleared her throat.

"He's not goin' to just leave us out in the cold, lass." Declan's deep voice was still cool and calm, amused.

"Well, it's hardly *that* cold," she said. "Although I'd thought this time of year it would be."

"It's the Gulf Stream," Declan said. "It keeps the climate here fairly temperate. Except during these short late fall and winter months, when some fairly nasty gales can come in off the Atlantic. Which is why Ry won't leave us stranded."

Ryder shook his head, knowing before it even began that he'd lost this battle. Declan was right. He wouldn't deny them, not now that they were here.

"Oh, my God. Look at this place." The woman's voice softened with awe. "It looks like something out of *Wuthering Heights.*"

Declan laughed. "Aye. Ry's great-grandfather Phelan built the place, hence the name Phelan's Keep. Look over there." Gravel crunched as they backed up a few steps. "That's an honest-to-God tower. Used for storage now, but at one time there was a bedroom at the top."

"Wow." A shadow passed by the window, and Ryder saw her walk by, her head thrown back as she looked up at the house. "Just how many rooms are there?"

"Seven bedrooms, five and a half baths. Old Phelan was ahead of his time and gave nearly all the bedrooms their own separate bathroom. All of the stone used to build the house was quarried from the island." Declan snorted. "Jaysus, Taite. I'm not a flippin' realtor. It'll be dark in another hour or so. Let's get inside."

She walked back toward the front door, then the door knocker creaked as it was lifted. The clunk of brass on brass reverberated through the foyer and filtered into the study. Ryder listened for Cobb's footsteps, frowning when they didn't sound.

"You were saying?" The woman's voice held a note of wry humor.

The knocker clanked again, and after another minute, Declan muttered, "Son of a . . . You wait here, Taite. I'll walk 'round to the other side of the house and see if they're in the kitchen. Be right back."

Declan walked past the study, pausing to jiggle the handle and peer through the doors. Ryder, needing a bit of time to come to grips with the emotions stirring within him, stayed in the corner, careful not to draw his friend's keen gaze in his direction. When Declan was apparently satisfied the study was empty, he went on around the side of the house.

Something thumped against the front door. Ryder grinned at the picture in his mind of Taite slamming her balled-up fist against the unforgiving wood. Another thump and a pithy comment. Then more thumping.

Cobb's footsteps sounded in the foyer, and the front door squeaked open. "Yes?" his employee asked in a bored, unwelcoming tone.

"Hi." Taite's voice was bright and friendly, in direct contrast to the dark comments muttered at his door mere moments before. "My name's Taite Gibson. I'm here with Declan—"

"Mr. Merrick is not at home to visitors, miss, which I believe he made very clear to Mr. O'Connell when he called." The door squeaked again, and Ryder knew Cobb was about to close it in the woman's face.

He sighed at Cobb's stubborn insistence on maintaining their privacy, even after Ryder had told him not to. When he heard a thud, he cracked open the door of the study to see Taite standing with one hand planted palm-down on the front door.

"Wait a minute. Please," she said, her smile still in place. "We've traveled all day."

"I'm sorry, miss. But if you leave now you'll reach St. Mary's before dark. It's not convenient for Mr. Merrick to have visitors at this time." Cobb's voice was cool and polite, but Ryder heard the underlying thread of steel. The little man didn't look like it, but he was quite the watchdog.

Even now, he chose to disobey Ryder's instructions in an effort to protect him. Cobb went on, "As I have said, Mr. Merrick is not available."

"But we've come all the way from the United States to talk to—"

Without a word or even a change of expression, the short, balding man closed the door. Ryder fully opened the study door and leaned one shoulder against the sturdy frame.

When Cobb turned, he caught sight of Ryder standing in the doorway of the study. At Ryder's raised eyebrow, Cobb said, "This isn't a good time, you said so yourself."

"I also said they'd have to at least stay the night. The sun will be fully set in another hour—I don't want them trying to get back to St. Mary's in the dark."

He wasn't sure why but, even knowing he couldn't have her, he needed to meet this woman. Nodding toward the front door, he said, "We'll just have to be sure the basement door stays locked at all times to avoid awkward questions. Let her in."

The older man sighed and turned back to the door. Pursing his lips, he swung open the door and stepped back as Taite's raised fist nearly caught him on the nose. "Come in, miss," he said in a long-suffering tone. He waited until she'd picked up her suitcases and walked into the house, then he went out and collected the other two suitcases Declan had left on the small portico.

Coming back inside, Cobb set the suitcases down and closed the door, shutting out the cool November wind.

Ryder could see the flecks of gold in her dark eyes, could smell her beguiling scent so much more clearly. Her lips were slightly parted, showing small, white teeth, and he clenched his fists against the desire that slammed into him with the force of a gale.

God, she was lovely. Why couldn't the person with Declan have been a man? He wouldn't have been tempted by a man. Oh, his *condition* would still flare but, without sexual arousal, it would have been . . . manageable. Throw his hard dick into the mix, and he wasn't so sure he could maintain control.

But as great and as immediate his need of her was, she was off-limits. He didn't trust himself with her, not with the time of his Change so close. More determined than ever to get her and Declan off the island in the morning, he moved forward.

Chapter 4

Taite's breath hitched in her throat as a tall, dark-haired man walked with sensual grace toward her. Cobalt blue eyes stared into hers from under the dark slash of heavy eyebrows. His hair, worn a little long, curled against the top of his shoulders, drawing her eyes to the strong column of his throat. A thin scar ran along his left jaw, from ear to chin, white against the dark stubble of his day-old beard.

Her lips parted. Her breath came faster. Some power she didn't understand—was it just physical attraction amplified?—tugged at her. She opened her mouth to say something, anything, but her voice seemed frozen.

Passion flared in his gaze for a moment before he hid it by dropping his lashes and looking at her from under hooded eyes. He was, without a doubt, one of the best-looking men she'd ever seen. And the sexiest.

Her nipples tightened, and she hugged her arms over her chest even though she knew neither man could see them through her jacket. The closer he got, the more her insides clenched until, when he stood directly in front of her, her core loosened and moistened, dampening her panties with the beginnings of arousal.

"Hello, Ms. Gibson." A large, square-fingered hand came out, and she automatically put hers in it. The slide of his palm against hers sent a shiver through her. He held her hand for a fraction longer than was necessary, his thumb brushing over her skin in a motion both soothing and arousing at the same time. "I'm Ryder Merrick. We weren't expecting you for another few days."

It was nice of him to phrase it like that. Especially since he'd told Declan not to come at all.

He slowly released her hand. She quickly folded her arms again. His mouth twitched. For a moment she thought he might smile, but he remained stony faced. "I'm afraid you've caught us a bit by surprise, and so our hospitality has been less than satisfactory. I hope you'll give us another chance to make a good first impression." His tone didn't suggest he meant it, yet she'd be surprised if he was a man who ever said something he didn't mean.

She didn't think he'd be bothered to put on a social face if it didn't benefit him in some way. And welcoming a stranger into his house—a woman uninvited and unannounced—would hardly bring him personal gain.

For such a handsome man, he looked harsh. Unyielding. But his deep voice enthralled her, holding her in a spell, dark and sexy and making her wonder what he'd sound like when he was lost in passion.

She had an image of sweat-slicked bodies on tangled sheets. Raw, earthy lust drove his cock into the clinging depths of her pussy. Taite clenched her thighs against the increasing arousal flowing from deep inside her body.

Her gaze flicked down, traveling over the knit turtleneck he wore. A leather belt with a large silver buckle bisected his middle and drew her eyes to the center of his body. His thick erection, clearly outlined beneath the material of his jeans, lay along one muscled thigh. She pulled her startled gaze back to his.

She had the nonsensical thought of asking, "Is that a gun in your pocket or are you happy to see me?" but wasn't sure he'd appreciate her calling attention to his arousal.

His eyes were narrowed, nostrils flared as if he were . . . Was he sniffing her?

Her overtaxed mind must be on the edge of toppling into oblivion, she decided. Why in the world would he sniff her? Unbidden, her gaze darted once more to his midsection.

Realizing he was waiting for a response from her, her cheeks heated even more. She looked into his face and stuttered, "I-I'm sorry. We, um—"

"We had to come on ahead," Declan interrupted from behind them. He walked into the foyer from a narrow hallway. After a quick glance at him, Taite kept her gaze fixed on Ryder and saw a frown darken his features before it was lightened by a genuine smile for his friend.

Seeing them together, Taite was struck by how similar the two men were. Both were tall with dark hair and muscular, fit bodies. It appeared that Ryder was an inch or two taller than Declan, which would put him somewhere around six-four or six-five. Nearly identical broad shoulders tapered to narrow waists and hips, down to long legs and big feet.

The two men grasped hands and briefly hugged, pounding each other on the back with their free hands. When they parted, Ryder asked, "How did you get in?"

Dark eyebrows rose and a grin crooked a corner of Declan's mouth. "Your back door isn't as secure as it should be, Ry." Looking past Taite, he added, "Good to see you again, Cobb."

Taite glanced at Cobb, too, and saw his lips tighten briefly before he assumed the solemn, bored expression he'd maintained with her. The little man matched the house, that was for sure.

Dark, somber, with understated but evident wealth in both the cut of his suit and the architecture of the mansion. She'd been impressed by the place from the outside. Now that she was inside . . .

The floor of the foyer was a beautiful gray shot through

with streaks of dark green. Crimson cushioned antique chairs lined one wall. Above the chairs were two crossed swords and a coat of arms that had a snarling wolf, his massive paw planted on a snake.

Even here, it seemed, she couldn't get away from wolves. At least this one was a normal one and not something right out of a horror movie.

"Mr. O'Connell." With a slight sniff, Cobb looked from Declan to Taite and said, "I assume you're hungry after your travels. I'll fix something straight away."

"Can I help?" Taite asked, not wanting to put the man to any trouble.

Cobb looked surprised, then thoughtful. He glanced at his employer and gave a nod. "Yes, miss, I would appreciate the assistance. The kitchen is this way." Without waiting to see if she followed, he turned and walked through the large foyer and down a hallway on the opposite side of the stairs that led to the second floor.

With a small shrug, Taite followed the little man. As she left the room, she felt eyes burning into her back and knew Ryder Merrick was staring at her. Trying to ignore the shiver of awareness that coursed through her, she quickened her pace to catch up to Cobb.

"Come into my study and let's talk," she heard Ryder say. Declan murmured something in response.

Now out of earshot, Taite wandered into a large, ultra-modern kitchen to see Cobb washing his hands at a double stainless steel sink. As she followed suit, he turned and pulled a large turkey and a loaf of bread out of the refrigerator.

She dried her hands, then took the bread from him and set it on the dark green and black marble countertop. Cobb put the turkey on an old-fashioned butcher's block that sat in the center of the kitchen. She looked around. A small table with an L-shaped bench sat beneath a large corner window, with two chairs on the sides opposite the bench. Glass-doored cupboards lined two walls, and all the appliances were modern brushed stainless steel.

"This is lovely," she murmured, running her hand along the counter. She thought of her little galley kitchen in her apartment in Tucson and squashed a surge of envy.

"Thank you, Miss Gibson." He handed her a bread knife. "If you would cut some bread, please. Enough for yourself and Mr. O'Connell."

"Oh, please, call me Taite." She watched Cobb set a knife efficiently to the turkey, cutting off large slices, then she turned her attention to the bread and began slicing it. "How long have you worked for Mr. Merrick?"

"Nearly thirty years now." Cobb placed the carving knife in the sink. Pulling open a drawer next to the stove, he pulled out a butter knife and two forks. "My father worked for his father, and I began my employment when young Mr. Merrick was still a teenager. Would you like salad cream or mustard on your sandwich?"

Salad cream? Did he mean salad dressing?

Cobb must have seen the confusion on her face, for he clarified, "I believe you Americans call it mayonnaise."

"Oh, both, please." Taite set her own knife down and picked up the slices of bread. Turning, she walked to the butcher's block where Cobb had set aside thick slices of turkey. She placed the bread on two plates, then added a few tomato slices from a third plate. "What's he like? Mr. Merrick, I mean."

Without looking at her, he said, "I don't discuss my employer, miss." He placed the sandwiches on a cornflower blue platter and carried it over to the small breakfast nook "Go ahead and eat I'll fetch Mr. O'Connell."

Taite pursed her lips and watched Cobb leave the kitchen. She hadn't scored any brownie points there. She might've even lost a few. And somehow she had the feeling she needed the little guy in her corner.

*   *   *

"Well, fuck. You could've been a bit more welcomin', boyo," Declan growled. "It's a damned good thing I told Taite you were a loner or she might think you're just plain rude."

Ryder stretched out his legs and laid one arm along the back of the sofa. He watched Declan pace in front of the bookcase-lined west wall of the study. "I told you not to come," he reminded his friend. "If you wanted to make up with Pelicia, you could've used an excuse other than werewolves."

A shot of color rode high on Declan's cheeks. He scowled. "It's not an excuse."

"Uh-huh." Ryder crossed his ankles. He'd never seen Declan so discomfited, and it was too good an opportunity to pass up. "You and she didn't exactly part on good terms, as I recall. You think she'll even talk to you?"

"Dry up," Declan muttered. He rubbed one hand over his cheek. "And stop tryin' to change the subject. We were discussin' you and this ridiculous excuse *you're* givin'."

Not having anything else to fall back on, Ryder returned to his original pretext. "I do have deadlines, Declan." He leaned his head back and closed his eyes.

"Fuck that." Declan's emotions rode close to the surface. Ryder detected frustration and anger. And fear, which he'd never before sensed from the former marine commando.

There was a sharp *crack*, and Ryder opened one eye to see Declan standing at the desk, both palms flat on the surface. The sound had been his friend slamming his hands onto the desk. He closed his eye again and concentrated on appearing unconcerned.

"Dammit, Ry. You don't understand. The thing that came after us was a werewolf. A goddamned werewolf!"

The last thing Ryder wanted anyone around him to believe was that werewolves actually existed. And so he went on the offensive. "Pull the other one, mate."

"I'm tellin' you what I saw." Declan stopped pacing, and

Ryder could feel his friend staring at him. "The fuckin' thing was at least seven feet tall, shaped like a man but covered in fur. And its face . . ." Declan dropped onto the other end of the sofa and sighed. "Its face looked like a fuckin' wolf's."

Without opening his eyes or changing his posture, Ryder said, "All I can say is my research has never suggested that werewolves are real. Especially as Hollywood would portray them."

"Shit." Declan's voice was deep and harsh. "Well, if it's no', I don't know what the hell it is. But it's no' human, I can tell you that much." His Irish brogue became more pronounced, clearly showing his agitation.

They were silent for a few moments, Declan muttering under his breath now and again. Knowing his friend would get back on the subject of werewolves, Ryder shoved to his feet and walked to the bookshelves. Running one finger along the top shelf, he followed it until he reached the book he was looking for. He handed the thick hardback to Declan. "Here. This fellow is supposedly the foremost expert on lycanthropy."

Declan frowned, though he took the book. "Jaysus! I don't want to look through some fuckin' book, Ry. Why won't you just tell me what you know?"

Ryder opened his mouth to respond, but was interrupted by Cobb.

"Pardon me, sir."

Ryder turned his head to see Cobb standing in the doorway. "Yes?"

Declan muttered something under his breath and tossed the book onto the sofa.

Cobb raised his eyebrows, but didn't comment other than to say, "I've made a sandwich for Mr. O'Connell. Ms. Gibson has already started eating, if you'd care to join her in the kitchen," he said, directing his last comment to Declan.

"Sure. Why not?" Declan slanted a look at Ryder that promised the conversation wasn't over. "You comin'?"

"In a minute," Ryder responded. He needed to talk to Cobb to make sure they were both following the same game plan. Waiting until he could no longer hear Declan's footsteps, he looked at his employee. "They won't be leaving tomorrow."

Cobb blinked. "You've decided to let them stay?"

With a sigh, Ryder scrubbed the back of his neck with his hand, kneading muscles gone taut with tension. "I know Declan. He's like a bear after honey. He won't leave until he knows how he can protect the woman. If I try to make him leave, it will cause him to be more suspicious than he already is."

He didn't want to look too closely at the more pressing reason for having them stay.

His bone-deep loneliness.

He'd missed Declan, that was a fact. It would be nice to catch up on old times with his friend. Ryder closed his mind off to thinking about his other houseguest. Perhaps if he didn't put a name to her and thought of her in more abstract ways, he wouldn't be so attracted to her.

"We had discussed sleeping arrangements," Cobb said. "However, now that I've seen them together, I wonder . . . Should I put them in the same room? I assume they're lovers."

Ryder clenched his jaw at the thought of Declan touching Taite, of the other man sliding into her slick heat. A snarl left his throat, startling him. *Dammit.* What the hell was wrong with him? He didn't even know her, yet she seemed intimately familiar, like the warmth of home.

"It appears it would be in Mr. O'Connell's best interests for them *not* to be lovers," Cobb observed wryly.

Ryder stared at Cobb, the beginnings of panic swirling in his gut. He had to fight this attraction he felt, because it could go nowhere. He couldn't *let* it go anywhere. Especially given what had happened with Marika. . . .

With a curse, he slammed the lid on that thought and ran his hand through his hair. God, he was in trouble.

"It doesn't matter one way or the other," he finally responded to his employee and friend. "I can't have her."

Declan walked into the kitchen, unable to shake the conviction Ryder was hiding something. His friend was secretive—always had been—but this was something more, an underlying desperation he'd not sensed before.

Seeing Taite sitting on the window bench at the small table by the back door, her hands wrapped around a thick sandwich, made his shoulders tense and his mind go back to his conversation with Ry. *Hand him a book and tell him to read it. What the fuck?*

If Mr. Horror Novelist thought Declan was just going to sit back and wait for him to decide to start sharing information about werewolves, he'd better think again. Declan loved this woman like a sister—a novel experience for him—and he'd be damned before he let some oversized furball hurt her.

He'd always been of the opinion that men couldn't be "just friends" with women—it wasn't in a man's genetic makeup to form a platonic relationship with someone who could potentially be a lover. But with Taite that kind of attraction had never fully materialized.

Oh, he'd noticed how beautiful she was and what a lovely body she had but, other than an aborted attempt to seduce her early on, he'd not been sexually tempted by her. And now her friendship was too important to him to risk it by trying to make something work that clearly wasn't meant to be.

He joined her at the table, pulling out one of the chairs and plopping down onto it with a sigh, his mind already back on Ryder's incomprehensible refusal to help.

"What?" Taite stared at him with a slight frown dipping between her brows.

Before Declan could reply, Cobb walked into the kitchen.

Picking up a dishrag, he started cleaning the knives in the sink.

Declan looked at the turkey sandwich in front of him, then at Cobb. "Only one?" He was starving, and one wasn't going to do it.

Without a word, Cobb opened the refrigerator. He took out the turkey, then jars of salad cream and mustard. "What would you like to drink, Mr. O'Connell?"

Declan glanced at the glass of water in front of Taite and frowned. "I don't suppose you've any iced tea?"

Cobb sniffed.

"I didn't think so." Declan shook his head and winked at Taite. "It's an American way of drinkin' tea, puttin' ice in it, and I've found I quite enjoy it. But it's somethin' you'd never do to a good cuppa, would you, Cobb?"

"It's a sacrilege, doing that to tea."

Declan grinned. "What did I tell you?" he said sotto voce to Taite. Looking at Cobb, he leaned back in his chair. "How 'bout a pint, then?"

"We have Guinness and Fuller's."

"Fuller's Ale?" Declan licked his lips. He hadn't had a Fuller's in years. At Cobb's nod, he said, "Give us a Fuller's, then."

Cobb pulled a bottle of the amber ale from the pantry. "Would you like one, miss?" he asked Taite.

She wrinkled her nose and shook her head. Cobb's lips twitched, and he popped the cap, then placed the ale in front of Declan. Turning back to the stove, he fitted an oven mitt over his right hand and picked up a platter from one of the burners. Spatula in his left hand, he carried the plate to the table and slid a pile of homemade chips onto Declan's plate.

"These are so good," Taite said as she bit into a chip. "How do you fix them, Mr. Cobb?"

"Just Cobb will do, miss." He carried the plate back to the

stove and set it down. "A good chef never reveals his culinary secrets."

"Ah, one of his famous Cobbisms," Declan murmured. When Cobb turned to the butcher's block and started preparing another sandwich, Declan said, "Go light on the mayo, all right?" He patted his stomach. "I've gotta watch my waistline." Grinning at Taite's snort, he leaned forward and snagged the remainder of the chip from her fingers. His grin widened at her—"Hey!"—and he dodged the swat of her hand. "Well, you weren't eating it," he said in defense of his action.

"You didn't give me a chance." She reached over and took a warm chip from his plate. "From now on, eat your own," she said around a mouthful of potato.

Cobb placed a second sandwich on Declan's plate, then put the turkey and condiments away.

Declan scooted his chair to the side to watch him. Now was the time to ask Cobb about Pelicia. Trying to ignore how his gut tightened at the thought of her, he asked, "How's Pel?"

"Fine." Cobb's voice was cool, even more so than his usual formal tones.

Taite leaned forward. "Pel?"

"My daughter." Cobb cleaned off the butcher's block. As he wiped his hands on the dishtowel, he said, "Should you require anything else, please let me know. I shall be next door in the laundry room." He neatly folded the towel and placed it on the butcher's block, then left the room.

Declan stared after him. The older man's reaction was not unexpected, and Declan felt the weight of his disapproval. It wasn't completely undeserved.

Realizing he'd tensed, he drew in a deep breath and rotated his shoulders. When he turned his chair back to the table, he saw Taite's raised eyebrows. He sighed. "Pel and I have a history."

"So I gathered." She glanced toward the kitchen doorway. "And it's one Cobb apparently isn't too happy about."

Declan took a swig from his bottle of ale. He set the bottle on the table with a thud. "No, that he's not." He didn't want to think about how he'd left things with Pel, much less talk about it. It was something he planned to set right, which was another reason he'd been so impatient to get to the Isles of Scilly.

Picking up his sandwich, he took a big bite. The mustard hit the back of his tongue and he groaned in ecstasy. "God, this is good," he said around a mouthful of food.

Taite propped her elbows on the table and put the last of her sandwich in her mouth. After a moment, she said, "Okay, I get that you don't want to talk about her. So, tell me what Ryder said."

She took a long drink of water, her gaze on his over the rim of the glass. Her look was full of hope, as if she expected him to impart some golden nugget shared by Ryder.

Son of a bitch.

"He told me to read a goddamned book." Declan bit into his sandwich with the savagery of a barbarian. He chewed and washed it down with a swig from his ale, then took another bite. Once he'd swallowed, he said, "Like we've time to do that."

Taite leaned her chin on one fist and frowned. "I don't understand. You explained what we saw? The werewolf?"

"Aye. But Ryder seems reluctant to help." He finished his sandwich and picked up the bottle of ale. Rolling it between his palms, he stared into the opening.

He was puzzled by Ryder's nonchalant attitude. If anything, he'd have expected his friend to look at him—and treat him—as if he suspected Declan needed to be fitted with a straightjacket. But the damned man had sat on the sofa with his eyes closed, sprawled comfortably and looking as if Declan was keeping him from a nap.

Setting the bottle down, he started in on his chips and the other sandwich. His years in covert operations told him something was up. He didn't know what—yet. But he wasn't going to be unprepared if—or, rather, when—the werewolf caught up to them, as he had no doubt it would.

Some stalker and now a werewolf had staked a claim on Taite, and Declan feared neither would give up until he had her or he was dead. Declan aimed to make sure the outcome was the latter of those two choices.

"Then I don't understand why he won't help," Taite said, her voice full of confusion. "We can't have come all this way for nothing. You're the one who said he knows this stuff, Declan. I mean, how hard is it?" She dropped her voice. "Ryder, me lad, what do you know about werewolves?" In an equally deep voice but with a crisp British inflection, she went on. "Oh, I know so much I'm considered to be an expert, old bean. Jolly good."

Shaking his head, Declan rolled his eyes. "That was a fair imitation of Ryder, darlin'. But you had me all wrong."

"Don't change the subject." She sighed and leaned her chin on one fist. "I just don't understand."

"Let me talk to him again. I'll get him to come 'round." Or he'd bloody the stubborn SOB's nose.

"Well, he's an expert, so make him . . . *expert* something. Would it help if *I* talked to him?" Her voice was taut and ended a little on the shrill side.

Declan sighed and rubbed one hand along the back of his neck. Remembering the way Ryder's hard-on had tented his pants when he'd first met Taite, Declan wasn't sure it was a good idea, especially since Ryder didn't seem very happy with his attraction to her.

Or maybe that was it. Ryder had been alone so long he probably didn't remember what to do with a woman. Declan grinned. Taite could be just the thing for his old friend.

Declan knew he had to get through to Ryder, or they were in deep shit. He couldn't shake the feeling that the werewolf would somehow find them here on the island. The damned thing had tracked them to Atlanta, after all. "Not if you're gonna be a fishwife, which is what you're soundin' like, darlin'," he said in answer to her question.

She frowned then her lips curved into a small grin. "I was sounding a bit shrewish there, wasn't I?" She inhaled deeply, letting the air out in a rush. "I just don't know how much more of this I can take."

"I know." Declan leaned forward and took her hands in his. They were soft and warm, and she gripped his fingers tightly. "Listen, I'll go back and talk to Ryder again. He used deadlines as an excuse for not bein' able to help, but I've a feelin' there's more to it than that." Releasing her hands, he stood and placed his palm on her slender shoulder. "Will you be okay on your own for a wee bit?"

She nodded, staring at the table. When she looked up, tears glazed her eyes. Frowning, she swiped at the moisture. "Dammit, this is making me a cry baby. Do what you can, Declan. If it turns out we have to read books, then we'd better get started."

"Chin up, darlin'." He leaned down and hugged her. Just as her arms wrapped around his waist and she pressed her face into his side, he heard footsteps behind him and a slight shuffle as if shoes had skidded to a stop.

Keeping one arm around her shoulders, he turned to see Ryder standing there, a dark scowl on his face.

"Just the man I wanted to see," Declan said, frowning right back at his friend. "We need to talk."

A muscle flexed in Ryder's jaw. Declan recognized that look—it meant the other man was irritated about something. Tough. He was liable to become even angrier before Declan was through with him.

"Is it all right if I take a walk around the grounds before it gets dark? I've been cooped up on an airplane most of the day." Taite started to slide off the bench.

Declan moved back so she'd have room. When she was standing, he slid his arm back around her shoulders and hugged her to his side, offering support in the only way he could for now.

Ryder's eyes narrowed and his lips thinned, though his voice sounded normal enough as he said, "If you go outside of the landscaped area, be careful, especially along the coves. The rocks can be slippery." He nodded toward the back door. "Cobb's hung your coat there on the hooks." With a glance at Declan, he turned on his heel. "Let's go back to my office."

Taite watched the two men as they left the kitchen. Biting her lower lip, she wondered at Ryder's reaction upon seeing her and Declan together. His face had suggested he was jealous of their proximity, but that couldn't be right. He didn't even know her, and he'd sure as hell made it clear they were unwelcome.

Even if he'd been aroused when she met him, she didn't *know* that she was the reason for it. And while part of her was thrilled to think she *could* cause such a strong reaction, another part of her hoped he'd just been watching porn or flipping through a girly magazine.

With her own personal stalker, she had enough problems with men and their desires. She didn't need another complication.

She wouldn't be surprised if Ryder asked them to leave first thing in the morning. And that little man Cobb would probably be down on the docks helping push the boat off. Oh, he was polite enough, but she suspected it was more a matter of professionalism than any genuinely felt courtesy.

God, she was tired. She'd gotten precious little sleep over the last several months, but especially this past week. Even so, she was too wired and it was too early to go to bed just yet. Getting some exercise should help.

Walking over to the back door, she took her coat from the peg and shrugged into it. Once she'd zipped it up, she reached into one of the big oversized front pockets and pulled out the pedometer she'd insisted on buying before they reached La-Guardia.

One thing she'd discovered about werewolves was they caused a lot of stress. And she dealt with stress by power walking. She was up to fifteen thousand steps a day, which was five thousand more than the recommended amount. Rain or shine, she walked. If the weather didn't permit her to be outdoors, she got on the treadmill or did stairs.

Today she'd be walking around an isolated island off the coast of Cornwall. "Who'd a-thunk it?" she muttered and pulled open the door.

Cool November wind gusted, scattering leaves around the small stone patio. Taite went outside and quickly closed the door behind her to keep anything from blowing inside the house. Cobb already didn't want them there—he'd be less than thrilled to walk into his pristine kitchen and find twigs and leaves on the floor.

A white cast aluminum bistro set squatted on one side of the patio, and a cobblestone path led through what would probably be a beautiful garden come spring. Taite set off down the path, hands in her pockets, starting at a leisurely pace until her muscles could warm up.

The little trail meandered through the garden where a few flowers still bloomed, then ran alongside the lawn, parallel to the woods. Once the lawn ended, however, the walkway became little more than a packed dirt footpath.

She loved it. Even from where she was, she could hear the crash of the ocean against the rock-strewn shore and the riotous cry of the seabirds. It even smelled different here, a combination of the salty sea in the air and something with an aroma remarkably like sage. Some native plant, she supposed. As the path became rougher, she pulled her hands out of her pockets so she could better balance herself.

Rounding a bend, she came upon a small inlet. She picked her way over and around rocks. The waves lapped gently against the shore, and she stopped at the sloping edge, staring out over an ocean that glittered in the sun as if the great width was covered in a mammoth, diamond-studded net.

Here at the water's edge it was colder. She huddled into her jacket, her hands once more in her pockets. In spite of the wildness of this place, she felt more at peace than she had in a long time. Maybe it was because she felt safe for the first time in weeks. Once she'd left Tucson she hadn't had to worry about her stalker, and she and Declan had given the werewolf the slip after he'd caught up with them in Atlanta. She only hoped the old myth about werewolves not being able to cross water was true.

She stopped, frowning. Or was that a myth about vampires?

Damn. She didn't have a clue about any of this crap. If Ryder didn't help, she didn't know what she'd do.

Ryder. A shiver that had nothing to do with the weather and everything to do with sex worked its way down her spine and wrapped deeply around her womb. Her nipples tightened and she squeezed her thighs together against the sudden ache in her core.

She did not need this complication, as much as she might want it. From the short time she'd been around Ryder, she could tell he would be hard to handle. And she just didn't have the energy.

Sighing, she stared around the cove, seeing fallen logs and moss-covered rocks. Here and there were varying types of flotsam—pieces of wreckage and trash littering the shoreline. Wind roared into the small cove and she huddled into her coat, drawing her collar up around her neck.

As beautiful as it was, Taite was reluctant to flounder around after dark. Turning, she retraced her steps. The sharp crack of a twig snapping made her stop before she'd gone very far. She looked around. There was no movement that she could see, but she couldn't shake the feeling that someone—or something—was out there.

Surely the werewolf couldn't have found her already. With

her heart slamming against her ribs, she started walking as fast as the terrain would allow, fighting the urge to look over her shoulder. If it were the werewolf, he would have already attacked her, wouldn't he?

But if it wasn't him, who was it? *What* was it?

She swallowed and picked up her pace. It *could* be the werewolf. Unlikely, since she'd only arrived an hour ago, but there was that possibility.

Or was it all her overtaxed imagination?

Chapter 5

Taite wouldn't be surprised if her imagination was working overtime. In the last several days she'd barely slept—either because when she closed her eyes all she could see was that freaking wolf-man charging Declan's car, or she woke after only half an hour or so of sleep, sure she'd heard something, afraid it was the stalker. Or the werewolf.

It hadn't mattered that Declan was close by, ready to protect her. Fear was an irrational thing and not easily absolved.

Another twig snapped somewhere behind her and her heart rate tripled. When she reached the lawn, she broke into a run. At the back door, she stopped and turned, looking behind her, scanning the forest for any movement at all. There was none.

Just as she reached for the door, it opened from the inside and she gave a little squeak. One hand over her pounding heart, she looked into the green eyes of the little Man Friday. "Oh, Cobb, you scared me."

"The way you came running up to the house, miss, I would say you were already frightened." He peered over her shoulder. "Is everything all right?"

Taite pressed her lips together, unsure how much to tell him. He already didn't seem too impressed with her—she really didn't want him to think she was crazy, too. "I thought I heard something. It was probably just my imagination."

"Are you sure, miss?" He stepped to one side to allow her to enter, but his gaze remained fixed on the woods. "There doesn't appear to be anyone else about, but perhaps we should inform Mr. Merrick."

"No, it's not necessary to bother him with this. Thank you." Trying to look nonchalant, she shrugged out of her coat and hooked the collar over the peg. "Are there animals on the island?"

"Other than small rodents and birds, no, miss." He continued to look toward the woods. "Did you see something?"

"No." She sighed, then cleared her throat. "I told you, I'm sure it was just my imagination. Comin' over me," she finished in a song, her voice shaking with remaining nerves.

When he looked at her without any change of expression, she pursed her lips. The man had no sense of humor, either.

Cobb closed the door. "I was about to make a spot of tea, miss. Would you like a cup?"

She stared at him. Just when she thought she'd figured him out—and knew he didn't like her—he offered tea. As much as she'd like to get warm quickly, she wanted even more to find out if Declan had been successful with Ryder. "Thanks, no," she said with a smile. No sense in alienating him by appearing ungrateful. "Maybe later?"

"As you wish."

She started to leave, but he called out to her. "Ah, miss?"

Taite stopped and glanced back at him.

"Your shoes. If you please."

Looking down, she saw her shoes were covered with dirt, and she'd already tracked it halfway across the kitchen. So much for not alienating the guy. "Oh, my God, Cobb. I am so sorry."

She toed them off, bent and picked them up, and carried them to the back door. Opening the door, she clapped the shoes together, knocking off as much dirt as possible, then shut the door and placed the shoes on the floor beneath her coat. "Let me clean this up."

Cobb had already retrieved a broom and dustpan. "I have it, miss."

"Oh." She stood there, watching him clean up her mess, discomfort at her faux pas rolling through her. "I really am sorry."

He straightened, the dirt-laden dustpan in his hand. A small smile creased his face, lightening his expression and making him seem almost boyish. "It's not a problem, miss, I assure you. I've cleaned up much worse." He turned and pulled open the door, throwing the dirt back outside. "The gentlemen are in the study, if you were wondering."

"I was. Thank you." She left the kitchen and padded down the hallway. As she approached Ryder's office, she slowed, trying to regain her calm. *It was just your imagination, girl,* she admonished. *Get a grip.* Drawing on meditation techniques she sometimes practiced, she started breathing deeply to restore her inner calm.

Just then she heard Ryder say, "It isn't a good time, Declan. I told you, I—"

"Have deadlines. Aye, I got that." Declan's deep sigh was loud, even to Taite where she lurked in the hallway. "What I don't get is why you're tryin' to fob me off with such a lame-ass excuse."

"It's not lame." Ryder's voice sounded near, as if he'd moved closer to the door. "Especially to my editor."

"Uh-huh." Declan sounded unimpressed. "And I know if the wildly successful horror novelist Alexander Ryder got on his satellite phone and called his editor, that editor would grant him an extension."

"It's not that simple." Ryder's deep tones held shades of irritation and aggravation. Considering he was talking to Declan, the master of both, she knew exactly how he felt.

"It *is* that simple." There was a thud, then Declan said, "I don't think you understand the urgency of the situation, Ry. Taite has a werewolf after her. We don't have time to read fuckin' books. We need information now. *Now,* dammit."

Taite felt a little guilty for eavesdropping. Though her intent had been to give herself time to get calm so she'd appear strong when she went into the room, the end result was that she'd lingered in the hallway longer than she should have. She moved to the doorway and cleared her throat. Both men looked toward the door, Declan with a welcoming expression, Ryder with . . . Well, it wasn't exactly welcoming.

If anything, he looked almost savage. Like a wild animal, frightened and cornered, and ready to lash out at anyone unwise enough to get too close.

Hoping to smooth things over, she put on her professional investigator persona. Walking into the study, she said in a calm, steady voice, "I understand we haven't arrived at a very convenient time, Mr. Merrick. But I hope you understand how important this is."

A muscle flexed in Ryder's jaw, and his sensual lips pressed together. He sat behind his desk and crossed his legs, one ankle resting on the opposite knee. His square-tipped fingers curled over his ankle, and she couldn't help but stare at his lean, masculine hand.

What would those hands feel like moving over her skin? Soft and strong or slightly rough? Realizing he hadn't responded to her, that he was just sitting there, staring at her, she cleared her throat and went on. "As crazy as it sounds—and believe me, I *know* it sounds *completely* insane—there's a werewolf . . ." She trailed off, looking at Declan, uncertain how to say this to a total stranger.

Declan shrugged, his handsome face still frowning from his argument with his friend.

"As I understand it," Ryder said, his voice deep and his tone sardonic, "you think you have a real live werewolf chasing you."

Taite couldn't stop the blush that heated her cheeks. "I said it sounded crazy." Pacing in front of the desk, she spread out her hands pleadingly. "But it's true. It's *real*." Then she said the three words that were the hardest she'd ever spoken. "Please help me."

His jaw flexed again. "I'm sorry, but I doubt you saw what you think you saw, Ms. Gibson." He paused, leaning back in his chair with his hands loosely clasped over his flat stomach. "I just don't think I have anything of value to you. What I write about are legends. Creatures that don't exist outside of myth. If you have a werewolf after you—and I still find that hard to believe—I can't help you."

"Bullshit!" Declan slammed his hands down on the desk. "I've known you a long time, boyo, and I know when you're blowin' smoke outta your arse. This is one of those times." He rocked back on his heels and crossed his arms. "Or maybe that's just a mighty thick stick you've got crammed up there."

A look passed through Ryder's eyes that Taite couldn't decipher, but a shiver went through her just the same because it was dark and dangerous and, for a moment, deadly.

Then he sighed and the moment was gone. "I can give you access to any books in the study," he said, ignoring Declan's outburst. He didn't sound happy about helping, merely resigned. "But I really can't spare any time myself."

Taite could see they were not making any progress. Declan started to argue, but she put one hand on his arm and talked over his objections. "Thank you. We'll take what we can get and stay out of your way. *If* you'll answer one question for me."

He raised one dark brow. "Yes?"

"Can werewolves cross over bodies of water? Or is that a vampire thing?"

That startled a laugh from Ryder. He rocked back in his chair, delighted with her in spite of himself. "As far as I know," he said, his lips twitching, "that's a vampire thing."

"Dammit." She heaved a sigh and wandered over to the bookshelves.

"Why?" He tried not to stare at her, but it was hopeless. *He* was hopeless. She was the first young, attractive woman to be in this house in years. That in itself was enough to make his cock perk up and take notice.

Leaning forward, she braced a forearm along a shelf. She swung one bent knee back and forth, which made her ass sway. He had a sudden vision of her naked and bent over his desk, her legs spread, her slick heat welcoming his surging cock. He clenched his fists as his erection sprang to life once more.

"Oh, look here." Not answering his question, she straightened and picked up a silver-framed photograph and tilted it briefly toward him.

It was a picture of him, Declan, and another mate of theirs from university taken . . . a lifetime ago.

"You were so young."

Declan wandered over and looked over her shoulder. "Aye. We were. I was nineteen, and Ry had just turned twenty. Sully was the babe of the group—only eighteen and in his first year."

"Sully?" She looked at Declan with such affection in her gaze that Ryder ground his jaw to keep from jumping up and shoving his friend away from her. He clenched his fists against the irrational surge of possessiveness.

"Rory Sullivan. Detective Chief Inspector Rory Sullivan now, that is. One of Scotland Yard's finest." Declan glanced at Ryder with a grin. "Who'd a-thought that lad would end up a cop?"

"Not me." Ryder knew his words were abrupt, but he was holding back a growl and it couldn't be helped.

Taite apparently decided he was irritated with her delving into his past, for she quickly set the frame down and looked back toward the books. "Which ones should we start with?" she asked. She turned her head to look at him over her shoulder, catching him with his gaze firmly fixed to her derrière. The sharp scent of her surprise mingled with the renewed musk of her arousal.

He was chagrined to feel heat spread along his cheek-bones. He'd not blushed since he was a schoolboy. To be caught and discomfited by a woman . . . He reacted the only way he knew how. "Any along the top shelf there will suit your purposes, Ms. Gibson," he said, his tone cool and disinterested.

He heard a snort from Declan, which he ignored.

An answering blush darkened her cheeks. "Apparently, anything will suit my purposes but you," she muttered, giving him a dark look, her voice tart and full of sass.

Even as he bit back a grin at her impudent response, he flipped open the cover to his laptop and pushed the power button. Without looking at her again, he said, "Take them to the parlor or your bedroom. Either is fine as long as I'm not disturbed."

"Oh, you're already plenty disturbed, boyo." Declan stalked over to the bookshelves and started taking down books, stacking them on the counter that was at waist level. Once he'd piled up half-a-dozen or so books, he picked them up and walked toward the door.

"Come on, Taite. We've lots of readin' to do." He shot a look at Ryder, which Ryder took in stride, knowing he deserved it, and more.

"In a minute." She picked up her pile of books and stopped in front of Ryder's desk, waiting until he looked up at her. The flush had left her cheeks, leaving her looking a little pale, freckles he hadn't noticed before trailing starkly over her nose.

"I *am* sorry we've interrupted your routine, Mr. Merrick. And I'm sorry I've bothered you with my problem." Her tone was more sarcastic than apologetic, and he got the message. It had been a long time since someone had taken him to task.

Her frown deepened. "I only hope we know what to do before it finds us. Here. On your island." She turned to leave and shot a hard look at him over one shoulder. "So, you see, it just might be in your best interest to help us, after all, instead of leaving us to blindly fend for ourselves."

Her reprimand was ruined by a wide yawn. He bit back a grin at the sheepish expression that crossed her face. She was not only pretty, she was cute. A deadly combination to any man's libido. Not to mention his emotions.

She walked across the foyer, her strides quick and purposeful, and Ryder knew it was another glimpse into her personality. Add feisty to cute.

He was in trouble.

Ryder got up from the desk and followed her to the parlor. He took the books out of her hands as she struggled to place them on a low table. "Look," he said, plopping the books down, addressing his comment to both her and Declan, who'd looked up when he'd entered the room. "Why don't you get a good night's sleep and start on all this in the morning?"

She shook her head. "I have to know what to do. We don't have time to sleep."

Declan stood and stretched his arms over his head. Ryder heard the bones of his back and shoulders crack. "He's right, darlin'. I've been sittin' here readin' for a couple of minutes, and I couldn't tell you one word of what I've read. We can pick this up in the mornin', after a good night's rest."

"But . . ." She looked at the stack of books, then picked up one and started reading the back cover.

"Of course," Declan went on with a glare at Ryder, "if Ry would agree to help us it would go much faster."

Ryder shook his head. "I can't. I've told you, I—"

"Have deadlines," Declan finished with a scowl.

Taite looked up. "It would only take a few minutes—"

"I'm sorry to keep hounding you on the subject," Ryder said. He slid his hands into his pants pockets and clenched his fists. Keep it up, and he'd spend more time arguing about not talking to them than a recitation of all things werewolf would take. "But the closer a writer gets to deadline, the more inaccessible he becomes. It's a fact of life."

Declan muttered a curse. "Which room am I in?"

"About that . . ." Ryder looked at his friend. His gut tightened in anticipation and, as he glanced at Taite, he trapped the territorial growl trying to make its way from deep inside. "Cobb wasn't sure if he should put the two of you in the same room or not."

Taite shook her head at the same time that Declan frowned and said, "Separate rooms."

Ryder tried not to let the relief he felt show. "I'll let him know that. Give him a few minutes, then come up to the second floor," he murmured and left the room.

Bypassing the small lift, he took the stairs to the guest quarters' floor two at a time. Cobb was in the first guest room on the right of the wide hallway, turning down the navy bedspread.

"Declan goes here," Ryder said. "Put Taite in the gold room."

Other than a slight lifting of his eyebrows, Cobb's placid expression didn't change. "They're not lovers, then."

Ryder frowned to realize that question really hadn't been answered. Not as definitively as he would like. Just because they weren't sharing a room didn't mean they weren't intimate with each other. What was the Yankee colloquialism?

Ah, yes. *Friends with benefits.*

A muscle in his jaw ticked. "Just put her in the gold room, Cobb."

"Of course, sir." Using a calm voice to go with the calm expression, Cobb turned and walked out of the bedroom. He crossed the hallway and went into the guest room that had been Ryder's mother's favorite.

Ryder followed behind and looked around the room. A gold comforter covered a queen-size bed, and gold brocade curtains hung from the ceiling to drape on the light blue carpeted floor. He glanced back at the bed as Cobb pulled off the comforter and began putting the bed linens on the mattress.

He had a very clear picture in his mind of Taite's hair, freed from its braid, spread out on the pillows. His head would rest on her full breasts, her scent invading his lungs and taking hold so he would always smell her.

With a slight snarl, Ryder turned and left the room. He heard the whir of the lift and, as he reached the landing, the doors slid open.

Taite stepped out, a book in her hand, followed by Declan. When she looked at Ryder, her eyes were wide. "I've never been in a house with an elevator before," she said. "Well, not one that wasn't a historic landmark."

Ryder shrugged, fighting back the sense of panic that always threatened whenever he thought about being in the small, cramped lift. "I haven't used it in years. I prefer the stairs." He swept his arm out, gesturing down the hallway. "Taite, you're in the gold room, which is the first room on the left. Declan, you're across the hall."

"Where's your room?" Taite asked. Almost immediately he saw a rush of color in her cheeks. "Never mind," she quickly added.

He shrugged. "I don't mind. My room is on the ground floor." Not that he'd be spending much time in it. If he couldn't get them to leave, he'd be chained up in the basement in another couple of nights. "At the back of the house. It's the master suite."

He tilted his head to read the title of the book she held. *Werewolves: Fact and Fiction,* by S. L. Gray. It actually was a rather accurate volume, a bit too accurate for his comfort. Of course she'd have chosen *that* one.

"A little light reading?" he asked, nodding toward the book.

She sighed. "I don't want to waste time."

Declan muttered something and started toward his room. "All you're gonna do is give yourself nightmares," he called over his shoulder. "You'd be better to get a good night's sleep and start in the mornin'."

Taite glanced at Ryder, looking as if she wanted to throw a

pointed barb his way, but restrained herself as she followed Declan down the hallway. "Declan, you know as well as I do that the werewolf could be out there, right now. We're not safe."

Declan stopped so suddenly she almost ran into him. Turning, he put his hands on her shoulders. Ryder stiffened at the sign of familiarity, fighting the urge to throw Declan's hands off her and growl *Mine!*

"We covered our tracks well, lass." Declan dropped a kiss on her forehead and turned her toward her room. He smacked her lightly on the ass, propelling her forward. "We've some time before it picks up the scent again."

She stopped in the doorway, half in and half out of the room. "You don't know that." Her voice was pitched low. Her eyes were shiny with tears Ryder could see she fought to control.

"Aye, I don't. But we've traveled over a rather large body of water, darlin'. Dogs can't track scent through water and, when you get right down to it, it *is* a dog." Declan turned and walked toward his room. Pausing in the doorway, he said, "Get some sleep. One night isn't gonna make a difference."

"It *could*." She bit her lip, her gaze going from Declan to Ryder, then back again. "You don't know for sure."

Declan came back to her and pulled her into his arms. Chin resting on her head, he murmured, "I'm just across the hall. One tiny little sound from you, and I'll be there. I'll keep my door open and you do the same, all right?"

She blinked and drew in a slow breath. "All right. Once I've gotten ready for bed, I'll open the door back up." Looking at Ryder, she gave a small smile and murmured, "Good night."

Declan gave Ryder a flinty look then went into his room. Within a few seconds, Ryder heard the water running in the adjoining bathroom. He stood in the hallway long moments, looking at Taite's closed door. He could hear her moving about the room and pictured her drawing off her clothing and pulling on her nightclothes. Wondering what she wore, he took a couple of steps and rested his forehead against the door.

He had to stop this . . . this obsession. He knew better. She couldn't be his. Ever.

With a sigh, he turned and walked away, more resolved than ever to make sure they left first thing in the morning. They could take all the books they wanted. He wasn't heartless enough to not help at all, but they couldn't find out about him.

They had to go.

Taite padded barefoot out of the adjoining bathroom. Wearing her favorite pajamas—a deep purple cotton tank top and matching boy boxers—she went back to the bedroom door and opened it a crack, just enough for a sliver of light from the hallway to permeate the room. Retracing her steps, she climbed up on the high bed and drew the covers over her legs. She positioned the pillows behind her back and picked up the reference book.

Flipping open to the beginning of the book, she read a few lines and frowned. The author suggested there were two distinct types of werewolves—those who were infected by a bite from another werewolf, and those who became werewolves due to a curse visited upon them. In those instances, the lycanthropy was not only transmittable by bite but also through bloodline.

Via children.

"So does a woman have a litter?" she wondered aloud. "And are they human or canine?" She read further, but saw no answer given to that particular question. "Well, whichever it is . . . No, thanks. I don't want to have any werewolf babies."

The author also wrote that being a werewolf in and of itself didn't make a person evil. It was the type of person an individual was prior to being turned that determined whether he was evil once he became a werewolf.

She read several more paragraphs, from which she gleaned that werewolves had an—for want of a better word—allergy to silver. If silver remained in their blood, it could prove to be fatal. Taite closed her eyes and leaned her head back against the headboard. "And just what do you do when you don't have any silver?" The long flight and stress caught up with her, and she yawned, her jaw cracking and tears squeezing from her eyes.

God, she had to get some sleep. Hoping she'd find the rest of her answers in the morning, she closed the book and placed it on the nightstand. She reached under the brocade-covered lampshade and clicked the light off, then pushed the pillows flat and lay down. The light coming in from the small opening between the door and doorframe was just enough to keep her irrational fear of the dark from taking over.

The wind had picked up, rustling the leaves on the trees outside her window and creating a roaring surf that pounded against the rocky shore below the house. She wondered if the beginning of an Atlantic gale was stirring, one like Declan had talked about when they'd first arrived. She hoped not. She wasn't crazy about storms, especially when they had the propensity to knock out power.

She was even less crazy about the dark.

She gritted her teeth against the memories of being shoved into a dark closet while her mother wined, *whined* and dined what inevitably turned out to be the latest in a long line of abusive husbands.

Taite turned on her side and tried to banish the past. Her mother was dead. Her last stepfather was dead. She was alone in the world, and she was fine with that. It meant her stalker had no leverage over her.

The loneliness she sometimes felt was better than having a family member available for him to use as bait.

And so here she was, thousands of miles away from home,

on a secluded island with an even more secluded host. She hadn't imagined Ryder's sexual interest in her, but he seemed reluctant to follow through on it. She had a healthy self-image, so she wasn't worried that it was something about her that was off-putting.

No, it had to be something else. Every instinct she had as an investigator prickled with awareness, telling her there was more going on here than that Ryder just didn't want guests. If she had more time—and one less werewolf—she'd be tempted to ferret out the truth of it.

But she had to focus all her energy on stopping the werewolf before he put a stop to her.

With a sigh, Taite flopped over onto her belly and scrunched the pillow under her head. What had she done to screw up her karma so badly that she'd ended up with an insane werewolf after her? And anyone would agree that a werewolf trumped a stalker in the worry department.

Of course, on the bright side—and she rolled her eyes that she could even think there *was* a bright side to all this—she finally got to see part of the U.K.

And she'd met Ryder Merrick.

She drew in a deep breath and exhaled noisily. Ryder. He was such a puzzle to her, blowing hot, then cold. He seemed irritated whenever Declan touched her, but didn't make any move to touch her himself.

Of course, they had just met, and he might be a more proper sort, what with the old stiff upper lip and all.

Well, stiff something, anyway.

Thoughts of that led her to thoughts of how that stiffness could be put to good use. Her breath caught in her throat. Closing her eyes, she fantasized Ryder was with her, his long, lean body pressed to hers, his hands touching her, his mouth tasting her.

Restless, she shifted onto her back. Her nipples beaded, and her body began thrumming with need. Conscious of her need to keep quiet, she bit her lip while she moved her right hand to her breasts, pinching and pulling on the hard tips. Sliding one hand down her torso, she slipped her fingers under the waistband of her boxers and into the swelling folds of her sex.

Her increasing arousal coated the lips of her pussy with slick cream. She pushed first one, then another finger into her wet sheath. It wasn't enough.

She wanted Ryder's thick cock plunging inside her grasping channel, wanted his fingers strumming her clit, his mouth sucking her nipples. Pulling her hand back, she rubbed the swollen bud of her pleasure, faster and faster, until a climax rolled through her. She clenched her teeth and tried not to make any noise.

With the release of her pent-up desire, her mind turned fuzzy, and she relaxed. As she slid further toward sleep, her breathing deepened. Images of Ryder and the werewolf, sometimes superimposed over each other, rolled back and forth until exhaustion finally claimed her.

Ryder turned over onto his back and laced his fingers behind his head. The mattress that usually hugged the contours of his body felt hard and lumpy. Staring up at the ceiling, he knew why.

She was two floors above him. This close to his Change, he could hear her sighing breaths as she dreamed, heard the rustle of the bedcovers as she twisted and turned.

Smelled the musky scent of her lingering arousal. It called to him, to his beast.

He was halfway up the stairs before he realized he'd left his room. But once his feet started moving, he couldn't seem to stop his progress until he reached her door.

Stretching out his hand, he placed his palm against the partially opened door. The door swung wide, and he stepped over the threshold.

Perhaps stepped over the line as well, but at this moment he was helpless to resist her allure, unknowing as she was.

With quiet treads he walked to stand beside the bed. Taite lay on her back, the bedcovers tangled around her hips. A tank top, dark against her pale skin, lay softly against her breasts, which rose and fell with her gentle breathing.

Her face was turned away from him, giving him a view of the strong tendons of her neck, the softness of her throat. A contrast as intriguing as the woman herself.

She sighed and shifted. Ryder pulled back his hand and curled his fingers into his palm, appalled that he had been reaching out to touch her. Good God. What was wrong with him? He'd gone without a woman too long, that's what. He'd turned into some kind of goddamned voyeur.

He backed out of the room and quietly pulled the door closed. When he turned, Declan stood in the open doorway of his room, arms crossed, one shoulder resting against the frame. With raised eyebrows, he asked, "Whatcha doin' there, Ry?" His voice was low, but Ryder caught the underlying tension in the soft tones.

Caught with his pants down. At least, that's how he felt. "Nothing," he muttered. Feeling ridiculous, like a teenager caught snogging with a girl, he shrugged and started down the hallway. "I didn't do anything."

"That's the only reason I didn't go in and give you a kick in the bollocks." When Ryder stopped and faced him, Declan tapped one finger against his ear. "Special Ops trainin'. I sleep light."

Ryder scowled. "Taite doesn't need to be protected from me." He paused, hoping against hope he wasn't lying. Clenching his jaw, he knew he couldn't rely on hope. The safest, *sanest* thing to do would be to get them off the island. "But it would be better if you left in the morning."

A muscle flexed in Declan's jaw. "Even with everythin' you know, you still want us to leave?" He straightened from his lounging position.

"You can take any books with you that you need." Ryder

steeled himself against the look of disbelief he saw on Declan's face. "But you can't stay here."

With that, he turned and went back down the stairs to his
room. Once he'd closed the door behind him, he leaned against
it with a sigh. God, what a mess. In order to keep his secret,
he was looking like an uncaring brute.

It couldn't be helped. Better to be thought a brute than to
prove himself one.

Chapter 6

The next morning, after a restless and sleepless night, Ryder walked into the kitchen, fully prepared to reiterate his demand that Declan and Taite leave. He was surprised to see only Taite sitting on the bench at the small table.

This morning she was dressed in a bright red T-shirt tucked into a worn pair of blue jeans. The shirt brought a strawberries and cream cast to her complexion, and his appetite for her sharpened.

He pulled out a chair and sat, trying to appear nonchalant, and concentrated on keeping his hands from shaking with need. Waiting until Cobb placed a steaming cup of coffee in front of him, he asked, "Where's Declan?"

"He left for St. Mary's just after dawn." Taite took a bite of toast and flipped a page of the book she had in front of her. "Said he was going to check with the boat rental places to make sure we haven't been followed."

Anger surged through him at Declan's delaying tactic. "Goddammit. He knew I wanted you out of here today."

"What?" She stared at him, her toast halfway to her mouth. "What do you mean? I thought we'd settled all that."

That was before he'd watched her sleep, before he'd realized how tenuous his control was where she was concerned. "I really can't spare any time, and I can't afford any more distractions." He took a gulp of coffee and tried to ignore the growing outrage in her eyes.

"Distractions? I'm running from a werewolf and you're worried about *distractions?*" She dropped her toast and pushed her plate forward. Scooting off the bench, she stood and planted her palms on her hips, glaring down at him. "You arrogant, uncaring, unfeeling son of a bitch."

She grabbed up the book, her grip so tight he could see her knuckles turning white. When she spoke again, her voice was thick with anger. "I am so sorry we've imposed upon you, Mr. Merrick. As soon as Declan gets back, you can be sure we'll be out of your hair. Then my werewolf will no longer be any concern of yours. Not, apparently, that it ever was."

Spinning, she nearly ran over Cobb in her rush to leave the kitchen. She muttered an apology and kept going, her sock-covered feet slipping on the hardwood floor.

The two men were silent for a moment. Cobb placed a large steak in a hot skillet. A loud sizzle preceded the mouth-watering aroma of the cooking meat. "She's running from a werewolf? A real one?"

"As opposed to a fake one?" Ryder asked, his tone dry. He grimaced. "Sorry." He pushed back his chair and got to his feet. Rubbing his nape, he paced to the back door and looked out over the garden. "Declan saw it, too, when it was in man-form. You know what that means."

"The werewolf is not one born, but one who's been bitten," Cobb answered. He clattered behind Ryder, the sound of eggs being stirred in a bowl. "They're the only ones who can take man-form."

"Don't remind me." Ryder scanned the forest beyond the garden, for once not feeling the peace he usually felt upon seeing the wildness of his home. All he could feel was an ever-increasing tightening in his gut.

And the sense of a noose tightening around his neck. He was damned if he did and damned if he didn't.

He sighed. "What do I do, Cobb?"

The other man chuckled. "This brings back fond memories, sir. You haven't asked for my advice in many years."

Ryder turned. The older man sounded wistful, and a small smile played on his lips. "I've asked for your advice plenty of times. Haven't I?"

Cobb shook his head. "No, sir. Not since you were a young man away at college. And once the Change happened, and then the situation with your ex-fiancée . . . Well, you've determined your own course since then."

From his tone, Ryder surmised it had been hurtful to Cobb to lose his role as advisor, though of course his loyal employee had said nothing. "So? What do you think I should do?"

"Only you can determine your path, sir." Cobb picked up Taite's plate and carried it to the sink. He gave a quick smile. "However," he went on before Ryder could respond, "since you asked, I have seen your interest in the young lady. I would recommend against sending her away."

"But you know what happened with Marika," Ryder muttered. He ran his hand through his hair in frustration. "I can't take the chance again."

"Take the chance that what? What are you afraid will happen?"

Ryder faced the windows again and stared unseeingly at the gardens beyond the house. All his life, he'd listened to his father lecture about how bad they were, that only evil could come from the wolf. His mother had never agreed, believing with all her heart that the evil was present only if the man started out that way, but Ryder figured his dad knew what he was talking about, since he was affected by the curse, too.

When Ryder was thirty, he'd met Marika Smythe-Parker, a shy, sweet young woman with blond hair and cornflower blue eyes. He'd fallen fast and he'd fallen hard. For the first time in his life, he'd believed he could be more than his beast. Marika had held him at arm's length, her beautiful face earnest as she told him she wanted to wait for marriage to have sex—just like the good Christian girl she'd been raised to be. And, like a fucking lunkhead, he'd fallen for it. He'd put a ring on her finger and dangled at the end of her line like a gasping fish taking its last breath.

He'd started to see the way she'd manipulated him with her wide eyes and soft touches, doling out kisses, letting him go so far but no farther, and had begun to wonder if he wasn't being played. Had begun to think she was more in love with his money than with him. She must have realized she was about to lose him, for she suddenly decided the time was right.

It was too near his Change, but he'd been denied for so long, he'd followed his cock's lead. And he'd lost control of his beast.

If he closed his eyes, he could see the look of horror on Marika's face as his beast broke free. His eyes had burned with the fire of bloodlust, his teeth elongated, aching to pierce flesh.

It could never happen again. "I'm afraid I'll lose control, like I did with Marika."

"She didn't love you." Cobb's voice was calm, unhurried. "Had she loved you, she would have accepted you, just as your mother accepted your father."

"I don't believe love conquers all," Ryder scoffed. "And neither do you." He turned and walked back to the table, sitting down as Cobb placed a plate with steak and eggs in front of him.

Ryder looked at the plate, seeing the blood from the rare meat running into the eggs. He knew most humans would find it revolting, but to his beast it was haute cuisine. The metamorphosis into the wolf used up a tremendous amount of energy, and the men in his family had found that if they ate a higher than normal amount of protein the few days before the Change, they were better able to make the transition.

Without another word, he dug into the eggs and had them eaten in three bites. He cut into the steak and forked a big, bloody piece into his mouth. Making short work of it, he had nearly finished the steak when the clang of the front door knocker reverberated through the foyer and down the hallway.

Cobb, busy cleaning the countertop, dropped his dishrag. "That's most likely young Robbie with this week's groceries. I'll be back shortly."

The little man left the room. Ryder forked up his last bite and carried his plate to the sink. He'd just rinsed it off when Cobb returned, followed by a dark-haired teenager. Ryder turned around and smiled in greeting. "Hello there, Robbie."

"Hullo, Mr. Merrick." The young man wheeled his small cart behind him. He started pulling paper sacks out of the cart, placing them on the counter.

"Young Master Robson was telling me he had news of happenings on the mainland," Cobb said.

When neither Robbie nor Cobb spoke, Ryder looked from one to the other. "Well? What's the news?" he prompted.

Robbie took a deep breath. "There's been a murder, Mr. Merrick. On the mainland, in Land's End. A murder!"

"What!" Ryder glanced at Cobb, who raised his eyebrows in surprise.

"Go on, Master Robson," Cobb said, busy putting away groceries.

Robbie's eyes widened, and he leaned on the counter. "It's unbelievable. A young woman was murdered. The news report said her time of death was somewhere around midnight last night." He looked at Ryder. "It was all over the news first thing," he said, as if they should already have heard about it.

"We haven't listened to the radio yet this morning." Ryder ignored the young man's expression of incredulity. "There *have* been murders in Cornwall before, Robbie."

"Aye, sir. And there will probably be more." He lowered his voice. "She was raped, too."

Ryder raised one eyebrow. He might not listen much to world news, but he knew rape wasn't that uncommon an event, either.

"And," Robbie went on, self-importance heavy in his voice, "they said she'd been bitten. Several times. They said parts of her were missing. Her boyfriend is what they call a 'person of interest.'"

Cobb loudly cleared his throat. "All right, young sir, that's quite enough." Cobb shooed the boy out of the kitchen. Ryder could hear him muttering all the way to the front door, telling the young man he needed an edit button.

After a few minutes, Cobb walked back into the kitchen. "Stupid boy," he murmured, shaking his head. "Why he felt it important to share that kind of grizzly news is beyond me."

"You did ask," Ryder reminded him.

"Yes, well, I like to hear news from outside this rock every now and again."

Ryder leaned against the butcher's block. His employee had never complained about the isolation, but after so many years it had to bother him. Ryder was ashamed he'd never thought about it before. "Cobb . . . I'm sorry. I hadn't thought—"

"No, no, sir. Please." Cobb placed his hand briefly on Ryder's shoulder, then resumed his task of putting groceries away. Opening the refrigerator, he stacked several steaks on a shelf. As he put milk and eggs inside, he went on. "I have enjoyed—and continue to enjoy—my time with you. I'm doing what I'm best at."

Ryder's lips twitched, but he fought back the threatening grin. He had a feeling he was about to be favored with one of the little man's Cobbisms. "And that is?"

"Anticipating someone's needs. In this case, yours. If you'll pardon my lack of humility, I am an exceptional employee."

This was said as a simple statement of fact, without any braggadocio at all.

"Yes, you are." Ryder clapped one hand on the other man's shoulder. "And I don't say it enough, but I appreciate you."

Cobb smiled. "I know you do, sir." He patted the hand still on his shoulder. "And now you have a decision to make." When Ryder looked at him with raised brows, the other man nodded toward the door. "Do they stay, or leave?"

Ryder sighed. He didn't know, dammit. He just didn't know. But he couldn't let Taite continue to think he was a heartless jerk. Dropping his hand from Cobb's shoulder, he turned and walked out of the kitchen.

Going down the hallway and into the foyer, he tried to formulate what he would say to her. The words wouldn't come. He scowled. He was a writer, for God's sake. He should be able to come up with *something*.

He paused at the doorway to the parlor. Taite sat cross-legged on the sofa with a book open on her lap, a slight frown of concentration on her face. "Declan hasn't made it back yet?" he asked, his voice husky.

"Nope." Not looking up from the book, she scribbled something on a small notepad on one knee, then flipped the page and continued to read.

"Hmm." He glanced at his watch. If Declan had left just after sunrise, he'd been gone three hours. What the hell could be taking him so long? "What was he doing?"

"I told you. He's checking to make sure the werewolf hasn't found us yet." Her voice was polite, cool. As unwelcoming as he'd been.

"Look, Ms. Gibson . . . Taite." He sat next to her, angling his body so that their knees touched. When she shifted slightly, pulling back from him, he wasn't surprised. What *did* surprise him was the sense of hurt he felt at the movement. But it was no more than he deserved. "I know I've

been . . . less than hospitable," he went on. "I'd like to apol-
ogize."

She did look at him then, her gaze solemn. She sighed and
rubbed her fingers across her forehead. "Mr. Merrick—"

"Ryder. Please." He stretched his arm along the back of
the sofa and leaned in toward her, just slightly, to gauge her
reaction. She stayed put, though her pupils dilated and her
lips parted.

After a moment, she broke his gaze and looked down at
the book, one hand coming up to push a thick strand of hair
behind her ear. "Ryder." Her voice was huskier than it had
been.

His name on her lips sizzled like lightning through him. He
wanted nothing more than to take her in his arms and protect her from the big bad wolf she was so afraid of.

But then who would protect her from *him?*

Meeting his gaze once more, she said, "I understand, really
I do. We've descended upon you without notice and, from
what I understand, against your wishes. And then we tell you
this incredible story. . . ." She sighed and played with her
hair, twirling a strand around and around her index finger.

"Still, it's no excuse for my poor behavior." He took her
hand in his, and they both went still. He heard her breath
catch and felt the thrumming of her pulse under his fingers.
Rubbing his thumb over the back of her hand, he tried to remember what he'd been about to say.

She leaned forward, her gaze fastened on his mouth, and
all thought fled his mind like water sliding down a drain. He
couldn't ignore his need any longer. He had to get a taste of
her. Setting his lips on hers, gently, Ryder sipped at her sweet-
ness, taking her sigh into his mouth and returning his own.

When she moaned, he pulled her fully into his arms and
leaned back, drawing her over top of him. Dimly he heard
the thud of the book as it fell to the floor and the flutter of

paper as the notepad followed it, but his entire focus remained on the woman in his embrace.

Ryder slid his tongue over her bottom lip then sucked on it, eliciting another moan from her. He nipped her lightly and then slanted his mouth over hers once more.

Her softness settled over his erection and, when she shimmied against him, he groaned and moved his hands to her hips to hold her in place. God, she felt so good, so right. Forcing himself to slow down, he moved his lips to her jaw, then down her throat to the curve where her neck met her shoulder. Sliding his mouth over her skin, he rested his lips against the pulse pounding there.

Well, he thought with self-deprecating humor, *this sort of behavior is certainly what one should expect from a host.* But then the heat and smell of her drew his mind back to more carnal thoughts.

Life thrummed beneath his tongue. Lust roared through him, tightening his body all over, drawing his beast closer to the surface. With a low growl, he twisted, sliding her under him, rocking his erection against the cleft of her body.

"Ryder." Her voice was a rasp in his ear, her hands gripping his shoulders with fierceness.

He took her mouth again, nipping and licking and sucking until she cried out and clasped his head, holding his face to hers. Her tongue twisted around his, surging into his mouth when he retreated. He sucked on it, drawing her deeper, making them both groan.

Her nipples pressed like hard diamonds against his chest, branding him through their layers of clothing. His entire body was taut, something dark and primal inside him urging him to strip her naked and mount her then and there. Make her his. Savage possessiveness surged through his blood. His hands tightened, holding her still, and he crushed his mouth to hers, needing—demanding—a response.

Taite was springtime in his hands—fresh and light, bringing him such a sense of renewal he felt it deep in his bones.

She was everything he wasn't—soft, giving. Not wanting to scare her with his passion, to lose her before they'd even begun, he tempered his response, gentled his touch.

Drawing slowly back, he rested his forehead against hers. "I've wanted to do that from the moment you walked through my front door. What you do to me . . ."

"Is no more than what you do to me." She rolled her forehead back and forth on his then turned her face to one side. "I can't do this."

"Can't do what?" When she pushed at his shoulders, trying to lever him off her, he settled his weight more completely on top of her. "Can't do what?" he asked again.

She made a vague gesture with her hand, indicating him, then her. "This." She pushed at him again, frowning when he wouldn't budge. "I've got enough trouble without adding to it."

Somehow, hearing her put his own feelings into words irritated him. "So, you think I'm trouble?"

Giving him a look that suggested not only was he trouble but he was also a bit on the slow side, she shoved against his chest. This time he moved, sitting in the place where she'd been.

She bent over and retrieved the book and notepad. He heard her deep breath as she sat up, saw the trembling in her hands. Her arousal was a sweet musk in his nostrils, and he started to reach for her.

One slender hand came up, palm outward, warding him off. "Don't." She fisted her hand and let it fall to her thigh. "Just . . . don't. Not now."

Ryder sat back and ran his hand through his hair. She was right. Of course she was right. He had to share what knowledge he could and then send them on their way. No matter how much he wanted to lose himself in her sweet warmth, it wasn't meant to be.

He drew in a steadying breath and pulled at his jeans, trying to relieve the pressure on his erection.

She followed the movement of his hands and blushed. "I . . . I, uh . . ." The muscles of her throat moved with her hard swallow. "Sorry," she finished softly.

"I don't suppose you'd care to help me with it." He grinned as her eyes widened. "I'm not serious, love."

"It's not funny." She stared at the book resting on her thighs.

He grimaced and adjusted his cock again. "Do you see me laughing?" When her blush deepened, he sighed. "I'm sorry, Taite. It's been a while since I've . . . Well, I guess I've forgotten how to act properly around a woman. I don't usually, ah, attack like this." Mainly because he'd kept himself isolated.

Yet because she intrigued him, he wasn't ready to let her disappear from his life just yet. Maybe, just this once, he'd follow through on his emotions. He bit back a sigh. He really *had* been bored with his life if he was this willing to let someone break the monotony of his isolation. A few days wouldn't matter one way or the other.

At least, that's what he tried to convince himself of.

He was an idiot. An idiot who had only himself to blame for his current discomfort.

Taite stared at him, trying to keep her gaze off his thick erection, cursing to herself when she kept glancing down. God, this was just not like her. She'd had that instant attraction to a man before, but she'd never been ready to have sex within a few seconds of kissing him.

What was it about *this* man? It was more than his dark good looks, more than the sadness he wore around him like a cloak. It certainly wasn't his personality—so far she'd seen him irritated, angry, and slightly more angry.

And aroused.

She fought back a shiver. *Don't go there,* she warned herself. *You don't have time and, like Grandma always lectured, you shouldn't borrow trouble.*

She had werewolf problems. That's what she should be focusing on, not how hard and thick Ryder's cock felt pressed against her.

"I told you I can't do this right now," she muttered. Getting to her feet, she put the book on the sofa. She needed to clear her head, put some space between her and Ryder so she could concentrate on the trouble at hand. And the best way she knew to deal with stress was exercise. "I'm going for a walk."

Ryder stood, too, and looked like he was about to say something.

She held up her hand, chagrined to see it shook. Fisting it, she dropped it to her side. "I . . . I have to go." Turning, she walked out of the room at a fast clip. By the time she reached the stairs, she was running. She climbed the stairs, trying to keep her mind blank.

She knew she needed to be researching her problem, but right now all she could think about was knocking Ryder to the floor and boffing his brains out. She felt the heat of his gaze on her and knew he'd come into the foyer and stood there, watching her run away from him. It took all her strength to keep from turning around and following through on her desire.

But she had to remember why she was here. She couldn't just say to hell with the consequences and forget about the werewolf. As much as she wanted to take a vacation from reality for a while, she couldn't.

That kiss had been soft, gentle, not one of domination or uncontrolled passion. It had held a flavor of uncertainty that had fired her desire even more than the wildest kiss would have. She'd started to imagine him visiting that soft touch all over her body and she'd gotten wet. Ready.

She needed to work off her frustrated energy. Pausing on the landing, she glanced down at the foyer where Ryder still stood. His dark hair fell over his forehead, his strong hands clenched into fists at his sides as if he fought his own urges.

Holy Hannah. Was she ever in trouble.

* * *

Ryder walked into his study and kicked the door closed behind him. Standing behind his desk, he tapped his fingers on the wood surface, then touched them to his mouth. He could still feel the touch of Taite's soft lips, her tongue twining with wet heat around his.

The kiss played through his mind, again and again. Her sweet scent and eager response clung to him. Desire thrummed through him and his cock pulsed in response, hard. Demanding.

Turning, he drew the curtains over the French doors, blocking out light from outside and, more importantly, giving himself some privacy. He then walked to the study door and flipped the lock. What he was about to do was best done in solitude. The last thing he wanted was for Declan or Cobb—or, God forbid, Taite—to walk in on him.

Ryder sat on the leather sofa and unzipped his pants. His thick cock, the ruddy tip already pushing above the waist of his briefs, throbbed demandingly for release. He pushed his underwear down, hooking it under his tight balls, and gripped his cock in his fist.

His hand slid up once, twice, then he ran it from the tip to the base, a quick brush. Imagined it was Taite touching him, light, soft hands moving slowly against his hard, pulsing shaft. With a sigh, he acknowledged he didn't need it slow and gentle. He needed it hard and fast.

He used some spit for lubrication and tightened his grip, gritting his teeth as pleasure streaked through him. Bringing up his left hand, he palmed the head of his cock, rubbing around and over the slitted tip. Then his fingers moved down to cup and finger his balls.

Painful need engorged his shaft to even greater proportions. He moaned, his hips pumping as he jacked harder. With each stroke of his hand he remembered how Taite tasted, smelled, felt. He pictured her as she would look bent over in front of him, her shapely ass thrust up for his possession, her pussy wet and swollen and inviting.

His hips jerked rhythmically. He drove his cock deep into his fist and bit his lip to hold back his shout as his release spewed from him.

It wasn't enough. He rolled his head against the back of the sofa. He needed to be buried inside Taite. But he couldn't. Not now.

He'd help where he could while still protecting his heart. And his secrets.

Good God. He was in trouble.

Chapter 7

The admirer leaned back in his chair and stared at the computer screen. His travel plans were confirmed. He would have preferred to be waiting for Taite on that little island, but matters on the mainland had demanded his attention first.

He allowed his lips to curl upward. He had moved his pawns into place. His smile widened. He would let them think they had control of the game for now—only when he revealed himself and his benefactor would they realize to what extent they had been manipulated. Only he knew, for now, that they didn't make a move without him. But soon enough they would understand just how cunning, how *superior,* he was.

Once things were lined up the way he'd planned—once he revealed himself for the powerful creature he was—he would make Taite understand one more thing.

She belonged to him. Only him.

Forever.

Chapter 8

Declan pulled back the throttle and eased the small rental boat up to the jetty on Phelan's Keep. After shutting off the engine, he jumped onto the wooden dock and secured the boat. Then he set off at an easy pace up the long, winding path that led to the house high up on the cliff.

His trip to St. Mary's had been successful on one front and highly unsuccessful on another. According to the rental places, no strangers had rented a boat recently. Of course, that assumed the bastard—whoever he was—would actually be honest rather than just take what he wanted. But Declan was confident someone would have told him if one of their boats had been stolen.

On the other hand, his brief—disappointingly brief—meeting with Pelicia had gone . . . Well, he'd like to say it had gone badly, because that would mean he'd at least been able to talk with her. But the truth was it hadn't gone at all. She'd seen him coming, her face had tightened, and he'd practically heard the hardening of her heart.

A couple of superficial pleasantries later and he'd found himself alone in the small foyer of the bed and breakfast she owned. That was when he'd decided a strategic retreat was called for while he planned another offensive.

Reaching the top of the cliff, he paused for a moment and gazed out over the ocean. The sun was directly overhead, telling him it was lunchtime. He could see dark clouds in the distance, which meant the gale warning he'd heard earlier was on the money. He'd go in and see what kind of progress Taite had made and help her continue the research.

And have another go at Ry.

He'd get his friend to tell him what was going on if he had to beat it out of him. And the way Declan felt, giving someone a solid thrashing would do wonders for his mood. He turned and walked the rest of the way to the house. Once inside, he started toward Ryder's closed study door.

"Excuse me, Mr. O'Connell." Cobb walked from the back of the house, a laundry basket full of folded towels in his hands. "When the door is closed, Mr. Merrick is not to be disturbed."

"Too late," Declan muttered. He glanced into the parlor and saw the reference books, but the room was empty of people. "Where's Taite?"

"Ms. Gibson went for a walk about"—Cobb twisted his left wrist to glance at his watch—"ten minutes ago." He started up the stairs.

"Cobb, wait." Declan walked forward, stopping when the older man paused and looked at him over one shoulder. "I . . ." He trailed off. What could he say? *I didn't mean to break your daughter's heart. Help me fix it?* He blew out a sigh. "Never mind."

Cobb gave a slight nod and continued up the stairs. Declan watched him go, then started up the stairs himself. He'd change into his running clothes and go find Taite. Maybe a run would clear his head and help him formulate a plan to get back his girl.

Twenty minutes later, he reached the first cove and found Taite picking her way over logs and rocks. He watched her for a few moments, frowning when she stopped and bent, poking at a pile of rocks. "What the hell are you doin'?"

She gasped and whirled to face him. "Don't *do* that!"

"Do what?" He started toward her, and she moved to meet him.

"Sneak up on me." She reached him and looked around the cove, hugging her arms around her middle. "I have that creepy feeling like I'm being watched, and it's starting to freak me out." She moved around him. As she started back toward the path, he followed.

"I'm fairly certain the werewolf's not here yet, Taite. Let's worry when we have to, all right?" Declan put his arm around her shoulder and squeezed. Glancing back at the cove, he asked, "What were you doin'?"

She slid one arm around his waist and looked over her shoulder, then looked at him. "I was just seeing if there was any interesting flotsam."

He gave her a one-armed hug. "It's hard to tell what you might find on these islands. This area had quite the reputation for bein' a smugglers' haven." He glanced around the cove. Wanting to take her mind off things, for a while at least, he dropped his voice, affecting the Hollywood speech of a pirate. "Aye, matey. I should think there's pirate booty in some of the caves 'round here. Aargh."

"You're a nut." Taite smiled at him, then grimaced and looked around nervously. "There are caves?"

"Aye. What's wrong?"

She shrugged and got the look she did whenever she was trying to appear tough but not feeling it. "I just don't like the dark very much."

"Well, then, stay out of the caves."

When she punched him lightly in the arm, he grinned and dropped one eyelid in a slow wink.

"You're such a smartass," she murmured. "I don't know why I put up with you sometimes."

His grin widened, and he laughed. "Sure you do, darlin'. You put up with me 'cause you love me."

She smiled and laid a hand on his arm. "I do, you know."

"Me, too." He wrapped his arms around her and pulled her close for a hug. That she clung to him, hard, told him more than words ever could. She was scared, her brave front held onto with a fragile thread of control.

Well, the one thing he could do for her was give her support as long as she needed it. He'd stand here until she decided she'd had enough.

Taite finally relaxed her hold, and he released her. She drew in a deep breath and blew it out from between her lips. "I think I'm going to finish my walk. Coming?"

Declan shook his head. "I'm gonna poke 'round here a bit." He needed something to take his mind off Pel.

Taite glanced down at the pedometer at her waist. "Well, I still have at least another two thousand steps to take before I can stop." She tightened her arm around his waist and then moved away from him. "So I'll see you back at the house."

"Keep an eye on those clouds." He pointed toward the western horizon. "We've a gale alert. Besides, aren't you takin' that a bit too far?" he asked, nodding toward the pedometer. "You're rather obsessive with the whole thing."

She raised her brows. "You've got a lot of room to talk, Mister I'm-going-for-a-run-so-I-can-think." When he laughed, she stuck her tongue out at him and walked away.

Declan watched her until she was out of sight then turned toward the cove. As he walked back to where Taite had been poking around, he scanned the ground. There was nothing here. Disappointing. He really wanted something to do—this waiting around was going to make him crazed.

Taite came across a second cove, one that looked much like the first one. She stopped for a few minutes to catch her breath, and checked her pedometer. Still over a thousand steps to go to meet her goal. At this rate she'd have to walk the entire island.

Well, that was okay by her. Going back to the house meant

going back to where Ryder was, and she wasn't sure she was ready for that. Not with her body still humming with need. When she'd been horsing around with Declan, she'd been able to push it to the back of her mind, but now . . . Now, it commandeered her thoughts to the point she wished she'd had time to pack her battery-operated boyfriend. And extra batteries.

She started back up again, glad to be out in the fresh air and still amazed at the temperate climate for this time of year. Before they'd left, Declan had told her she wouldn't need heavy clothing, but she hadn't really believed him.

Yet here she was, on an island off the coast of Cornwall in mid-November, wearing jeans, a T-shirt, and a light jacket. Last night she'd gotten the best night's sleep she'd had in weeks, and the salty sea air refreshed her further.

Taite rounded a bend and came to another cove. This one was completely in shadows cast by the trees. Even with the increasing wind, it felt . . . quiet. Calm.

A balm to her tired and battered soul.

She continued to walk, soon making her way toward the center of the island. Here she found a grassy clearing, surrounded by woods on each side. The wild, clean beauty spread out before her like a visual banquet. With every step she took, serenity returned, until she finally just had to stop and close her eyes.

The wind blew through her hair, a strong breeze with the tang of the sea. Cries of birds drifted in from the ocean. Taite smiled. God, this was so incredible. She could stay here forever.

A scent of sage wafted through the air and she opened her eyes. Drawing in a deep breath, she held it for a moment, then exhaled and began walking around the clearing, looking for the source of the smell.

As she reached the portion of the clearing farthest from the path she used to get there, the aroma became stronger. She gazed at the ground, searching for a plant that looked enough like sage to perhaps have the same smell. But she found nothing, not even when she bent over to sniff a few plants.

Just as she turned to head back toward the path, the undergrowth behind her rustled. She stiffened and jumped around, expecting to see a mouse or squirrel. When the rustle sounded again, she realized it was deeper into the undergrowth, in the woods. Backing up a few steps, she searched the area.

A crackle of twigs sent her back even farther. Turning, she started to run. Expecting to hear pounding footsteps following her, she ran until she reached the opposite edge of the clearing. When the chase failed to occur, she faltered, then stopped.

Turning around, she gulped for air and stared at the area from which the rustling had come. Nothing stirred. It seemed as if even the air had quieted. "Declan? If that's you, it's not funny."

There was no response.

"I so do not need this right now." Taite gave one last look, then spun around and started down the path. With her elbows bent, she pumped her arms and got into the fast gait of a power walker.

"There's nothing there," she muttered. "There's nothing there." When she reached the area where the path narrowed and became rockier, she was forced to slow down. She tried to keep her breathing slow and steady so she could hear the sounds around her.

Once she'd passed the first cove, she couldn't resist looking over her shoulder. Though nothing moved except the leaves on the upper branches of the trees, that feeling of being watched was back in full force. And when she heard the sharp crunch of twigs snapping, Taite decided enough was enough.

Whirling around, she took off at a run. She bounded over the rocky path and past the middle cove with her surroundings a blur. At the last cove, she slowed enough to glance around for Declan but, once she determined he wasn't in view, she picked up speed again.

God. What if Declan was wrong? What if they *had* been followed? She wasn't even close to being able to defend herself and, now, being here, she'd placed two more people in jeopardy.

By the time she went through the garden and reached the back of the house, she was completely out of breath and had worked herself into a frenetic near-hysteria. She grabbed the doorknob, almost sobbing with frustration when she had trouble opening it. Finally she managed and entered the house, slamming the door and locking it behind her.

She leaned against it, shaking, trying to regain control. Never before had she felt this level of fear and unease. She wasn't handling this situation with her normal professional indifference, because now it was personal.

She should've been able to ferret the information from Ryder by now. Instead, when he'd refused to help, she'd closed down, accepting his decision without much of a fight.

That wasn't like her, dammit. She never gave up.

Ever.

She wasn't known at the office as Taite the Terrier for nothing.

Closing her eyes, she drew in a deep breath and held it, feeling her pulse pounding in her neck. She exhaled noisily.

"Taite?"

She jumped and opened her eyes.

Ryder stood a few feet away, a coffee cup in one big hand, a question in his blue eyes. "Are you all right?" he asked, continuing to the counter. He set the cup in the sink and then walked closer to her.

He wore black jeans and a deep burgundy long-sleeved shirt with the sleeves rolled up over brawny forearms. The top two buttons were undone, crisp dark hair curling in the opening.

Trying to catch her breath and trying hard to tough it out, Taite told herself it was her imagination. She had a hard time believing it. As much as she might like to have a shoulder to lean on, she waved him off.

"What's wrong?" He stopped in front of her and placed his hands lightly on her shoulders. "What happened?"

She shook her head. "It was nothing. Probably some damned bunny."

One dark brow rose. "Somehow I don't see you as the type who falls to pieces over a rabbit."

Well, thank you for that. "It's just . . ."

When she didn't go on, he pulled her into his arms and held her in a loose hug. It felt so good she couldn't do anything else except wrap her arms around his waist and rest her cheek against his chest.

"Declan told me no one's rented any boats from St. Mary's, so the chances that your . . . werewolf has caught up to you are slim." He brought one hand up and palmed the back of her head, then stroked it down her hair.

Taite sighed. "Thanks for not saying 'alleged' werewolf," she murmured and closed her eyes. "Even though I know you were probably thinking it."

It felt so good to just stand there, held in his embrace, the heat of his big frame permeating her body. For the moment, she didn't feel the need to appear strong and independent. For the moment, she wanted to enjoy being held by another human being.

"But Declan can't be sure," she said. "What if he stole a boat, or he went to Tresco or one of the other islands and took a boat from there? What if he chartered a helicopter? Did Declan check that?"

"We would've heard a helicopter."

She noticed he didn't say anything about renting a boat from one of the other islands. Granted, St. Mary's was the largest and closest and, therefore, the most logical choice, but still . . . Her mind raced, and even as she said the words she knew she was being silly, but she couldn't help it. "What if he gets scuba gear and swims here? We wouldn't know!"

"Let's worry about him when the time is right, okay? For right now, just know that Declan and I won't let him hurt you, honey." Ryder tightened his arms, and she felt his lips on the top of her head.

Her breath quickened at the endearment and the touch. But she reminded herself that being with him was a bad idea and pushed him away. "I've got to get back to work." She sidled around him. "So many books, so little time."

"Taite . . ."

She stopped in the doorway and turned back at him. She shook her head. "You can't have it both ways, Ryder. I came here for a reason and, as tempting as you are, sex wasn't it." She brushed hair away from her cheek. "Unless you're ready now to tell me something about werewolves?"

Ryder knew he needed to give her something. But carefully. "According to what I've read, there's no way to ward off a werewolf like you would, say, a vampire with garlic or crucifixes." He gave a shrug. "The only thing you can do is kill them."

She frowned. "I don't necessarily want to kill it. I just want it to leave me alone."

"Someone inflicted with lycanthropy—allegedly," he stressed, "descends completely into bloodlust when the moon is full. The only remedy is death." When she shook her head, he asked, "Are you saying you wouldn't be able to kill it if that's what it came down to?"

Her frown deepened. "I don't want it to get close enough so that's the only option I'm left with." She heaved a sigh. "Isn't there a spell or herbs or something I can use to, I don't know, put some sort of invisible shield around myself?"

"You really don't know anything about this, do you?"

Her shoulders slumped. "Nope. Not a bit." When she looked at him, she appeared resigned. Defeated.

He didn't like that look at all.

And that it bothered him after such a short amount of time disturbed him even more.

"So how does one go about killing a werewolf? One of the books had something about silver."

Ryder chose his words carefully. "According to legend, werewolves have the ability to heal themselves at an incredible rate. Going through a shift—changing from man to wolf or vice versa—accelerates the process." He moved to the kitchen counter and leaned his hip against it. "It's said that silver or a derivative thereof, like silver nitrate, for example, in the bloodstream will kill them. Something about silver keeps the lycan from regenerating, and so they would die from a severe enough wound."

"So the book was right. A silver bullet would do the trick, then."

"Only if you managed to lodge it in the creature." He folded his arms across his chest. "If the bullet passes through the body, only a miniscule amount of silver would remain in the wound tract, and the werewolf would be able to heal that injury."

Taite's eyebrows rose. "Even if it went through its heart?"

"That would certainly weaken the werewolf, but not kill it. But it would give you time to decapitate it."

Her nose crinkled. "Ew. I'm not sure I could do that." Her chin dipped. "Would it really be necessary?"

"Even a werewolf can't recover from having its head chopped off," he said wryly.

"But . . ." She shook her head. "Where do they come from to begin with? How does someone become a werewolf? Or can they? I mean, for all I know, werewolves could just be another species and you're either born one or not. That one book said as much."

This conversation needed to end, and end now. *You have work to do*, he reminded himself, though he knew that wasn't the reason he needed to redirect her. "Most werewolves have been bitten by a werewolf and that's how the . . . disease is transmitted."

"Okay. But then who was the first werewolf? He couldn't have been bitten, so how did it get started?"

"I really can't say." Ryder pushed away from the counter and walked toward her, intending to go to his study.

She didn't move out of his way. "Can't say? Or won't?" Those intelligent eyes stared at him, trying to see past his carefully constructed façade.

"Pick one." Even knowing he was being an ass, he went on in a cool and disinterested tone. "If you need more information, any of the books you've already selected will do."

A blush darkened her cheeks. "Like I've said before, I'm sorry we've interrupted your routine. But I have to be able to kill a werewolf, because it looks like that's the only way to stop it." She turned and started down the hallway, her derrière swaying with her quick strides.

Immediately his arousal returned. Ryder stomped toward his study while she entered the parlor. God, his cock was like a third leg, hard and throbbing against his thigh. Once again, he'd have to take matters into his own hand before he'd have a hope of getting any work done.

He glanced toward the parlor and saw her sitting on the settee, legs curled under her, a notepad on one thigh and a book in her hand. A muscle in his jaw flexed as he ground his teeth. He understood her hesitancy to get involved—he had the same goddamned reluctance himself—but it didn't mean he had to like it.

If they could forget themselves and allow their desire to control them, they'd both probably be a lot happier. They'd be a hell of a lot more satisfied, at any rate.

As he watched, she closed her eyes and leaned her head on the back of the settee. The creamy skin of her throat moved, and he had the urge to put his mouth on the softness of her neck, his hands on the sweet curves of her body.

She turned her head toward the foyer and opened her eyes. Seeing him standing there, watching her, she flushed and her tongue slid over her lips, leaving them shiny. When he took a reflexive step forward, she jerked upright and looked down at her book.

Ryder drew in a quick breath and released it, and turned toward his study. Just as he started around his desk, Taite came to the doorway.

"I need another book," she said. "Do you have *Good Werewolves Gone Bad*? It was referenced in one of the other books."

"Top shelf." He motioned toward the bookshelves.

Her gaze flicked over him, lingering on his erection. With a soft sound, she looked away and went over to the bookcase.

Ryder reached down and cupped his erection and tried to unobtrusively adjust it under his now too-tight jeans. What was it about this woman that he had such an immediate reaction to her? He had to figure it out before she drove him 'round the bend.

She looked up then and caught him with his hand on his cock. Even though her blush returned, one eyebrow rose and she pursed her lips. "You know, you seem to do that more than any man I've ever known. You should see a doctor."

Sass. Through her embarrassment, she was sassing him. He grinned. Yet another layer of her personality he was seeing, and it strengthened his attraction to her even more.

He'd always loved a woman who was sassy.

"Yes, well, you do seem to have a certain effect on me, Taite." Ryder straightened and walked slowly over to her. He reached out to take the book she held, and she tightened her grip. They played tug-of-war with it for a few seconds and then, with a slight jerk, he got it away from her and set it on the counter.

He put his arms around her, loosely clasping his hands at the small of her back. Looking down, he traced the freckles on her nose with his gaze, finally coming to rest on her full lips before moving back up.

Her gaze met his, brown eyes searching, hesitant yet soft with promise. "Ryder . . ." She drew in a deep breath. Her hands came up to rest on his shirtfront, and she stroked her thumbs back and forth just above his nipples. Her light touch stoked the fire of his arousal, making his cock twitch with need.

"This isn't a good idea." She wet her lips, tempting him with their moist surface.

"Probably not." He drew her closer and covered her mouth with his.

Her lips parted for the thrust of his tongue. She canted her hips and pressed into him, pushing against his erection. What he had meant to be a gentle kiss quickly turned to one of rough hunger. Ryder groaned and cupped his hands around her head, the tips of his fingers resting against her thick braid. Her hair was like silk, and it made him wonder about the rest of her, if she'd be this damned soft all over. Tilting her head, he slid his tongue along the seam of her mouth.

She made a low, eager sound, her hands sliding around to clutch at his back.

This is insane, he told himself, even as he held her head still and deepened the kiss. Her mouth was sweet and moist, her tongue stroking over his.

He rocked against her, pumping his erection against her softness, wanting her touch in the most intimate of places. When he finally came up for air, he sighed and leaned over until he could rest his forehead against hers. "What is this . . . this *thing* between us, Taite? Why am I so drawn to you?"

Her sigh drifted over his lips. "Because you've been alone a long time, and you're horny."

A bark of laughter escaped him. "That's true enough," he agreed, rolling his forehead back and forth. He dragged in a breath, drawing her sweet honeysuckle and vanilla scent deep into his lungs. "But there's more to it. You make me want to tell you—"

"There you are." Declan's voice came from the doorway, and they broke apart. He cocked an eyebrow. "Sorry. Am I interruptin' somethin'?" His lips twitched as he crossed his arms.

"Yes," Ryder muttered at the same time that Taite said, "No!" and moved away from him.

Ryder scowled and went to the sofa, sitting down and propping his ankle over his knee. When Declan looked pointedly at his erection, Ryder's scowl deepened, and he dragged a pillow onto his lap.

"Uh-huh." After looking from one to the other, Declan moved farther into the room.

Chapter 9

Declan walked to the French doors behind Ryder's desk and peered out. "Well, looks like we're in for a rough ride."

Taite walked over and stood next to him. When she saw the dark gray clouds rolling in over the ocean, she gave a low whistle. "Wow. Those came in fast."

Ryder joined them at the French doors. When he caught sight of the clouds, he frowned. "Damn. I didn't know we were due a gale. That looks to be a big one."

"Gale?" Taite looked at him, then at Declan. "Is that like a hurricane?"

"Landlubber," Declan teased, grinning when she elbowed him lightly in the ribs.

"Hurricanes have stronger winds than gales," Ryder said. He frowned at Declan, looking displeased with the easy banter between him and Taite. "But gale force winds can be as high as ninety kilometers an hour." He turned away and walked back toward the sofa.

She scowled. "That doesn't tell me anything. How fast is that in miles per hour?"

Declan shook his head. "You Americans really need to get with the times. The rest of the world uses metric and you just keep goin' on your merry way usin' a sub-standard measurin' system."

When she threatened him with her elbow again, he laughed and protected his side with his arm, ducking away from her. "It's somewhere over fifty miles an hour. I don't know the exact conversion." He sobered and lifted his chin, motioning to the credenza behind her. His gaze darted to Ryder then, in a hushed voice, he said to Taite, "Take a look at that."

She turned and noticed two thick journals lying on the edge of the credenza. The book on the bottom had dark green binding, the one on top a deep burgundy. The uppermost journal had the same motif as the crest in the foyer—a snarling wolf, his massive paw planted on a snake. In beautiful hand-written script it read *Beware of the wolf*.

At the upper edge of the journal rested an old photograph. She reached out and picked it up. Two small boys stood side by side, one dark-haired and somber, the other with lighter hair and a crooked grin. The dark-haired boy was Ryder—she could see the resemblance to the man in the young features. The smaller boy looked familiar to her, but she couldn't place him. Though, how could he be? She'd never been here before, and up until now Declan had been the only non-American she'd ever met.

"This is you?" she asked, flipping the photo over to show Ryder.

He nodded. "Me and my cousin Miles. He left when he was nineteen."

A dark note in his voice made her raise her eyebrows. There was a story here, but the expression on his face told her it was a painful one. She didn't pursue it. Instead, she reached out and stroked one finger over the uppermost journal.

Before she could do anything more, Ryder was at her side, snatching both journals away and holding them in the crook of one arm. "These are private." Flags of color streaked his high cheekbones. "I'll just put them in the basement for safekeeping." His gaze met hers, apology and something else in the depths of his eyes, something like . . .

Regret.

Without another word, he strode from the room.

Taite looked at Declan.

He shrugged. "Ryder's dad was always lookin' at his grand-father's, Ryder's great-grandfather's journal—the green one—and writin' in his own. Ryder would never let me see either of them, but I suspect that a lot of Ryder's early research came right from those books."

She frowned. "His research?" Understanding dawned. "On werewolves, you mean?" She shook her head and sighed, feeling—not for the first time—completely overwhelmed by the whole thing.

Declan pulled her into his arms and rubbed his hands up and down her back. "You're not in this alone, darlin'. You've got me. And Ryder."

"Oh, yeah. Ryder." Taite heaved another sigh and pulled away from him. She walked over to the bookcase. Planting her hands on the counter, she leaned over, her head bowed. "This is so not a good idea."

"He's a good man, Taite, if a bit stubborn. But I doubt that's your problem with him, is it?" Declan walked over to her and took her by the shoulders, turning her gently to face him.

Her gaze searched his. "I have a werewolf after me, Declan, and I don't know how to stop it." She shrugged his hands off and started pacing. "Well, other than shooting it with a silver bullet and, wouldn't you know, I left all of mine at home. Damn."

He grinned at her dry wit.

She stopped and faced him. "I don't have time to be dis-tracted with . . . with *sex*."

"I think maybe sex is just what you need right now," he said and turned toward the bookshelves. "To take your mind off things for a while." A slow smile lifted his lips. "You should go after him."

"Go after . . . But—"

"Go. Now. Before he comes back upstairs." He tilted his

head toward the door. "Go on. Maybe you can find out what's in those journals."

Maybe she'd do just that. Taite walked down the hallway to the left of the foyer. She'd only been down the right side to the kitchen—she hadn't been down this way yet, to Ryder's bedroom. The open door at the end of the hallway piqued her curiosity, and she went all the way down until she stood in the doorway.

A king-sized four-poster sat squarely in the center of the room. Matching end tables framed the head of the bed, and two large dressers stood side by side along the wall opposite the foot of the large bed.

The room was decorated in hunter green and burgundy. Very much a man's room. On one side of a set of French doors was a plaid love seat covered with plump pillows, balanced by an antique rolltop desk on the other side.

Her gaze drifted back to the bed, and a flush of heat spiraled up from deep inside. Even though the bed was neatly made—no doubt by the remarkable Cobb—she had no trouble picturing Ryder sprawled over its surface.

Ryder, naked and aroused, waiting for . . . her.

The flush became a slow burn. Liquid heat slid from her core to lie slickly along the soft folds of her sex. She rubbed her thighs together to try to alleviate the growing ache. She clenched her hands and, with a last, wistful look at the bed, turned and started back down the hallway. Stopping at a door to her right, she opened it and peered inside. At seeing a vacuum cleaner, a couple of brooms, and various and sundry cleaning products, she frowned. "Broom closet."

Taite closed the door and crossed the narrow hallway to a door under the main stairs. Opening that door, she saw a dimly lit staircase. She started down the steps, holding on to the railing with her right hand.

At the bottom, she paused and looked around. It didn't smell like a basement, musty and slightly damp. No, this one smelled fresh and clean, just like the upstairs. She shook her head in amazement. "Geez, Cobb needs to get a life, if he keeps the *basement* this clean."

On the left was what looked to be a workbench. Hammers, screwdrivers, and wrenches were lined neatly on a pegboard on the wall above it. A large gray metal storage cabinet stood to one side.

To her right was an old cream-on-gray sofa covered with plastic. The style reminded her of something she'd seen once in a historic Victorian parlor. It was probably a family heirloom, passed down to Ryder and stored away here.

There was also a fully stocked floor-to-ceiling wine rack, at least eight feet wide. She walked over and pulled out a bottle. After blowing a light coating of dust off it, she looked at the label and gave a soft whistle. "Eighteen ninety cognac. Nice." She replaced the bottle and drew out another one farther up the rack. "Nineteen forty Armagnac." She put the bottle back and stepped away from the wine. "Impressive collection."

Turning, she didn't see Ryder and assumed he must be in a room that lay behind the door at the far end of the basement. Just as she reached it, her hand out to turn the knob, it swung open. She jumped and yelled, her hand flying to cover her rapidly beating heart.

Ryder stood there, a startled look on his face that quickly darkened to irritation. "What are you doing down here?" As the bare bulb hanging from the ceiling flipped off, she saw a small bed against the wall and wondered at it.

He closed the door behind him, but not before she saw something that made her eyes widen.

Manacles. There were manacles attached to the wall above the bed, just at the height of someone sitting on the bed with his hands raised above his head. Manacles that looked like they'd been there a very long time.

Oh. My. God. Why the hell would he have wall manacles in his basement?

There was something going on here that she didn't want to look at too closely. She really didn't. But every instinct she had prompted her to probe further.

Did this have something to do with Ryder's reluctance to have her on the island? His locking away of his family's journals? His unease at helping her with her werewolf problem? "I don't want to know," she muttered and turned away from the door. She hugged her waist and started walking toward the stairs. "I really don't want to know. I'm attracted to him, so of course he's gotta be some kind of weirdo, right?"

Taite heard Ryder's steps behind her and quickened her pace. She'd happily ignore her instincts this time. She had one short-term goal in mind.

Get upstairs, away from the creepy basement with its expensive alcohol and sturdy wall manacles.

"Taite?" Ryder called, his voice deep and husky and so sexy it made her entire body clench with need.

She whirled to face him. She didn't want to know. She did *not* want to know. "What the hell were those?" she demanded, her voice as shaky as the finger she pointed toward the door.

Dammit. What happened to not wanting to know?

His face closed up, his lids dropping to shutter his eyes. A muscle in his lean jaw flexed. "Manacles."

His response was truthful but brief. Too much so, and it pissed her off.

"And just why do you have manacles in your wine cellar?" Her tone was acerbic, and she didn't care. She didn't care that she'd known Ryder for all of two days and it was really none of her business. The kisses they'd shared were more than just fleeting caresses. She had a connection to this man that was hard to explain, even to herself.

And she didn't care if he was offended at her prying into his personal life. He owed her an explanation, and she was damned well going to get it. She'd been acting like some weak-spirited, spineless child, but no more. He was going to talk to her or have to physically move her out of his way.

No more Ms. Nice Guy. It was time to bring Taite Gibson, tough criminal investigator, out to play. She'd been hiding for the past few weeks, but considering she had a mean-assed stalker and a werewolf after her, it was no wonder.

But no more.

The cowering stopped now.

"It's really none of your business, Taite." Ryder started to walk by her. She moved, blocking his path.

That really had been the worst thing he could've said to her. "Not my business? When you've had your tongue down my throat? Try again."

He sighed. A muscle in his jaw started up in a steady tic. Eyes dark with irritation and some other emotion she couldn't define, he muttered, "Just because we've kissed a couple of times doesn't mean anything."

She blinked. Who the hell did he think he was? That seemed like a reasonable question to her, so she asked it. "Just who the hell do you think you are? Remember this? 'Why am I so drawn to you?'" She poked him in the chest. "You asked me that not ten minutes ago, bub. So don't go acting like this is all one-sided on my part."

He had the grace to look chagrined. "It's . . . complicated."

Her eyebrows rose. "So? Uncomplicate it. I'm a fairly intelligent person," she said with pointed sarcasm. "I'm sure I'll be able to grasp it."

"Taite . . ." He sighed. "I can't. It's not just me that's involved. My family . . ."

"Your family . . . what? Is involved? Wouldn't understand? Would kick your ass? What?" Frustrated, she poked him in the chest again. "What's so bad you can't tell me? And is it in those journals you don't want me to see?"

He sighed again, and one hand came up to the back of his neck. She watched the play of muscles as his biceps strained against the material of his dress shirt, and she suddenly and irrationally didn't care anymore.

He had been irascible and irritating, but never frightening. Even in his passion he had held her gently and with such care she'd not once felt threatened by him. She wanted to feel loved, cherished, for once in her life. That didn't need to mean a lifetime commitment, just a promise not to hurt her in the short time they'd be together.

He had secrets to hide, things he held deep inside that he didn't want anyone else to see—so did she.

"Just tell me that, whatever it is, it won't make a difference to *us*."

"I can't." He tried to sidestep her, and she blocked him again. "Dammit, Taite. Get out of the way."

He didn't want to talk about the journals or those manacles? Well, he'd have to go through her to get away. "Make me."

Oh, God. She didn't know where that came from, but by the look on his face, he wasn't going to let her take it back.

"You just don't know when to stop, do you?" His eyes narrowed and big hands went around her waist, hoisting her into the air. A few steps brought him to the antique sofa and, even though his grip on her was hard, he settled her with care on the cushions, his body a welcome, warm weight over hers. "What's it going to take for you to leave well enough alone?"

"More than you've got." Her voice came out throaty, low. When his eyes flared with heat, the ache low in her belly started up again.

"Hmm. We'll just see about that." With those darkly muttered words, his mouth came down over hers.

Chapter 10

The admirer glanced at the sky. Roiling black clouds loomed overhead. Lightning forked across the darkness. A boom of thunder rumbled. The strength of the wind had increased, making the branches of the trees whip back and forth. The wildness called to him. Closing his eyes, he lifted his face to the oncoming storm.

He'd guess the winds were gusting at around thirty miles an hour. Looking again at the storm clouds, he knew it wouldn't be long until the little island was engulfed in the full-blown gale the weather reports had described.

He'd like to have *something* full-blown, and it sure as hell wasn't a gale. In response to the carnal turn his thoughts had taken, his cock jerked to life. He closed his eyes again, imagining Taite on her knees, her hands tied behind her back, her lips stretched thin by the thick wedge of his shaft. His mouth curved in a satisfied smile.

But at the thought of his would-be love, his smile faded. The dark-haired woman would be his whether she wanted it or not. Once he tamed her, taught her the consequences of her defiance, she would settle into the new life he'd planned.

Or she'd die.

The first thing he had to do was get rid of the usurper. Merrick would pay for his interference. He should never have touched her, never even had the thought that she could be *his*. She belonged to the admirer only.

He licked his lips in anticipation. Gutting the other man would leave him vulnerable, weak, unable to fight—lucid enough to merely watch as the admirer claimed his woman. Just the thought of all that hot, sticky blood had his cock burgeoning thicker with lust.

To him, this was what being a werewolf was all about—the power, the blood.

The sex.

Taite was his, and anyone who got in his way would die.

He edged closer to the house. Peering through the window of the kitchen, he saw Cobb, a short apron around his waist, an oven mitt over his hand. The man hummed a song under his breath, slightly off-key. He opened the oven and drew out a metal sheet.

The admirer's nostrils flared at the sweet scent of scones. His eyes went from the scones to the little man. While both would be tasty, he'd much prefer to feast on man-flesh than pastries.

It had been too long since that little tart in Land's End.

Wait, he cautioned himself. *Be patient. Your chance will come.*

Chapter 11

Ryder had lost all good sense. That was the only explanation for his actions. Even as he thought that, his body took over. Feelings long denied took control, and he could no longer fight them. His mouth slid to the softness of Taite's throat, tongue tasting the saltiness of her skin over the pounding of her pulse.

She sighed and moved against him, slender legs sliding under his, softly rounded belly pressing against his erection. "Ryder." Her voice had the same throaty sound that had gotten him into this predicament to begin with, and he was powerless to resist her allure. "What about the manacles . . ."

He started to explain, but held back. He should tell her, but this had been his secret for so long the words wouldn't come. So he did the only thing his lust-muddled mind allowed. He kissed her again.

Her soft lips parted for his tongue, and he swept inside the dark cavern of her mouth. She tasted sweet and needy. When she pulled his tongue deeper, suckling him gently, eagerly, he groaned and settled his weight more fully onto her.

Slender hands clutched at his back, kneading the hard muscles there. She slowly pumped her hips against him, making his cock as stiff as an iron pike.

What she did to him . . . he didn't want to look at too closely. While he didn't believe in love at first sight—hell, he wasn't even sure he believed in love, period—there was *some* emotion roiling deep inside him that made him think she was right for him.

The woman of his soul. The woman he *needed* as much as desired.

He'd never felt hunger like this. Demanding. Pulsating with a life all its own.

Her soft, sweet scent wrapped around his senses and put him in overdrive. He concentrated on keeping the beast under control. He didn't want this kiss to end, not yet. Not until he could satiate the sensual hunger in some small way.

Dear God, he wanted her like he'd wanted no other. Possessiveness—raw, sharp, and primitive as hell—surged inside him with astonishing strength.

He worked his way down her throat once more, pausing where her heartbeat pounded under her skin, wanting to go on tasting her as long as she'd let him. For surely once she knew what he was, she would run from him.

He needed to make this special for her so that later, if he had even a snowball's chance in hell with her, he could remind her of the way it was between them. Great sex might be the only hold he'd have on her.

With a groan, he stripped the T-shirt up over her head and stared down at her near nakedness. Pale, freckled skin framed by a dusty rose bra beckoned him. He buried his face in the valley of her breasts, then rested his cheek on the soft mounds.

Her heartbeat thudded in frantic rhythm against his face. Taite gulped air and then suspended her breath, and he realized she was waiting for his next move.

Ryder ran the tip of his tongue along the upper edge of her bra. She squirmed under him, her hands coming up to fist in his hair. When he slid open the front catch and pushed the silky material away from her breasts, her breath hitched in her throat, then eased from her in a long sigh.

"You're so lovely," he murmured, and latched onto the peach-tinted tip of one breast.

Her body arched and she cried out, her fingers twisting in his hair. He winced at the painful tug, but decided it was a small price to pay for her enthusiasm. The spicy aroma of her arousal wafted to him, and he drew in a deep breath. He wanted to sear his lungs with her scent so that, long after she was gone, he would remember what she smelled like.

Moving his mouth to her other nipple, he sucked it deep. She was soft and silky in his mouth, and he wanted to taste her all over, but especially the wet folds between her thighs.

"Ryder, please . . ."

He raised his head and looked down at her. She had the prettiest breasts, plump and pale and soft. Her nipples were tight and red, wet from his mouth. Full lips parted with her quickened breathing, dark eyes wide and needy.

Taite belonged to him.

Based on their short acquaintance, the possessiveness was unrealistic, absurd even. But he knew he'd felt it from the moment he'd first seen her.

Now, seeing her spread underneath him, her body soft and willing, his hunger was understandable. His cock, thick and heavy, strained against his jeans and pulsed with each heartbeat.

He wanted to be buried balls-deep inside her so much he was close to losing it and embarrassing himself. He hadn't spewed inside his pants since he was a teenager, but he felt closer to the edge than he ever had before.

The light from the stairwell illuminated her except for where his body cast her in shadow. The rise of her breasts, the curve of her cheek, the stubborn point of her chin.

The hint of uncertainty in her eyes.

That, more than anything else could have, tempered his desire. He would make this good for her, so good she would look back on him with favor. Eventually.

He didn't even want to think about how Taite would feel about him making love to her without telling her what he truly was.

All he knew was that not touching her was no longer an option.

But . . . Dammit. She deserved to know, regardless that it wasn't just his secret to tell. He drew a deep breath and held it a moment, then blew it out. "Taite, there's something I need to tell you."

"Will it spoil the mood?"

He sighed. "Probably."

Her gaze searched his. "Will it change the way you feel about me?"

Ryder shook his head. "Absolutely not."

"Will it change the way I feel about you?"

His long, slow breath lifted his shoulders. Above all else, he owed her honesty. "I'd like to think not, but more than likely . . . yes."

That stubborn chin lifted. "Then I don't want to know right now. Right now I want you to make love to me."

It showed a certain weakness in his character that he gave up so easily. He would tell her, but not now. Not when she was so soft and willing under his hands. Giving a low groan, Ryder pulled off her shoes. He unfastened her jeans and slid them down her legs. Dropping the denim to the floor, he placed one hand on her belly, low, the tip of his thumb resting just above the elastic of her skimpy panties.

He slid both hands under the waistband of her panties and stripped them off. Her legs fell open. Immediately, the scent of her arousal became stronger, drawing him like a bee to the sweetest of flowers.

Short dark hair triangled above her labia, beckoning him to uncover her feminine secrets. He wedged between her thighs, draping her legs over his shoulders. With his thumbs, he spread her folds, then he pressed his mouth to her soft flesh.

The plastic on the sofa creaked with their movements. He had the fleeting thought that he should take the covering off but, looking down at her, the thought quickly fled, to be replaced by pure instinct.

She was deliciously wet and swollen, and he groaned again with the excitement of it, at the taste of her. His tongue speared deep, drawing her tangy essence down his throat.

Taite gasped and her hips rose to meet his mouth. With each thrust of his tongue, she shuddered against him, begging and moaning.

His chest expanded, his heart burgeoning with something much more than affection, something that cracked the walls he'd built so carefully over the years. Feeling his control nearing an end, he closed his mouth over her clit and suckled her, gently at first, then with increasing demand.

He pushed two fingers deep inside her slick channel and started pumping in and out. Her orgasm exploded through her, the contractions around his fingers strong and steady. Her cry was muffled, and he glanced up to see she'd bitten down on her fist.

Her release fired his own impending climax and, once she'd quieted beneath him, he unzipped his jeans and sighed with relief when his cock was freed from its prison of metal and cloth.

Holding her gaze, he took her hand and wrapped her fingers around his erection. When she gently squeezed, he closed his eyes and bucked his hips against her hand. A few strokes later, he placed his fingers over hers and halted her movements.

"Stop." His voice was strangled, lust and need nearly overwhelming his ability to use the higher functions of his brain.

"Why?" Even though he'd stopped her hand, he couldn't control her fingers. She kept softly squeezing his shaft.

"I don't have a condom, and I'm about ready to come." When her thumb swept over the tip of his cock, spreading pre-come over the ruddy head, he groaned and clenched his jaw against the exquisite pleasure. "I need to wait."

He could, and he would, but it would be pure torture.

"Why?" Taite repeated. Her thumb made that maddening sweep over his cock head again, lingering at the sensitive slit. "We don't have to . . . you know. Go all the way. Let me do this for you."

Ryder looked at her, his breath catching at the sight she presented. She was partially sitting up, bracing herself on one hand, her breasts softly swaying as she shifted her weight. Her sweet pussy, still flushed and swollen from her orgasm, glistened with her juices.

Without a word, he released his grip and leaned back against the arm of the sofa. He raised his right leg until his foot rested on the seat cushions. She moved around until she was between his legs, her hand never leaving his cock.

"Lift your hips," she whispered, and once he'd complied, she slid his jeans and boxers to his thighs. One hand returned to his cock. The other went between her thighs. When she withdrew it, it was wet with her cream. She clasped his cock at the base and stroked up, spreading the natural lubricant over his length.

She kept her touch light. Too light.

"Harder, honey." Ryder spoke through clenched teeth. His breath came harsh and fast. "Do me harder. Faster."

She picked up the pace, tightening her grip. His hips pumped, thrusting his thick length through the ring of her fingers. Another stroke, then another, and his climax erupted.

He threw his head back against the arm of the sofa, his neck tight with strain, his body as rigid as his shaft as he held in his shout of release.

Through it all, Taite kept milking his cock. He groaned and shuddered with each new stroke. Finally spent, he put his hand over hers. "Stop. It's too much."

A cute pout curved her sensuous lips before they tilted in a smile. Combined with the sleepy, sultry look in her cocoa-colored eyes, it was the expression of a woman realizing her power, and on Taite it was damned sexy.

He looked down at her and saw his ejaculate on her breasts and stomach. Without a word he unbuttoned his shirt and pulled it off. First he wiped her hand, then mopped up her belly and breasts. He leaned down and kissed her mouth, gently, softly.

"What do you say we move this upstairs?" he asked. "I have a perfectly good bed that's going to waste."

She nodded. Looking down, she fastened her bra and grabbed her jeans and top. "Where're my panties?"

Ryder pulled his underwear and jeans back up and fastened them, and got to his feet. Just as he bent to pick up the rose panties that were halfway under the sofa, he heard Cobb's voice from the top of the stairs.

"Mr. Merrick? Are you still down there, sir?"

Taite's eyes widened. With jerky movements, she pulled on her jeans and fastened them. Muttering, she shoved her head and arms through the openings of her T-shirt.

"We're just on our way up, Cobb," he called, amusement tugging the corners of his mouth. His inestimable employee no doubt knew exactly what was going on and would never be so gauche as to venture down. He was letting Ryder know they needed to get upstairs.

"Very well, sir."

Seeing that Taite was already dressed, Ryder stuffed her panties into the back pocket of his jeans. He reached out and smoothed her hair. "Looks like we'll have to wait on round two."

Dark eyebrows rose. "Round two? You make it sound like a wrestling match."

He grinned. "A wrestling match of the best kind."

She went up the stairs ahead of him, her shapely ass swaying, and his beast yowled at being denied more of her.

Soon, he promised himself. Soon he would plunge into the tight clasp of her body and satisfy them both.

Taite reached the top of the stairs and fought a blush at seeing Cobb patiently waiting. When one of his eyelids came down in a wink, she lost the battle. Heat flooded her face, and she pressed her lips together.

When Cobb spoke, it was directed at Ryder. "Mr. O'Connell was making noises about coming to find you, sir. I thought you would rather I interrupt you than him."

"Yes, thank you, Cobb." Ryder pressed a kiss to Taite's temple and whispered, "Wait here."

He walked into his room. She heard a creak, then a plop like a lid falling down. He came back into view, sliding his arms into a royal blue shirt. Walking toward her, he buttoned a few buttons and left the tails of the shirt hanging over his jeans.

When he reached her, he stroked the back of his hand over her hot cheek before moving it to the small of her back. Even that light touch electrified her. She'd just had an explosive orgasm, but it had barely taken the edge off. She wanted him, now.

Fast and deep and as hard as possible.

Not his fingers. Not his mouth. His cock. Inside her. Claiming her.

It wasn't very twenty-first century of her, she supposed. But it was what it was. She wanted him so deep she couldn't tell where he ended and she began.

They walked into the study, and she went straight to the bookshelves, ignoring Declan and the mocking look he sent her way. She could tell from his expression he saw Ryder had on a different shirt than the last time he was in the study.

"You two get lost?" Declan asked, the lilt heavy in his voice. When she glanced at him, he winked, letting her know his anger was for show. Good thing, too, since going after

Ryder had been his idea. "Just what was it you were doin' down there?"

She rolled her eyes. Good God. She was thirty-three years old, way too old to need a father figure, but there he was, pretending to be an enraged parent.

"That's between me and Taite," Ryder drawled.

She bit her lip against a grin. Even when he spoke with lazy grace, his voice still had a crisp British inflection, and it drove her wild.

"Well." Declan cleared his throat and apparently decided to let it drop. For now. She had no doubts he'd bring it up later, and she and Ryder would be mercilessly teased. Declan huffed out a sigh. "It's lookin' like this gale is gonna last a while. It's a big one."

She glanced out the window, astonished to see it was nearly dark outside and rain was lashing the windows. "When did it start to rain?" Even as the words left her mouth, she wished she hadn't spoken them, for it gave Declan another opening.

His grin told her he saw it, but all he said was, "When you were in the basement."

She pursed her lips and started to look back to the bookshelves when something from outside caught her eye. Squinting, she peered past Declan, then walked closer to the French doors.

For the briefest of moments, a face appeared, out of focus and cloaked in darkness, but she knew she'd seen it. She yelled and jumped back.

Both men ran to her. "What?" they asked in unison.

"I saw something. Someone. A face. A man's face." She wrapped her arms around her waist and forced herself to approach the doors again. When Declan reached behind him and flipped off the desk lamp, the room was plunged into darkness except for the light coming in from the foyer.

Ryder pushed open the door and peered outside. When he

turned, his face and hair were soaked. "There's no one there now," he said.

"There was." Taite cleared her throat, trying to keep her voice from trembling. "I know what I saw."

"I'm not saying you didn't see it, honey." Ryder looked at Declan, who nodded. "We'll take a quick look around, all right?" He called for Cobb, who quickly came to the door.

Declan flipped the desk light back on as Ryder explained what they were going to do. Then Ryder asked, "Where are the torches?"

"And the guns," Declan added. When everyone looked at him, he shrugged. "It'll even up the odds."

"What odds?" Taite asked. "It was one guy." Her heart thudded against her ribs. "You don't think it was . . ."

"The werewolf?" Declan finished when she trailed off. "Did it look like him?"

"I don't know. It happened too fast." She thought back. "It seemed . . . human."

"There you are, then." Declan glanced back through the window. "As far as I know, the bloody beast hadn't found us as of this mornin'." He shook his head. "At any rate, I think bein' armed is a good idea."

Cobb nodded. "I agree. We have a few large torches in the cupboard under the stairs, Mr. O'Connell, if you would be so good as to get them. I will fetch the weapons." The little man turned and left the room, his footsteps echoing in the foyer.

"I'll get the flashlights and be right back." Declan walked out of the study as well.

Ryder went to Taite and drew her into his arms. His chin came to rest on the top of her head. "Stay in here with Cobb, all right?"

"But—"

"Taite, I need to know you're safe." He leaned back and stared down at her. She met his gaze and saw concern and affection reflected back at her.

"I don't want you out there traipsing around looking for God knows what."

She huffed a sigh. Now wasn't the time to argue about it, but he was going to learn she wasn't the type to sit around, wringing her hands, while the menfolk saved the day.

"Fine. But I want a gun. I'm licensed to carry," she insisted. "I'm probably a better shot than you are."

His lips tilted on one side. "Oh, you think so, do you?"

"I'm a crack shot." She looped her arms around his neck and pulled his face down to hers. "I have very good aim. And I always get my man."

Ryder's mouth curved into a full smile. "Oh, I don't doubt that for a moment, love."

Taite's heart lurched at the endearment. She knew he used it lightly, like Declan used 'darling,' but her foolish heart didn't care.

"None of that, now," Declan said, walking back into the room. He carried two flashlights, one of which he handed to Ryder. "We've work to do."

Refusing to be embarrassed, Taite pulled away from Ryder. They'd only been hugging, after all. It wasn't as if Declan had caught them making out on the desk.

She glanced at the big desk and shivered. God!

Ryder leaned over and put his mouth by her ear. "And none of that, either," he whispered. "At least not until we can be sure we won't be interrupted."

Her gaze flew to him and he grinned. "It's written all over your face, love. Besides . . ." He gave her a wink. "I've had a picture in my mind for some time now of you sprawled over my desk."

She did blush then, and laughed. So what if what she felt was showing? She was a healthy woman with desires and had a handsome, sexy man to fulfill her needs. It beat the hell out of a vibrator any day.

Declan walked to her and looped an arm around her neck. "Haven't heard that in a while, darlin'. It's nice to hear."

She saw Ryder stiffen for a moment, then relax. Keeping her gaze on him, she asked Declan, "Hear what?"

"You laughin'." Declan tightened his arm for a moment before dropping it to his side.

"Yeah, well, I haven't had a lot to laugh about lately." She turned as Cobb came into the room.

He held a shotgun under each arm, a box of ammunition in one hand, and his unbuttoned suit jacket revealed a pistol tucked into the waistband of his trousers.

"Hope you've got the safety on there, boyo." Declan walked forward and took one of the shotguns. Ryder took the other.

Cobb frowned. "Of course I have the safety on, Mr. O'Connell. *I* am not an imbecile." He looked Declan up and down, his message clear. When Declan only grinned, Cobb sniffed.

"Give that extra gun to Taite." Ryder took several cartridges and put them in his pocket.

Cobb pulled the pistol from his waistband and handed it, grip first, to Taite. Taking it, she opened the cylinder and checked the rounds in the chambers, then spun the cylinder a couple of times and clicked it closed.

When she looked up, all three men were staring at her. She shrugged. "I like the way that sounds. I'm used to a semi-automatic, so I don't get to do that very often."

"How many rounds does your gun hold?" Cobb reached behind his back, under his jacket, and pulled out another revolver. He went through the same routine she had and she grinned, thankful for a brief respite from the worry and fear gnawing at her gut.

"The magazine holds ten, but I usually rachet one into the chamber and put another round in the magazine." Taite carefully slid the barrel of the gun under her waistband at the small of her back.

"Well, aren't you two surprisin'?" Declan took a handful of cartridges from the box Cobb had placed on the desk and slid them into the right front pocket of his jeans. "Just be sure you don't shoot *me.*"

Cobb looked intrigued with the idea, and Taite bit back another grin. Once Ryder had taken extra cartridges for his shotgun, she sobered and put a hand on each man's shoulder. "Please be careful out there."

"You be careful, too, love," Ryder murmured, and placed a tender kiss on her forehead. "We'll be right back."

"You'd better be," she muttered. Once they'd gone out into the storm, she closed the doors behind them and looked at Cobb. She blew out a heavy sigh.

"Now we wait," Cobb murmured and sat on the sofa, his gun in his hand.

Taite couldn't sit still. Instead, she paced back and forth from the French doors, down the length of the bookshelves, and back again. She jumped with each lightning strike, then started counting the seconds between the flash of light and the corresponding roll of thunder.

The center of the storm was roughly four miles away, by her estimate. Gusts of wind shook the windowpanes in the French doors. The storm would only worsen. Not crazy about being left in the dark, she fervently hoped the generator would hold out.

After what seemed like at least an hour but was in reality maybe fifteen minutes, the two men opened the doors and came back into the room. Their clothing was drenched, dark hair plastered to their skulls.

"No one's out there that we could see." Ryder swiped his hand over his wet face. "No footprints, either."

"Course, it's rainin' so hard, just about everything's under a couple of inches of water," Declan added. He ran his fingers through his hair, pushing the long strands off his forehead.

"Here, you're dripping water over everything." Cobb walked around the desk. "And please return the weapons to me." Once they had all complied, he began shooing the men out of the room. "Go change, now."

Declan allowed Cobb to push him out of the study. Ryder walked up to Taite and touched her gently on the cheek. "Want to give me a hand?" His blue eyes were dark and intent, and she shivered at the carnal promise she saw in his gaze.

Reaching out, she took his hand.

Chapter 12

The door to Ryder's bedroom closed behind them. Taite couldn't contain the shiver that raced through her at the heated look in Ryder's eyes. The room was dim from the storm, shadows shifting with the movement of the clouds outside.

His face hardened with desire, yet something softer shone in his eyes. Jagged streaks of lightning illuminated the rugged contours of his features in quick flashes. The wildness of the storm worked its way inside her soul, and she forced thoughts of stalkers and werewolves to the back of her mind. She would deal with them later. She would also deal later with whatever it was Ryder had wanted to tell her. For now . . . now she needed him.

Her gaze dragged over every inch of his body, her breath snagging in her throat. He looked savage, every hard, carved muscle delineated beneath his clinging, wet clothes. His dark hair hugged his head, the ends slightly curling. Blue eyes glittered, and his jaw flexed.

Brutal lust slammed off him in waves, strong enough that she could feel it. He began stalking toward her, his movements so graceful and primitively male she couldn't help but respond with a shiver.

Her pulse seemed to slow and center between her thighs, her clit throbbing in a rhythm in direct contrast to her quickened breathing. As he continued to approach her, she involuntarily stepped backward until he'd trapped her against the door.

Ryder placed his hands flat on either side of her head and leaned into her. His hips pressed against hers. He was fully aroused, his cock a long, stiff ridge between their bodies.

Her breath hitched. Her pulse hammered wildly in her throat. *Oh, sweet Jesus.* His mouth slanted over hers with a small twist, coaxing her lips apart, and his tongue slid into her mouth. It was an invasion of hot, wet silk, one that set off a burst of sensation that arrowed straight to her sex.

Taite rose up on her toes and opened her mouth wider. Her eyes slid shut.

He put a hand on the back of her neck and clamped down, holding her head immobile at the angle he wanted it. The sensation of being restrained, dominated, intensified the arousal streaking like lightning to her belly.

He lifted his head. She opened her eyes to find him staring down at her, his breath coming fast and hard. Heat rolled off him, even through the sodden state of his clothing. Amazed the water on his skin wasn't steaming, she tracked the progress of a droplet of water as it trailed down his throat. With a small sigh, she leaned forward and lapped at his skin.

Contact with his clothes soon had her own clothing soaked. A fine trembling started in her hands and gained strength. Soon her entire body shook with need. She moaned, certain she'd never been so turned on in her entire life. Her lips felt bruised from his hard kiss, and her pussy was so wet she could feel her juices along the lips of her sex.

Outside, the wind howled and lightning flashed. A roll of thunder echoed the need rioting throughout her body.

"Easy, love," Ryder soothed her, his voice husky, deep. "We've all the time in the world."

They didn't; she knew that. She also knew the time they did have would be precious, and she didn't want to waste a minute of it.

Taite wanted him inside her. Now.

Her fingers went to the buttons of his shirt, and she unfastened them. She pushed the shirt off him. Staring at his chest, she concentrated on breathing. In. Out. In. Out.

God. He was the most beautiful man. Gorgeous muscled chest, but not overly bulky like a bodybuilder. Strong collarbones. Dark hair spread over his pecs and tapered down in a tempting little trail that disappeared into the waistband of his jeans.

She brought her gaze back up to his wide shoulders. Her palms went to the taut tendons on either side of his neck, rubbing them gently. She slid her hands over his shoulders and down his arms to wrap as much of her fingers around his biceps as she could.

"I love the feel of you," she whispered, flicking her tongue out to wet suddenly dry lips. It didn't surprise her, not really, since all the moisture in her body seemed to have pooled between her thighs. "So hard. So hot." Looking up, she was caught by the dark shimmer of his gaze. At this moment he was pure, basic male, and it called to her on an instinctive level.

Taite licked her lips again and drew a deep breath. Assaulted immediately by the musky scent of Ryder's wet, heated body, she involuntarily clenched her fingers, her nails digging into his skin. When his eyes darkened at the small bite of pain, she loosened her grip and stroked her fingers over the grooves left by her nails.

Her hands moved to his chest, fingers sliding through rough hair to his hard nipples. He drew in a sharp breath and his eyes became heavy-lidded. She trailed her hands across the contours of his abdomen and lower to the waistband of his jeans.

With shaking fingers she freed his belt from the buckle. She popped the button of his jeans and carefully slid the zipper down, making sure she caressed the hard ridge of his cock with her knuckles.

"God!" Apparently impatient with her slow progress, Ryder

shoved his pants and boxers over his hips and kicked the wet clothing away. His cock rose full and proud from his groin, a clear drop of liquid clinging to the slitted tip. He was so hard he throbbed, the reddened head bobbing gently.

He looked huge and delicious. She thought about how it would feel, taking his thick cock inside her body, and her pussy began to flood in earnest. Taite couldn't breathe, staring at his masculine beauty.

His bottom half was even better than the top half. And his top half was absolutely yummy.

"One of us is overdressed," he muttered. His hands went to the hem of her T-shirt.

She raised her arms. He drew the shirt off her, dropping it to the floor with careless ease. His fingers unclasped her bra and she shrugged it off, letting it fall to her feet.

His lids dropped to half-mast over glittering eyes, and his face tightened. The thin scar along his jaw line stood in white relief against the tanned skin.

Taite reached out and stroked her fingers over it, dropping her hand to her side as he moved closer.

Holding her gaze captive with his own, Ryder closed one big hand over her breast while the other hand went to the curve of her buttocks and pulled her lower body against his.

Gently he caressed her, his palm shaping her. When his fingers brushed over her beaded nipple, they both gasped. His eyes closed briefly. He groaned, a harsh, low sound drawn from deep in his chest, then opened his eyes and stared at her nudity.

"You're so beautiful," he murmured, his voice a low rasp. "So soft, so sweet." Leaning down, he kissed her shoulder, her throat. His mouth was hot against her skin, his tongue hotter, leaving a burning trail wherever he touched.

His kiss branded her in the valley of her breasts. Taite laced both hands into his sodden hair and urged him toward her nipple. Both peaks were painfully tight, and she needed his mouth on her. "Ryder, please. Suck my nipples."

"Easy, love." He gentled her with his dark voice while his hips, pumping steadily against hers, ramped her need. He brought both hands to her breasts and plumped them together. She made an urgent sound that he responded to by rubbing his thumbs over the distended tips.

Sparks fired along her nerve endings. She felt as if the storm outside was mirrored in her body, all the wild, wet fury of it. Taite moaned and pressed into his hands, wanting the pressure to be harder. Ryder closed his fingers and thumbs around the tips and tugged. She arched, crying out. More hot, slick liquid slid from her core to lie thickly along her labia.

"You like that?" he asked. "You'll like this even better." His tongue stroked over one taut nipple. She groaned.

He laughed softly, the sound one of triumph. And then he drew her nipple into the wet heat of his mouth. He suckled her gently, his tongue curling around her, his mouth pulling, drawing a response from deep within her core. Her legs became unsteady even as the rest of her body seemed to tighten unbearably.

Ryder moved one arm under her bottom and lifted her. She wrapped her legs around him, fitting the cleft of her body to the hardness of his erection. His head lifted from her breast and he stared down at her, his chest rising and falling with his harsh breaths.

Without breaking eye contact, he turned and walked to the bed, letting her slide to the floor when he stopped. He quickly stripped her damp jeans off, then urged her back until her legs hit the side of the bed.

A gentle nudge made her sit. He knelt on the floor. His hands on her knees coaxed her to move until his wide shoulders could wedge between her thighs. He stared at the wet folds of her sex. His sensual mouth held firm for a moment before it softened, the lips parting on a sigh. "God, you're pretty here. All soft cream and blushing pinks."

His hands swept up Taite's legs, fingers sparking sensations through the nerve endings in her inner thighs. He covered her mons with one large palm in an almost protective gesture. When his gaze came up to meet hers, her breath caught at the stark desire in his eyes.

"I need you now, Taite." Ryder pressed his mouth to the slight mound of her belly, his eyes closing. "Tell me you're ready."

His hot breath wafted over her skin, and she shivered in response. "God, if I was any more ready, I'd be done."

He laughed and pressed a kiss to the top of her thigh. "Let me just get one taste first. . . ." His tongue dipped between her folds and took a long, slow swipe.

Taite arched against him, the air hissing from between clenched teeth. When his mouth closed over her clit and gently suckled, her arms buckled. She fell back onto the bed.

Big hands grasped her hips and flipped her over onto her stomach. He lifted her and slipped a pillow under her belly, canting her hips higher. With her legs hanging over the edge, her sex was wide open to him.

She felt exposed, vulnerable, and wildly turned on.

Taite struggled up onto her elbows and looked over one shoulder. Ryder reached toward the bedside table and yanked open the drawer. He pulled out a square packet and looked back at her, his face a mask of concentration, his eyes dark with lust and desire as he kneed her legs further apart.

He held the packet between his teeth and ripped it open. She watched avidly as he grasped his rigid shaft and rolled the condom over his thick length. With a tight smile, he guided himself to her slick folds. Rubbing his cock through her wetness, he groaned and closed his eyes. The tendons on his neck corded, and his teeth bit down on his full lower lip.

The twisted position she held herself in put too much strain on her neck, and Taite turned back to face the bed, her head down. She felt the fat tip of his cock at her channel. Then he started the long, slow glide into her pussy.

When he was snug against her, his tight balls resting against her swollen sex, they both groaned at the exquisite pressure. Taite helplessly pushed her hips back to meet him. Her head dipped even further until her cheek rested against the mattress.

Ryder groaned as her movement dragged his cock deeper into her snug channel. He paused, savoring the feel of her wet heat surrounding him and then, unable to hold off any longer, he began to move.

The wildness of the storm permeated the room even though the doors remained locked. His beast felt the fury of nature and responded.

The drag of his cock through the tight clasp of her cunt had him howling inside. He clenched his teeth against an overriding urge to mark her, to fit his teeth into the muscled area where neck met shoulder, to show her and anyone else who saw her that she belonged to him.

But he couldn't. Because she didn't. And because he wouldn't twine her fate so irrevocably to his. She deserved better than to be made into a beast like him.

No, she was his only for this moment. He couldn't count on anything else. He pushed the surge of sorrow aside with ruthless resolve. If this was all he could have of her, he would damned well focus on this moment.

Gripping her hips with bruising fingers, Ryder slammed into her, brutal, hard. The control he exerted over his beast cost him, and his thrusts soon became wild and unrestrained.

Taite responded with equal abandon, sobbing and shoving back to meet his plunging hips. She dropped her shoulders onto the bed, her arms stretched out in front of her, fingers clutching at the bed linens.

His balls were already drawn tight against the base of his shaft, and a shivery sensation along his spine signaled his impending climax. Determined to take her with him, Ryder slid one hand under her belly and found her clit.

When he snagged it between two fingers, she groaned, then

undulated her hips. Her hands slid under her body to her breasts, and he knew she was rolling her nipples between slender fingers.

God. What he wouldn't give for another set of hands. His balls drew up even further, and he rubbed her clit harder. "Come with me, love. Come!"

Taite sobbed and writhed beneath him, slamming her hips backward. The hard slap of his flesh, the even harder drive of his rigid cock into her tight pussy spiked his arousal.

She let out a long wail. The walls of her cunt clamped down as she quaked beneath him.

Ryder gave a loud groan. One final plunge and his cock exploded. He threw his head back and howled his release. His hips jerked convulsively as he jetted into her, the smooth muscles of her cunt milking him of every last drop of semen.

When the last spasm faded, he collapsed against Taite, driving her completely down onto the mattress. Knowing he was too heavy to remain like that, with the last of his strength, he rolled off her.

Once he'd disposed of the condom in a bedside waste bin, he gripped her under her arms and drew her farther up on the bed, and flopped beside her. He gathered her into his embrace, gratified when her arms wrapped around him and she buried her face in his neck. He rested his cheek against the top of her head, breathing in the fresh scent of her and the heady smell of sex, thick in the air. Bringing up one leg, he curled it around hers and drew her lower body flush with his.

His sated cock flexed, then subsided.

"You smell good." Taite's voice was soft and husky, sleepy. "Kinda like a combination of citrus and sage." She nuzzled his throat, flicking her tongue against his skin. "Mmm. You taste good, too."

He tightened his embrace. "You feel good in my arms." He clenched his teeth against saying more. He wanted to say those three words he'd never said to another woman.

It was insane, feeling this way after only a few days. But there it was, inescapable.

The storm raged, both outside and in his mind. Here he was, lying in bed with a woman he was certain couldn't accept his beast.

Why would she want to trade one monster for another?

Chapter 13

The admirer drew back from the window, his entire body taut with fury. How dare she? How dare the little bitch fuck someone else?

Fuck another werewolf.

Even though she didn't yet know that Merrick was a werewolf. But that didn't matter. She was boning the other man to spite him, to throw yet another rejection in his face.

And she would pay.

Yes.

She. Would. Pay.

They would all pay.

When he was certain he was out of sight, he turned and ran through the rain to the large boathouse that also housed the industrial-sized generator.

He didn't want to try to take them on while they were together in the house, especially since they had armed themselves. While he was confident of his success, he was prudent as well. He would take care to keep his own injuries to a minimum.

So he must divide and conquer.

Once inside the boathouse, he shook the rain out of his fur and transformed back into his human form. He'd just as soon stay a werewolf all the time, but some things called for the dexterity only smaller fingers had.

He barely noticed anymore being naked after he shifted. It had become second nature to him, and he found he enjoyed the freedom.

He searched through the various storage cabinets until he found what he was looking for: a pair of wire cutters, a sledge-hammer, a wrench, and a screwdriver. Then he set to work.

By the time he was done, the boat was disabled and the generator was leaking fuel at a rapid rate. Thunder boomed outside, and he smiled. Once the storm dissipated, someone would come to investigate.

And that person would die.

He settled into the corner to wait.

Chapter 14

The next morning, Declan stood in front of the French doors in Ryder's study and watched dark clouds roll in once more. The outer fringe of the second gale had reached Phelan's Keep; already big drops of water splattered against the window panes.

Sitting around and doing nothing had always been hard for him—it made him antsy. Even though as a Royal Marines Commando he'd spent many hours hunkered down waiting for bad guys, he didn't do patience easily.

The weight of the revolver tucked into his waistband pressed against the small of his back. Taite wasn't given to hysterics—if she said she saw someone outside, she saw someone. Plus there was that little matter of the werewolf.

Declan crossed his arms and drummed his fingers against his elbow. If her stalker—or that damned mutt—had been able to track them to Cornwall, the storm should keep him away from the island a little longer. But Declan didn't like the idea of being trapped here, too.

Dammit. When they'd been in Tucson, starting their run from the werewolf, his only thought had been to get to Ryder and find out how to get the furry bastard off their tail.

Declan had allowed Ryder to sidetrack him with bloody books. He should've kept his eye on the ball—the nasty *fur*ball on Taite's trail.

The rain began to fall harder. He glanced around the yard and saw the damage from the earlier heavy winds: tree limbs littered the area, and several roof tiles had been blown free and now lay on the ground. They'd have some work to do once the storm ended.

His stomach grumbled, telling him to hunt up something to eat. He hadn't heard any movement from anyone else in the house, but he'd be surprised if Cobb hadn't already been up for a few hours. The man was nothing if not dedicated.

He scrubbed one hand over his face, the whiskers on his jaw rasping against his palm. *Probably should've shaved this morning.* But, then, why? There was no one here who cared if he looked a little scruffy.

Well, maybe Cobb, because he was such a proper sort. But that was it.

Hearing movement from the hall, he turned just as Ryder and Taite walked into the room. Ryder's head was bent, and he was laughing at something she'd said. When he looked up, he caught Declan's eye and a flash of red slashed across his cheeks.

Gratified to see his friends happy, Declan still couldn't resist teasing them. "Well, it looks like you two have patched up your differences. Or have you just agreed to disagree?"

A soft flush stole over Taite's face, pinkening her cheeks and neck. "Just shut up," she grumbled good-naturedly and headed straight for the bookshelves.

"Or, maybe not," Declan muttered with a glare at Ryder. "Are you still makin' her read through books instead of tellin' her what she needs to know?"

Taite muttered something he didn't catch, and he looked at her. "What was that?" he asked.

"I said, I haven't asked him again."

"You shouldn't have to, lass." Declan glanced back at Ryder. All this waiting around was driving him 'round the bend, and he was spoiling for a fight. "We need to be lookin' for that damned werewolf. We don't have time for this shit." He motioned toward the bookshelves.

Ryder's eyes narrowed, and he started to give the same tired excuses to them that he had before.

Declan scowled and made a slashing motion with one hand. "Just save it, boyo. I'm not buyin' what you're shovelin' anymore."

Ryder scowled. "The last thing I need right now is for you to be on my ass about this."

"Better me on your arse than a werewolf," Declan shot back. He started to say more but, when Ryder jerked and his nostrils flared, his head turning toward the door, Declan stopped. "What is it?"

"I thought I heard . . ." Ryder strode from the room and headed to the front door. Declan pulled the gun from his waistband and followed with Taite close behind.

Ryder pulled open the door. "What the . . ." He went down on his haunches on the small portico.

Declan squatted beside him. There on the concrete lay the mutilated body of a rabbit. He glanced around. "What the bloody hell?" He looked back down at the rabbit. "Since when do you have predators on the Keep?"

"We don't." With a speed that was startling, Ryder picked up the carcass and stood. He strode outside to the edge of the bluff and tossed the rabbit over. Then he came back into the house.

Declan trailed after Ryder toward the kitchen, exchanging a glance with Taite. "So what do you think did this?"

Ryder kept going. "What do *you* think did?" he threw over his shoulder.

Taite drew in a sharp breath and grabbed Declan's arm. "You don't think . . . the werewolf?" Her fingernails dug into his biceps through the material of his shirt.

"Easy there, lass, or I'll be needin' to trim *your* claws." He eased her hand away from his arm and held it, squeezing her fingers reassuringly. He walked with her into the kitchen, where Ryder was pouring a cup of coffee and Cobb stood at the stove, a short apron tied around his waist.

"And if I said I think it's the werewolf?" Declan asked in response to Ryder's question.

Ryder paused for a moment, then set the carafe on the counter and picked up his mug. He turned and stared at them. "Then I'd say we're out of time and there's something I need to tell you." His gaze went to Taite. "Both of you."

The lights in the kitchen flickered, then went out. Lightning streaked, briefly illuminating the room. A boom of thunder rattled the windows, making Taite and Cobb jump.

Ryder heard a low hum from deep in the house. The lights came back on.

Cobb straightened his tie and walked toward the hallway. "I believe, sir," he said to Ryder as he passed him, "that was the small emergency generator taking over. I'll check and be right back."

"I can look," Ryder protested, thinking to give the older man a rest.

Cobb appeared insulted. "It *is* my job, sir, to look after the house." He yanked at the bottom of his suit jacket. "I *can* manage to go downstairs and check on Junior." He left the room with a slow, dignified walk.

"Junior?"

Ryder glanced at Taite and saw her biting her bottom lip, trying—quite unsuccessfully—to hold back a grin. He didn't bother hiding his amusement. "The small emergency generator," he said. Raising his voice so it would carry, he added, "Cobb's little, but he's tough."

"I heard that." Cobb's voice came from farther in the house, and the three remaining in the kitchen laughed.

"It's nice to see him bending a little," Taite murmured as she sat down on one of the kitchen chairs. "He's way too uptight."

Ryder nodded and took a sip of coffee. "Cobb was raised to be very proper around people whom he believes are his superiors."

"Whoa, wait a minute there." Taite pushed her chair around until her back was toward the table. "His *superiors?*"

Ryder held up one hand. "Don't yell at me, sweetheart. I said people *he* considers to be his superiors. I've never treated him with anything other than respect. I certainly don't think of myself as better than him."

Far from it, he thought, trying not to let the bitterness show on his face. For while his mother believed he and his father were fine, respectable men, Ryder and his dad both knew better.

They were animals masquerading as men. Cobb was worth ten of him. Probably more.

Ryder had already regretted his earlier words. When Taite felt she was safe, she'd go back to her life in America. There was no need for her to know what he was. He couldn't keep himself from touching her, as if her purity of spirit could somehow tame his beast. He crouched in front of her and rested his hands on her thighs. "You doing all right?"

She slipped one hand around his nape. His skin warmed at the touch of her soft palm, at her fingers sifting gently through his hair. "I'm fine." She leaned forward and kissed him, her mouth moving softly over his.

It wasn't enough.

He took control of the kiss, parting her lips so his tongue could surge inside to mate with hers. The only thing that kept him from dragging her down onto the floor was knowing Declan sat there, probably watching with a fool's grin on his face.

Ryder drew back from Taite's sweet mouth. Turning his head, he saw his friend doing exactly what he'd suspected. Taite turned to look, too, and he was delighted to see a soft blush flood her cheeks.

"You're adorable," he whispered and placed a kiss at the corner of her upturned lips.

Ryder rose to his feet and sat in the chair next to Taite's. She turned back around to face the table, and he took her hand in his, lacing their fingers together.

Cobb entered the room carrying a large torch. "We're now using electricity supplied by the emergency generator, Mr. Merrick. I suggest we turn off all nonessential lights. I'll check the main generator to see what the problem is."

Ryder glanced out the window. Wind gusted through the trees while rain fell heavily against the glass panes. "Not until we have some respite from this storm, Cobb."

"But, sir—"

"No. It won't hurt us if we have to sit around in the dark for a few hours." Beside him, Taite stiffened, her fingers curling tighter around his for a moment before she relaxed.

"I don't want you stumbling around out there and getting yourself hurt. *And*," he stressed when Cobb made to voice another protest, "I'll be going with you."

Cobb sighed and set the torch on the counter by the sink. "Very well, sir. We shall wait."

An hour later, after they'd all had breakfast, what they'd been hoping for arrived—a slight lull in the storm. The clouds were still gray and angry, but the rain had lessened for the moment. Standing in the foyer, Ryder and Cobb pulled on heavy boots and rain slickers, and grabbed the portable torches.

"We shouldn't be gone long," Ryder said.

Taite and Declan stood side by side, watching them. Declan glanced at Cobb, then looked back at Ryder with a raised eyebrow. "You sure you don't want me to go with you? Especially if there *is* a werewolf out there."

Ryder shook his head. "It takes two sets of hands to get the thing recalibrated and restarted. Cobb knows the workings of the generator the best and can get the job done the quickest," Ryder said in a quiet voice. "Besides, I need you to watch after Taite. Just in case."

"Hey!" Taite crossed her arms. Tilting her stubborn chin, she scowled. "I can take care of myself, thank you very much."

"I know you can. It'll make *me* feel better. Humor me, all right?" Ryder walked over to her and cupped her face between his palms. He pressed his lips lightly to hers. "All right?" he whispered against her mouth.

She sighed. "All right. But . . ." She wrapped her arms around him and buried her face against his chest. "If it *is* the werewolf out there, you and Cobb could be in danger." She gasped and pushed away from him. "He could be trying to lure someone out of the house."

"It's probably just the storm, sweetheart." Ryder pulled her into his arms and rocked her. He wasn't sure he believed it, but he didn't want her upset more than was necessary.

He glanced at Declan. The Irishman was the closest thing to a brother he'd ever had. Ryder's gaze went back to the woman in his arms. And now here was Taite, burrowing her way into his life, into his heart.

His jaw clenched. As much as he was beginning to care for her, he knew there could be no future. Given the revulsion she expressed toward the werewolf, he could only assume she'd feel the same way about him.

After all, a werewolf was a werewolf was a werewolf.

So he'd keep her safe until the time came that he had to let her go.

An old saying went through his head. *If you love something, set it free; if it comes back to you, it's yours.* He grimaced and gently set her away from him. He would let her go, but he had about as much chance of her coming back to him, once she knew him for what he truly was, as a snowstorm in July.

And he knew he had to tell her, as much as he tried to convince himself he didn't. It was the right thing to do. He just didn't want to do it yet. He wanted to hold onto what he had because, when she found out, she'd slip through his fingers like water through a sieve.

Ryder realized Taite was speaking to him while Declan looked on with an amused expression. "I'm sorry, love," Ryder responded with a soft smile for her. "What did you say?"

"I told you to be careful." She touched him gently on one cheek.

Ryder cupped her hand in his and, turning his head, placed a kiss in her soft palm. He wanted to drag her into his arms and make love to her until the entire world coalesced to just the two of them.

Uncaring of their audience, he took her mouth, branding her as his—at least temporarily—in the only way open to him.

She sighed and leaned into him, twining her arms around his neck. When she stroked her fingers over his nape, sifting through his hair with a light, sensuous touch, his cock started to grow long and thick.

With a soft moan of regret, he pushed her gently away. A couple of deep breaths didn't help calm his erection, so he tried to focus on the problem at hand. "We'll be back, hopefully soon."

"Well, we'll be here," Declan piped up before Taite could respond.

Ryder knew his friend had seen his body's helpless response to her, and he braced himself for a bout of teasing.

"Ready and waitin' eagerly for your return." Declan winked and added, "Some of us more than others."

"Oh, bugger off." Ryder grinned at Declan's laugh and turned toward the door. As soon as he opened it, the smell of water-soaked ground wafted into the house. Rain fell in big drops, but without the driving force of an hour earlier.

They didn't have a lot of time to get to the boathouse and back before the storm picked up its fury once again.

Cobb closed the door behind them. They set off along the gravel walkway. Soon they were on the dirt path that led down to the beach. Their boots squished in the mud.

At one point Ryder heard a curse from Cobb, and turned just in time to catch him as he stumbled. "You all right?"

"Yes, sir." Cobb straightened and pulled the hood of his slicker under his chin.

Ryder nodded and kept going. After a few more slips and slides, they reached the dock. The boards under their feet creaked, and water from the storm-tossed ocean washed over their boots.

He paused at the boathouse door, fighting with the knob as it slipped in his wet grasp. Finally getting a good grip, he twisted it and pushed the door open. He flicked on his torch, shining the beam around the enclosure, then toward the generator.

Just as he stepped forward and Cobb came into the boathouse behind him, Ryder smelled something that brought him to a stop.

Wet-dog odor.

Sharp scent of anger and hate.

Intruder.

Enemy.

With a snarl, he pushed Cobb back outside and whirled to face the man-wolf hurtling toward him. He had an impression of reddened eyes, wide-open mouth, and clawed hands before the thing slammed into him, bearing him to the floor.

Sharp teeth sank into his shoulder, and he yelled in a mixture of pain and rage. He managed to get his feet under the body of the werewolf and shoved it off him. With one heartbeat Ryder felt his bones shifting, lengthening, drawing screaming muscles with them. He groaned and doubled over. Pain sliced through him with every labored breath he took. Another heartbeat and fur erupted over his skin. On the third heartbeat and with the loud rending of his clothes, his transformation to wolf was complete.

He planted his paws and growled a warning at the wolfman standing before him. With another growl, he hurled himself at the beast, knocking him to the floor. His teeth bit into the vulnerable throat but, before he could establish a killing grip, he was knocked away.

"You damned usurper!" The wolf-man scrambled to his feet and stood tall, panting, his clawed hands clenched into fists at his sides. Spittle dripped from his snout, still short from his partial transformation. His eyes reflected the weak beam of the torch on the floor. His voice was guttural, nearly unrecognizable as human. "She's mine. You had no right to touch her. To fuck her."

Ryder drew his lips back in a snarl.

Mine.

My mate.

Not yours.

He tucked his ears down and raised his hackles. Who touched Taite was her decision, not anyone else's.

And she'd made her choice.

The wolf-man bent and groaned. Fur receded, claws retracted. A brown-haired man with a white-blond streak at his part stood naked before him. He straightened and flashed a grim smile. "So you're the great and mighty Ryder Merrick."

Ryder paused and tilted his head, trying to figure out what the man was saying, what he meant with the anger ringing in his tones. Ryder had no idea who he was.

"I'm John Sumner. You don't know me, but you do know the man I work for, the man who gifted me with lycanthropy. Of course, it's been twenty years since he left the Keep, and you've probably forced him out of your mind." Seemingly unconcerned with his nudity, he crossed his arms. When Ryder gave a low growl, a slow grin curved the man's lips. "Your cousin Miles wanted me to take out your friend Declan, which I'll get to soon enough."

He took a few steps to one side. Ryder kept his gaze fixed on the man, waiting to see what his next move would be.

Sumner dropped his arms with a sweeping gesture. "I was

destined to be like this. Like you and Miles. And as soon as you're out of the way, I'll have Taite."

Unable to speak in his wolf form, Ryder instead growled again.

Sumner got the message. His eyes narrowed. "You don't think I'm worthy, do you? Anymore than you thought your cousin was worthy." He shrugged. "No matter. He found someone in New York who was more than happy to turn him—for a price. That seventy-five thousand pound inheritance from your dad came in handy. For that amount, he was worthy enough." A grin curved his mouth. "And now I am, too."

There was nothing to be worthy of, as far as Ryder was concerned. Miles had always wanted to be lycan, from the time he was a little boy and had seen Ryder's father during his Change. The elder Merrick had never thought it was a good idea, nor had Ryder as he got older and understood more. After his parents had died, Ryder had kicked Miles out for his own good.

It seemed, though, that Miles had finally gotten what he'd wanted. And he'd brought someone else into this damned way of life as well.

"Taite will see it, too," Sumner said.

Ryder jerked his head up and stared at him.

"I've been courting her, you see." Sumner rubbed his tongue over his lower lip. "When I first started trailing O'Connell, I saw her and loved her immediately. She's everything I want in a woman—she's smart, funny. Strong. Pretty, too." His smile faded. "She doesn't appreciate me, not like she should. I've given her gifts that she's thrown into the trash, tried to talk to her, to get her to understand we're meant for each other, but she wouldn't listen. She's too stubborn— that's a definite flaw. But when she sees *I'm* the dominant one, she'll come around." His eyes narrowed. "Though I will have to punish her for her indiscretion with you."

Sumner was her stalker? And, obviously, he was the were-wolf she'd seen. But how did he know her?

"I've known Taite for almost a year now," Sumner went on as if he'd heard Ryder's silent question. "Coworkers first, then friends. Tried to be more, but she wouldn't go out on more than a few dates with me. Wouldn't give me a real chance to show her the kind of man I am. She won't have a choice, not after this." Sumner took a small step forward. His left leg twitched, then his right arm, and Ryder saw the fur begin to sprout in ripples along the other man's skin.

From the corner of his eye, he saw Cobb inch into the boathouse and head toward the back. Ryder growled at Sumner, keeping his attention on him and off his friend.

Suddenly, Cobb rushed forward, a heavy oar in his hands. He swung at Sumner, who now was once again in his wolf-man form. Sumner jerked to one side, dodging the blow. Cobb jumped back out of the beast's reach.

With a roar of rage, the big wolf-man bent and, picking up a screwdriver, threw it at Cobb. The sharp metal drove into the side of Cobb's left calf.

Cobb cried out and fell back, hands clutching his injury.

"I'll get back to you later, little man," Sumner growled.

Ryder began to circle around, trying to get in front of Cobb, his foremost thought to protect what was his.

His pack-mate.

Sumner's left shoulder twitched. He groaned, dropping to his knees. A second later, his transformation was complete. A large brown-furred wolf with one white-tipped ear stood in his place. With barely a pause, he charged Ryder.

The force of his attack slammed Ryder back into the un-forgiving housing of the generator. Sumner's teeth clamped down on the heavy muscle in his rear flank.

Ryder growled through the pain and fought back, forcing Sumner away from him. They careened into the side of the building, knocking over old fishing poles and boating supplies with a loud crash. A hard thwack to his shoulder made Ryder yelp, and he jumped back.

"Sorry, sir," Cobb said. He stood a few feet away, holding the oar like a baseball bat. Blood made a dark, wet swath down his pant leg, the screwdriver still deeply embedded. Through clenched teeth, he muttered, "I shall try again."

He swung at Sumner and caught him under the chin.

Ryder heard the snap of the other wolf's teeth as his mouth was driven shut. Ryder sprang toward Sumner, who eluded him and went for Cobb.

The older man shouted in fear and jabbed at the advancing wolf with the flat end of the oar. Sumner grabbed it in his teeth and gave it a mighty shake, dislodging it from Cobb's hands.

Ryder lunged and bit down into the ruff at Sumner's neck, holding him back. The acrid taste of blood filled his mouth, slid down his throat. The sharp coppery scent saturated the air. As the flavor and odor heightened his bloodlust, he growled.

Sumner yelped, then snarled and tried to wriggle out of the grasp of Ryder's strong jaws. Ryder shifted his stance to try to hold firm, but the other wolf was finally able to knock him off-balance. Ryder skidded across the floor, his claws scrambling for a hold on the wooden surface.

He attacked again, and this time was successful in forcing Sumner to the floor. A nip to Sumner's right shoulder, then a fierce hold on his throat kept him down.

Blood streamed down Ryder's throat, over his fur as his teeth punctured veins and tore through muscles in Sumner's neck. He felt the rumble of the other wolf's growling yelp beneath his jaws, heard the sound become higher pitched as he tightened his hold.

With a forceful twist, Sumner shoved Ryder away. Ryder opened his mouth, dropping fur and flesh onto the floor. His tongue snaked out and swiped at the blood on his muzzle.

Enemy.

Eyes narrowed, hackles up, he prowled toward the wounded wolf, which backed up, blood gushing from the gaping wound in his throat. The dark brown wolf gave a low snarl, his fierce gaze fixed on Ryder with a clear promise of revenge. He turned and leaped through the window, shattering the glass.

With a loud growl, Ryder jumped out after him. Slipping in the blood the wounded wolf left behind, he stood, panting heavily, and watched Sumner skitter down the dock and head deeper into the island. The other wolf was bleeding heavily. With part of his throat ripped out, he would most likely need the better part of a full day to recuperate enough to be anything remotely resembling a threat.

Had Cobb not been wounded, Ryder would have gone after Sumner to finish the job. But he needed to see to his friend.

They were safe. For now.

Ryder closed his eyes and panted through the pain from the multiple bite and claw marks. With a shudder, he forced the transformation back to human, grateful it was daylight and he was able to do so. Come moonrise, he would be trapped in the wolf's body.

And now, knowing for sure who it was that was after Taite, Ryder had to tell her the truth. About how he felt.

About what *he* was.

It wouldn't be easy. This near a full moon, the closer it got to sunset the more the beast would claw to get out. With the taste of blood in his mouth, the scent of it in his nostrils, the beast roared with fury, wanting out again even now.

Ryder limped back inside the boathouse to Cobb, who sat on the floor where he'd fallen. His hands were on his calf, pressing down around the screwdriver. He looked up at Ryder and whatever he saw on his face made him blanch.

Ryder halted, clenching his fists. He'd never seen that look on his longtime employee's face, because always before he'd been securely locked up in the basement, allowing Cobb to feel safe. Now . . .

Now Cobb was face to face with a beast who looked like a man, and he was scared.

The sharp vinegary odor of fear and the coppery smell of blood only served to make Ryder's struggle for control that much harder. He closed his eyes and concentrated on breathing, calming his heart rate.

Once he felt he had himself much more under control, he looked at Cobb and smiled reassuringly. "It's me, Cobb. Just me."

Cobb nodded and started to struggle to his feet.

"Stay put." Ryder knelt beside him and pressed down on his shoulder. "I need to get this screwdriver out."

"Yes, sir," the older man said, his voice tight. "But we must get to the house and warn Miss Gibson."

"Yes, you're right." Ryder went to a wall cabinet and pulled open the door. Finding clean cloths on a high shelf, he pulled them down and went back to Cobb. He folded one cloth into a thick square and handed it to his friend.

"When I pull the screwdriver out, I need you to hold that to the wound while I bind it." He took a deep breath. "This is going to hurt."

"Just do it." Cobb's eyes squeezed shut, and he held his breath.

Ryder made sure he had a good grip on the screwdriver and yanked it out.

Cobb shouted in pain and slapped the folded cloth over the wound. With quick motions, Ryder wrapped the other cloths around Cobb's calf, tying them off to hold the makeshift pad in place.

He took Cobb's hands and pulled him to his feet. Positioning himself at Cobb's side, he put one arm around his shoulders and walked him toward the door. The older man limped heavily, his jaw clenched and groans escaping him every time he put weight on his injured leg.

Ryder reached for the door. "Once Sumner's injuries heal, he'll be back. We've got to get to the house and get ready. There's too much damage here to repair quickly. The generator will have to wait."

"Uh, sir?"

Stopping at Cobb's uncertain tone, Ryder looked down at his employee.

Cobb motioned in Ryder's direction. More specifically, toward his groin. "You should put something on, Mr. Merrick. This will be difficult enough to explain without you going back to the house naked."

Ryder was so used to being nude after a shift from his wolf form that he hadn't even thought about putting on clothes. But Cobb was right.

After propping Cobb against the wall, Ryder grabbed one of the slickers hanging on a peg by the broken window. He yanked it over his head and, looking around, located his boots. Once he'd shoved his feet into them, he opened the door. A slash of rain mixed with small pellets of hail pelted him.

Knowing Cobb would never be able to navigate the stairs that ran up the side of the bluff, he swung the man up in his arms and went outside. The wind howled through the trees, and the rain fell at an almost horizontal angle. The gale had once again gained strength.

The wind blew his hood back, and he bent his head against the sting of rain against his face. He stumbled at the edge of the dock, going down on one knee, hard. With an oath, he struggled to his feet and shifted Cobb more securely in his arms.

"Sir," Cobb shouted above the wind. "Put me down. I can walk."

"Not with that calf, you can't." Ryder started up the stairs and tried to ignore the pain streaking up his thigh and through his shoulder. When the stairs ended and he was on firmer footing, he picked up the pace. But the rain had turned the ground to slick muck, turning a slight incline into what felt like a battle to climb a mountain. He muttered a curse as he slid back several feet.

"Mr. Merrick." Cobb's voice was tight with stress and residual fear from the attack. "You've an injured leg yourself. You should put me down."

Ryder paused and drew in a deep breath. Looking up the muddy path, he knew he'd never make it to the house without being able to grab a few handholds along the way. Cobb wouldn't like what he was about to do, but no one would see the indignity of him slung over Ryder's shoulder like a sack of potatoes. "Hang on." Ignoring the sputtering protests, he moved Cobb into place.

"Sir!" Cobb's voice came from behind him. The little man put his hands on Ryder's rear and levered himself up. Seeming to realize where he'd placed his hands, he quickly moved them, grabbing fistfuls of the slicker at Ryder's waist.

"Just hang on." Ryder started up the path.

After several minutes of struggling for every foot and handhold, he made it to the edge of the lawn and paused to catch his breath. Knowing they were pressed for time, he broke into a jog and headed toward the front of the house.

"Sir, not the front," Cobb protested, his voice shaking as he bounced up and down on Ryder's shoulder. "You're too muddy."

"Oh, for God's sake, Cobb." Rather than argue with him, Ryder switched direction and headed around back. "We can clean it up, you know."

"It is *my* responsibility—*oof!*" That last sound was wrenched from him when Ryder slipped in the wet grass and jerked to keep his balance.

As Ryder rounded the house, he saw Declan climbing down a ladder that extended up to the top floor. He was coming down fast, cursing as the ladder shuddered against the wind and his feet skidded on the wet, slippery wood. When Declan saw them, a startled look crossed his face, and he climbed down even faster. "What the hell happened?" He jumped down the last few feet and started toward them.

Ryder reached the back door and flung it open, tracking mud onto the pristine floor as he walked over and placed Cobb on one of the kitchen chairs. "I was about to ask you the same thing, mate," he said to Declan as the other man closed the kitchen door.

"When the wind picked up again, it knocked a limb down onto the house." Declan toed off his filthy shoes, keeping them on the mat in front of the door. "It broke a window in Taite's room. I thought I'd better board it up before the storm flooded the place."

Ryder limped over to the cabinet where the medical supplies were kept and dragged everything out. He snagged a few clean kitchen towels as well. Before Declan could repeat his question, he said, "The werewolf is here."

Declan swore under his breath and raked one hand through his wet hair. "You're sure?"

"Well, I just pulled a screwdriver out of Cobb's leg. I sure as hell didn't put it there." Ryder plunked the supply kit on the table. "Where's Taite?"

"She's mopping up the bedroom."

Ryder felt a sense of relief he couldn't quash. Perhaps once he'd taken care of Cobb, he could get himself cleaned up, and she wouldn't see the mess *he* was in.

Wouldn't see his wounds heal faster than normal.

He grimaced at himself. He still needed to tell her what he was, and it really didn't matter if he was wounded or not. She deserved the truth.

Declan went to the back door and shoved his feet into his shoes.

"Where're you going?" Ryder asked.

"I'm movin' the ladder before that damned furball gets it into his head to use it. Be right back."

Ryder turned back to Cobb. Kneeling on the floor, Ryder

pulled off Cobb's boots, taking particular care with his wounded leg. "How're you doing, Cobb?"

"Fine, sir." Cobb's voice was tight and, when Ryder glanced up at his face, he saw the older man's skin was pale.

"Well, we'll get you fixed up in no time." Ryder bent and pulled off his own boots, tossing them toward the mat by the kitchen door. Then he went to the sink and washed the mud off his hands. Going back to the table, he opened the medical kit and began pulling out supplies.

He'd just lined everything up, ready for use, when Declan came back in.

"I've stowed the ladder back in the shed and locked it, though if he's determined enough that won't stop him." Declan toed off his shoes and padded over to them. "By the way," he said, peering at Cobb's leg over Ryder's shoulder. "How'd you manage to get away from him?"

Ryder briefly closed his eyes. How did he tell his best friend what he was, what he'd been hiding from the beginning of their friendship? He'd hoped it wouldn't come to this. He couldn't help but think that, once Declan knew, their friendship would be over.

And he'd be all alone, except for Cobb.

"I'll tell you later," he finally muttered. "I need to see to Cobb first." He didn't see how he could tell Declan who the werewolf was without pointing the finger right back at himself because of the connection with his cousin. So, for now, he'd keep that information to himself. He looked up at Cobb and said, "I'll take these bloody cloths off, then you need to roll up your pants' leg so we can get at that wound."

A flush rose along Cobb's cheeks and he glanced at Declan, then back at Ryder. "Sir, could we not do this in the privacy of my rooms?"

"Oh, for cryin' out loud." Declan gave a short burst of laughter. "It's only your leg. Don't be such a prissy little miss."

Ryder ignored him and shook his head. "No," he said to

his employee. He glanced at Declan. "Do me a favor and go to Cobb's room. Grab his bathrobe."

"It's hanging on a hook inside my closet door." Cobb's voice was strained with a chord of resignation.

Declan obligingly left the room, though he muttered something under his breath about damned persnickety blokes.

Ryder unwrapped the cloths tied around Cobb's leg, dropping them to the floor. "The medical supplies are all here in the kitchen," he said in response to Cobb's request for privacy, "and we need to take care of this and get the bleeding stopped now. So roll up your pants."

Declan returned and tossed the robe over the back of one of the chairs. "What else do you want me to do?"

"Get me a hot, wet towel, would you?" Ryder asked him. "I need to wipe off this blood."

While Cobb fumbled with his trousers, gingerly rolling the hem up to his knee, Declan went to the sink and turned on the faucet, waiting until steam rose before he plunged a towel under the stream. He gingerly wrung it out and handed it to Ryder, asking, "What about the werewolf?"

Ryder tossed the hot towel from one hand to another, his sensitive palms feeling the heat keenly. "I managed to wound him badly. There are oars and such in the boathouse," he quickly added at Declan's questioning look. "But until we get him taken care of for good, we need to stay together."

When he applied the towel to Cobb's leg, the little man drew in a sharp breath. Ryder heard his knuckles crack and looked down to see him gripping the bottom of the chair so tightly his fingers were red.

Ryder washed the blood away from Cobb's wound, relieved to see the bleeding had already slowed. "This isn't too bad," he said, trying to alleviate Cobb's fears.

"If you say so, sir." Cobb's voice sounded thin and reedy. White lines around his lips indicated the pain he suffered. "But I suspect you're merely trying to pacify me."

Ryder continued to work on Cobb's leg. Other than a few gasps from Cobb, there was silence in the kitchen until Declan leaned over his shoulder and said, "That's gonna need stitches."

Cobb's faced paled even more, leaving his skin looking like fine parchment. "Oh, dear," was all he said.

Declan rummaged through the medical kit and pulled out a needle, a pair of scissors, and a length of thread. Taking a bottle of rubbing alcohol from the box, he went to the sink and poured some of it into one palm and rubbed his hands together to disinfect them. Then he poured some of the disinfectant over the needle and turned back toward Ryder and Cobb.

"Here," he said, walking over and kneeling beside Ryder. "I've field medical training. Let me." He looked up at Cobb and said softly, "This will hurt a bit."

Cobb nodded and swallowed. His hands gripped the chair by his thighs, but he remained silent as Declan's steady fingers put in three neat stitches.

"You'll need to stay off that a few days." Declan got to his feet and went back to the sink. He removed the remaining thread from the needle. Once he'd poured more alcohol over the needle and cleaned it, he placed the items back into the medical kit.

"Nice job," Ryder said. Hearing a noise from the foyer, he turned his head. Taite's perfume wafted to him. He knew Cobb would be mortified were she to walk into the kitchen and see him in a rumpled state. "Declan, would you go head off Taite? I don't want her coming in here just yet."

Cobb straightened and his hands fluttered nervously. "Sir!" His voice sounded strangled. "Miss Gibson cannot see me like this."

"I know, Cobb." Ryder tried to soothe him. "That's why I'm asking Declan to take her upstairs to her room and stay with her until I can get you up there." He looked at Declan and caught the other man's nod.

"Sure thing," Declan said. "Just answer one question for me."

When he didn't go on, Ryder asked, "Yes?"

"What the hell happened to your clothes?"

Chapter 15

Taite heard Declan's question and quickened her pace. Just as she reached the door, she heard Ryder tell Declan to get out, and she very nearly ran into him.

"Ah, you can't go in there, lass." Declan blocked her way and, when she tried to duck around him, he grabbed the doorframe and refused to let her in.

"What's going on?" Taite tried to peer around him but couldn't see a thing. "Declan, move."

She heard Cobb moan, "Oh, my God," followed by a heartfelt, "sir, do something!"

"Stay out of here, Taite." Ryder's deep voice was filled with amusement. "You'll give Cobb a heart attack."

"But . . ." Taite tried a twist and duck maneuver, but Declan wrapped one brawny arm around her waist. She managed to get a glimpse into the kitchen and saw bloody rags on the floor and Cobb's bare leg.

"What's going on? Is Cobb hurt? Let me in there."

She looked at Declan, who started to respond but stopped when Cobb groaned out, "Oh, God." His voice sounded strangled. A chair scraped across the floor.

Ryder muttered a curse and then laughed, a short expulsion of sound that held a mixture of humor and frustration. "Taite, just give us a minute, would you?"

She crossed her arms and tapped one foot. "What the hell is going on?"

"That bloody beast is here," Declan said. His tone was flat and as serious as she'd ever heard it. "He put a screwdriver through Cobb's leg."

Her heart thumped, hard, and her mouth went dry. Reflexively, she took a step back and put one hand up to her mouth in shock.

Why she should feel so surprised was beyond her. She'd known it was only a matter of time before the bastard tracked her down. But she'd been lulled into a sense of security by Ryder and her own tangled emotions.

"Ryder? Is he all right?" she asked, trying to get around Declan again. If Ryder had been hurt . . . "Declan, get the hell out of my way."

From behind Declan she heard Ryder's voice. "It's all right. You can let her in now."

Declan stepped back and, as she passed him, she smacked him in the stomach with the back of her hand. "What is wrong with you?" she muttered.

"Hey!" he protested. "I was only doin' as I was told."

Taite grimaced, shooting him a glance over her shoulder. "Since when?"

She watched Ryder lift Cobb into his arms. Cobb reached out and grabbed the robe from a chair. Taite frowned to see blood on the floor and streaking down one of Ryder's bare legs.

She blinked and tilted her head to one side. Was Ryder naked under that raincoat? What happened to his clothes?

One of Cobb's pant legs was stained with the red stuff as well. There were more immediate things to worry about now than where Ryder's clothes had gone.

"Oh, my God. Are you guys all right?" She rolled her eyes and answered her own question. "You're both covered in blood. Of course you're not all right. Just ignore me."

Ryder's smile was a quick flash of white teeth and he said, "Oh, I could never do that, sweetheart." He walked toward her, limping slightly.

Realization struck her cold. Her heart thudded heavily in her chest. If the werewolf had bitten Ryder—or Cobb—then, according to legend, they would become werewolves themselves.

Oh. Dear. God.

"We'll be fine." Ryder leaned to one side and kissed her, his touch meant to be reassuring, no doubt. But when she saw him wince as he straightened, she knew he was just trying to fool her into thinking he was unhurt.

"Ryder—"

"Let me get Cobb settled," he interrupted.

She could see how pale and drawn the other man's face was, not to mention the way he clutched the white terry cloth robe like a precious possession, so she moved out of their way without a word.

As Ryder brushed by her, she saw the strain on his face and knew his injuries were worse than he was letting on. She followed him out of the room and up the stairs.

Cobb was fretting. "Sir, why not just take me back to my rooms?"

"I don't want anyone on the ground floor tonight," Ryder responded to his employee. "You'll all stay in the same room, sleeping in shifts."

"I'll just stay here and clean up the mess, then," Declan called after them, humor and disgruntlement in his voice.

Taite ignored his little sulk. Her arms were sore from mopping up the water in her bedroom. She'd clean up the kitchen if she had to, but Declan was completely capable of it, so she left him to it.

"So you think the werewolf will attack again tonight?" she asked Ryder.

"He's hurt, too." His jaw was held rigidly, and she could

see pain etched across his face. "Badly enough I can tell you he'll need at least overnight to recuperate." Ryder hefted Cobb higher in his arms and winced. "He lost a lot of blood."

"How do you know that? Nothing I read suggested anything even remotely like that." Taite stayed close behind, ready to help him if he needed it. As soon as they got Cobb settled she was taking care of her man.

And if he's been bitten? a little voice inside her head whispered. *What will you do then?*

God help her, she just didn't know. Her experience with werewolves was limited. But if the books were right and a good man remained unchanged by being bitten—well, except for the part about being furry once a month—perhaps she could still love him.

Perhaps.

She realized Ryder hadn't answered her question. "Ryder?"

"I promise you I'll answer your questions as soon as I get Cobb settled." Ryder paused on the landing. "Can you just give me a few minutes?" His breath came harsh and heavy, and she saw a fine trembling in his arms.

She narrowed her eyes but nodded her agreement. "Why didn't you take the elevator?" she asked, touching him lightly on one shoulder.

Ryder shook his head. "I don't like cramped spaces, never have."

"Why?" Taite knew why she didn't like the dark, and she was interested to hear the reason behind Ryder's phobia. That he even had one made him seem a little less perfect.

"I was trapped in a cave-in when I was a kid," he said. His voice held the flavor of that long-ago fear even now. "I was stuck in a space barely big enough to sit up in. It was two days before they could dig me out." He shifted Cobb in his arms.

"Why not just put him in a room on the first floor?"

"I want us up as high as possible."

To make it harder for the werewolf to get to them.

When they reached the top of the stairs, Taite squeezed around him and went ahead to get the door. "How about my room?" she asked, glancing back at him. "The window's boarded up, so the werewolf won't be able to get in that way." She left the *I hope* unspoken.

"That's fine."

She opened the door and went straight to the bed, turning down the covers. Ryder headed toward the bed, and Cobb started protesting.

"Mr. Merrick, you cannot put me on the bed."

"Cobb, we've been through this already."

"No, really, I must insist. The blood will ruin the bed linens." Cobb struggled to be put down, and Ryder stumbled. He muttered a curse and Cobb stilled, but continued his protest. "I need to clean up, and so do you."

With a scowl, Ryder carried him on to the bathroom. He set Cobb carefully on the side of the bathtub then left the room, pulling the door closed behind him. As he walked toward Taite, she saw that he still limped.

Her gaze tracked up the shiny surface of the slicker until she reached his face. Lines of pain and weariness bracketed his mouth. She touched his cheek gently, smiling when he cupped her hand in his and turned his face to plant a kiss in her palm.

"You need to be seen to, too, you know." Taite turned her hand around, linked her fingers with his and dropped their hands to her side. As big and handsome as he was, dressed in his yellow raincoat, he reminded her of Christopher Robin. Her heart squeezed. He needed her, whether he wanted to admit it or not. "As soon as Cobb is finished in the bathroom and we get him settled, we'll get you looked after."

And we'll just see what that wound looks like.

"I'll be all right," Ryder murmured. His gaze wouldn't meet hers, and she frowned. Was he just trying to be all stoic and manly for her benefit, or was he trying to hide something?

"Yes, you will," she agreed. "Because I'm going to make sure of it." She paused, then asked the question burning in her brain. "Ryder, did he bite you? Or Cobb?"

"He didn't bite Cobb." Ryder moved away from her, heading toward the door. "Stay here, would you, and look after him? I have to . . . clean up."

"Ryder, wait!" Taite stared at the empty doorway. For such a big guy, he sure could move fast. "Well, don't think that's the end of it, buddy," she muttered. As soon as she got Cobb settled, she and Ryder were going to have a conversation, whether he wanted to or not.

"Miss Gibson?"

She whirled toward the bathroom, one hand over her heart. "Cobb. You scared me."

"Sorry, miss." He limped out into the bedroom. He wore the robe, clutching the lapels over his chest. Seeing his embarrassed expression, she almost made a joke about his modesty being safe with her. His face, white with fatigue except for the bright flags of color on his cheekbones, changed her mind.

She hurried over and put an arm around his waist to support him. When they reached the bed, he collapsed onto it with a sigh.

Taite pulled the covers up over him. "Can I get you anything?"

He shook his head, his eyes closing tiredly. "No, thank you, miss. I just need a bit of rest."

She heard Declan yell her name. "In here," she called out.

Heavy footsteps came down the hall. He stopped in the doorway. "Is everythin' all right?"

"Ryder doesn't want any of us to be left alone," she said. "Would you stay with Cobb while I go check on Ryder?"

Declan nodded and came into the room. "Sure thing, lass."

He thumbed over his shoulder. "I passed Ry as I was comin' up the stairs. I think he was headed back down to ground level on his way to his room."

"Thanks." Taite paused beside him. "Behave yourself," she whispered with a nod of her head toward Cobb. "Don't upset him."

Declan raised his eyebrows. "Now, and why would you think I'd go and upset him?" He kept his voice pitched low.

"Declan." Taite narrowed her eyes. "He already has a problem with you. Don't aggravate him." She started to leave, then stopped and looked back over her shoulder. "Why is that, anyway?" She kept her voice low so as not to be overheard by Cobb.

"That he has a problem with me?" At her nod, Declan shrugged one shoulder and shoved his hands into the front pockets of his jeans. His voice was pitched as soft as hers. "I was involved with his daughter, Pelicia."

"I already figured that much out," she muttered. "There's something else, though."

A look of chagrin and something very much like self-loathing crossed his face. "I really don't want to go into it now, lass."

Taite would have pursued it, but Cobb was leaning toward them, trying to hear the conversation. She didn't want to press the issue in front of him, or lower her voice even more and take the chance that, in his curiosity, Cobb would fall out of bed.

"Well, just behave yourself," she repeated.

Declan nodded and entered the room. She watched him pull a chair up next to the bed. Before he sat down, he reached behind his back and grabbed the gun tucked into his waistband. Then he sat, the gun in one big hand resting on his thigh.

She went downstairs and straight to Ryder's bedroom. He wasn't there. She was just about to turn and leave when she heard water splashing in the bathroom.

Peeking in, she realized he was finishing up a shower. Steam had fogged the glass door of the stall, giving her only a glimpse of his silhouette. The blood-stained raincoat lay in a heap on the floor. She bent and picked it up. There were no other clothes there, not even underwear.

Oh, yeah, they were going to talk about this.

Taite backed up and put the lid down on the toilet, and sat down.

When Ryder opened the door of the shower and stepped out, she let her gaze travel over him, searching for wounds. She couldn't help but admire his body, the long, strong lines of his muscles, the part of him that made him male resting in its nest of curls.

"Taite, I asked you to stay with Cobb."

She frowned at him. "No, you *told* me to stay with Cobb. There's a difference, Mr. Bossy." When he opened his mouth for a retort, she waved him off. "Don't worry. Declan is with him, and he's armed."

She saw a wound high on his shoulder and another one on his thigh. With all the blood she'd seen on his leg, she'd expected the thigh wound to look deeper than it did. It was nasty-looking all right, the edges ragged and bruised, but nowhere near as bad as she thought it should look.

Then it hit her. He *had* been bitten. By a werewolf.

Dear God in heaven.

Taite shot off the toilet seat so fast she lost her balance and fell on her ass. When Ryder reached for her, she scrambled backward until she slammed into the wall. She put one hand palm out, waving him off, the other pressed against the floor as she tried to stand.

He moved toward her. "Taite—"

"Don't!" she screamed. "Don't touch me." With her back against the wall, she pushed herself to her feet. "You . . . you . . . Oh, God."

She edged through the doorway, not taking her eyes off

him. Her lover. The man who was going to turn into a werewolf.

Remembering what the werewolf in Tucson had looked like, his bulk covered in fur, his eyes glowing maniacally . . . She'd never been so scared in her life.

No. Not scared. Terrified.

She'd run from a werewolf and brought him straight to Ryder.

This was all her fault. Ryder, the man who'd been nothing but gentle with her, the man she was very much afraid she'd fallen in love with, was going to become a monster because of her.

Tears blurred her vision, and she blinked them away. She was cold, then hot, then cold again. Guilt and misery and fear roiled through her, making her legs and hands tremble. But her overriding emotion was fear, allowing little room for remorse.

Ryder reached out and she flinched, then bit her lip as he only snagged a towel from the rack. He wrapped the soft terry cloth around his lean waist.

Her gaze followed his inherently sensual movement. Seeing the bulge of his cock under the knobby burgundy cloth, remembering his touch, the feel of his shaft plunging into her—the memory now brought terror to her heart. She raised her horrified gaze to his.

His lips tightened, and his eyes darkened. Taite saw resignation and deep sadness in his eyes before he shuttered them with his lashes. Motioning toward the bedroom, he said, "We should talk."

Taite backed further into the bedroom. She bumped into the edge of the bed and almost fell over the corner of the mattress. Catching herself, she kept her gaze glued to him as she inched toward the door. Only when she bumped into the doorframe did she stop.

Ryder sighed and sat on the bed. "I don't know how to tell you this," he began.

Taite shook her head. She wrapped her fingers around the doorframe behind her back, clutching it so tightly her knuckles ached. "I know, Ryder."

His head jerked up. Wary eyes met her gaze. "You do?"

She nodded. Two fat tears rolled down her cheeks. "He bit you. You're going to turn into a werewolf."

His gaze became shuttered once more. "And it's pretty obvious to me how you feel about that. About me being a werewolf."

Taite swallowed, hard. Her throat was tight, her mouth dry. What did he expect her to say? *We had great sex, and since this is all my fault, I'm okay with you being a monster?*

She shook her head, unable to respond. Her fingers trembled as she wiped at the tears on her face.

He sighed. When he spoke, his voice was harsh and low. "Taite . . . First of all, I know who the werewolf is. So do you."

She frowned. "I do?"

"He said his name is John Sumner and that he used to work with you. That you dated."

"John!" She brushed a stray strand of hair off her cheek. Her frown deepened. She couldn't quite wrap her brain around what Ryder was telling her. "That can't be right."

"He's a bit shorter than me, with medium brown hair with a white-blond streak at his part."

Her heart thudded behind her ribs. "A streak . . ." Good God. Could it be . . . "That sounds like John." Taite shook her head. "But . . . I thought he was my friend." She cleared her throat, hating how whiny she sounded but unable to stop herself. "How could he do this? *Why* would he do this?"

"It sounded to me like he and your stalker are the same person. So you've not been pursued by a stalker *and* a werewolf. You've been stalked by one creature."

"Oh, what a relief. Knowing my stalker is a werewolf makes me feel so much better." She'd never realized before how sarcastic she got when she was scared, but she'd never been this scared before. And she'd dragged Ryder right into the middle of it. "I'm sorry. I never thought . . . And now you've been bitten. . . ." She trailed off, fighting back tears.

"Sumner biting me isn't going to change what I already am."

She frowned. "But . . ."

All the books she'd read had indicated that anyone bitten by a werewolf was infected and would become a werewolf, too. Unless the werewolf had become a lycanthrope because of a curse. That type wasn't contagious.

That must be what Ryder meant, that John's bite wouldn't change him. Her fingers loosened from the doorframe, and she heaved a sigh of relief. A tremulous smile formed on her lips, and she walked forward a few steps. "Oh, thank God. I was so afraid you'd . . ."

Ryder was shaking his head.

Then she realized she had misremembered the text. She replayed in her mind exactly what he'd said. *Sumner biting me isn't going to change what I already am.*

What I already am.

Taite gasped and jerked back, slamming into the doorframe, cracking her funny bone on the hard wood. Grabbing her elbow, she rubbed at the sting while she stared in renewed horror at Ryder. He had gotten to his feet but didn't move toward her.

So many clues had been there, if she'd only pieced them together sooner.

His unwillingness to talk about werewolves.

The manacles in the basement.

Bloody wounds that were nearly healed.

What I already am.

"I tried to tell you," he murmured. He held out one hand. Instead of his long fingers and broad palm, in her mind's eye she saw superimposed over it a wide paw-like hand of the werewolf. She threw one last horrified look at him, then turned and ran from his room. Her thoughts churned, rolling and bumping together, but one fact was agonizingly clear.

She'd run from one werewolf straight into the arms of another.

Chapter 16

Taite pressed a shaking finger to the control button and stepped into the elevator as soon as the doors swooshed open. Somewhere between the ground floor and the uppermost floor, she went from being terrified to being terrified and angry. Once the elevator stopped and the doors opened, she ran down the hallway to her room.

As she burst into the room, both Declan and Cobb looked up. Declan was still sitting in the chair with his feet propped on the bed, and Cobb leaned against the headboard, a book in his hands. He placed his finger in his book.

Declan jumped to his feet. "What is it, Taite?" He looked over her shoulder, gun in his big hand. "Is it the werewolf?"

"No!" she said in a near-shout. "Just tell me you didn't know."

He frowned. The set of his shoulders relaxed, no doubt because he realized there was no immediate danger. "Didn't know what?"

She looked at Cobb. "I know *you* knew."

"Knew what?" Declan asked, bewilderment sketched on his face.

Cobb sighed and placed the book on the bedspread. "It wasn't my place to tell you, miss."

Taite buried her face in her hands, pressing her fingertips to her closed eyes. Her world had been completely turned upside down. "The whole time, he knew. He knew what he was and he . . ." She fought back a sob. *God*. How stupid she had been, not letting him tell her when he'd wanted to. He was right—he *had* tried to tell her. But she hadn't wanted to spoil the moment.

"Tell what?" Declan looked from one to the other. "Somebody tell me what the hell is goin' on."

Taite glared at him. "Your boyhood chum is a frickin' werewolf!"

Declan narrowed his eyes. "You're fuckin' with me," he said as he tucked the gun into the waistband of his jeans.

"No. I'm not." Taite crossed her arms and began pacing at the side of the bed. "He was bitten by John. My friend, John Sumner—you remember him?—is the werewolf. And, apparently, he's also the one who's been stalking me." She drew in a shaking breath.

"God." Declan plopped down onto the chair he'd vacated earlier. His expression was stunned. "I knew the guy was a smarmy bastard, but I never thought he had the balls to . . . Wait. You're saying Ryder's become infected. He'll turn into a werewolf the next full moon." He looked up, his face paling. "Is there anything we can do? That's tonight."

"I'm not saying he'll *become* a werewolf. I'm saying he *is* one." She stared at him and felt tears begin to well. Her entire body started to shake, and she wrapped her arms around her waist. "He has been all along."

"What the . . . No fuckin' way!"

"Yes fucking way." She swiped at her face and tried to stem the tears that wouldn't stop. Fisting her hand, she dropped it to her side.

Declan got up. Walking over to her, he pulled her into his arms. "I didn't know, sweetheart. Swear to God." His big hands swept up and down her back. "I didn't know."

Taite buried her face in his chest, needing his comfort, the familiarity of his solid bulk in a world turned completely upside down. "The whole time, Declan, he knew. He knew what he was and he . . ." She fought back a sob. *God*. "How could he not have told me what he was before we . . ."

Declan's arms tightened around her. "I'm gonna kill the son of a bitch."

"No!" Cobb started to push the covers off, and Taite and Declan both turned toward him. "You cannot. Mr. Merrick was merely trying to protect himself. Protect his family."

He swung his legs over the edge of the bed, wincing as he did so. His hands held the robe securely around him, preserving his modesty. "I know he never meant to hurt either of you. He isn't a bad man."

"The hell he isn't," Declan muttered. "He's a soddin' werewolf."

"He's ashamed."

"Well, he bloody well should be."

"No," Cobb said with a shake of his head. "You misunderstand me. Mr. Merrick is ashamed of what he is. He always has been, since he was a child and was first told of the family curse."

"Family curse?" Taite reached up and swiped at the tears wetting her cheeks. "What family curse?"

Cobb sighed. "I really wish Mr. Merrick had told you himself."

She burrowed back against Declan, needing his warmth, his strength. Rubbing her forehead over his chest, she muttered, "He tried. I wouldn't . . . I couldn't stay."

Declan patted her back. His chest moved under her face as he drew in a deep breath and let it out slowly.

"I understand." Cobb's voice was calm but held an underlying layer of sadness.

She glanced over at him to see him studying his clasped hands.

He looked back up at her. "From the time he reaches his twenty-fifth birthday, every male in the Merrick line becomes a werewolf at each full moon. While they can control the Change during the rest of the month, at the full moon they're

helpless and shift to their wolf form as soon as the sun sets."
Cobb's hands twisted together. "Mr. Merrick is so very afraid
he'll hurt someone when his wolf comes upon him."

"Well, he could, couldn't he?" She gazed at Cobb. The fear
she'd felt earlier was creeping back over her. "He *is* a werewolf."

Cobb's eyes grew moist, his expression pleading. "But he
hasn't. Miss Gibson, you must understand. What a man is
before he becomes a werewolf is what he is after. While
Mr. Merrick can't control the Change during the time of the
full moon, he very much can control his beast, though he
fears he cannot."

"What the hell are you talkin' about?" Declan asked.

Not sure she wanted to hear Cobb's answer, even knowing
she needed to, Taite pulled out of Declan's arms and went
over to Cobb. "You should have that leg up."

When she started to bend to help him, he placed a hand on
her shoulder. "Please, miss." He waited until she looked up
at him. "Postponing the inevitable is futile."

She grimaced and nodded. "You still need to have that leg
up."

Once she'd helped him swing his legs back onto the mattress, she sat in the chair beside the bed. "Go on."

Cobb drew in a breath through his nose and huffed it out.
"From the time he was a boy, Mr. Merrick's father told him
he was an animal. A beast. For that's what Mr. Alexander believed to the day he died." He rolled his head against the pillow. "And that's likely why he murdered his wife and then
took his own life. Because he feared the beast would break
free and hurt her, yet he couldn't bring himself to allow her to
go on without him."

Declan grabbed a matching chair from against the wall
and placed it beside hers. "He and his father were very close.
Ryder was devastated when that happened."

Cobb nodded. "It's unfortunate that the elder Mr. Merrick
chose to isolate himself—and his family—in much the same

way that Ryder has. I fear they travel the same path need-lessly."

"How so?" Declan reached over and took one of Taite's hands in his. She was grateful for the warmth of his long fingers wrapped around hers.

"Mr. Merrick has always believed he needed to be locked up during the full moon so he would not hurt anyone, for that's what his father did and his father before him. However, I've never believed it to be so. And, down in the boathouse after he fought the other werewolf, he was able to come down from the bloodlust. He didn't hurt me."

Taite saw a look pass through his eyes. "But you thought he would, didn't you?"

"I did, just for a moment." He shook his head. "I'm most disappointed in myself."

Declan sat back in his chair and crossed one leg over the other, resting an ankle on the opposite knee. His dark brows rose. "You're disappointed in yourself? Not in Ry?"

"How am I to convince Mr. Merrick he's not a danger to others in his wolf form if I cringe in fear of him myself?"

Taite closed her eyes and rolled her head on her shoulders, trying to loosen tight muscles. This was all so bizarre, like something out of a dream.

No, a nightmare.

A childhood song flitted through her mind, though with lyrics far different than she'd sung as a kid. *Here a wolf, there a wolf, everywhere a wolf-wolf.*

"I'm sure Mr. Merrick is in the basement even now, trying to get himself fastened into the manacles."

Declan snorted. "You have manacles in the basement?"

"I saw them," Taite said, as Cobb gave a short nod. "Attached to the wall above a narrow bed."

Cobb went on, "There's one that goes around his neck, and one for each wrist. The wrist ones fall off once he changes to a wolf, of course—"

"Of course," Declan muttered.

Cobb eyed him balefully. "Once he has attached one of the wrist manacles, he can't reach the other one."

"If they fall off, why bother?" Taite asked. Her stomach clenched, and she fought back a wave of nausea. She'd had sex with a werewolf.

Her eyes widened. Had they used protection? *Ohgodohgod.* She couldn't get pregnant. She'd have a litter, wouldn't she? Remembering the condom Ryder had rolled over his erection, she breathed a sigh of relief and slumped in her chair.

Now was not the time to panic.

Hell. If ever there was a time to panic, it would be now.

"It's to keep him from being able to reach and unlatch the neck manacle. Human fingers are more nimble than wolf paws," Cobb said. "Normally I am the one to go down and help him, but . . ." He trailed off and motioned toward his wounded leg.

Declan scowled. "I'd be more than happy to go down and chain the bugger up," he muttered with narrowed eyes. "Then he'd have no choice but to listen to the few well-chosen words I have for him."

"There is also the matter of securing the door. It locks from the outside." Cobb's gaze slid to Taite. He started to say something, then shook his head and looked down at his lap.

"What?" Taite asked.

"Nothing."

"You were going to say something. What?"

He glanced up at her, his green eyes holding that pleading look again. "I just think it would be best if *you* were the one to go downstairs."

"Why me?" She had a feeling she knew what he was going to say, and she was just as sure she wasn't going to like it.

"You need to show him that you, too, are unafraid."

Taite's hand clenched around Declan's so hard his fingers went numb. "Easy there, lass," he murmured and gently pried her fingers loose. He flexed his hand and looked at her. "I take it you're not too thrilled with the idea."

She stared at him with wide, dark eyes. "How can I show him I'm unafraid when I'm frickin' freaked out of my mind?"

He reached out and swiped at a tear that slid down her cheek. "I'll go, sweetheart." Keeping a secure hold on Taite's hand, he stood and looked down at Cobb. "Is there anythin' else I should know before I go and face the big, bad wolf?"

Declan was only partially kidding. He had a very vivid memory of that bastard Sumner charging his car back in Tucson. If that's what he was going to confront when he went to the basement, he wanted to be prepared.

"He's *not* bad," Cobb insisted. Pushing himself up against the headboard, he adjusted his position and glared at Declan. "I keep telling you—"

"Yeah, yeah," Declan muttered. "He's really one of the *good* werewolves."

"He is." Cobb crossed his arms and stared mutinously at them. "If you would only see beyond the beast and see the man. . . ." He shrugged and sighed. "But it may be too much to ask of you, to see your friend instead of the wolf."

Declan scowled. That was below the belt. How the hell was he supposed to feel, finding out his best mate was a fucking monster? And that Declan hadn't had a clue?

He hated being clueless.

"I'll go." Taite pulled her hand away from Declan's and stood up with a deep breath. "Someone needs to stay with Cobb in case John comes."

Declan raised a brow. "Oh, I see. And you'd rather it be me who faces him, I take it?"

She grimaced and shrugged. "Better the devil you know . . ."

"Than the one you don't," he finished for her.

"I don't believe your John will come tonight," Cobb responded.

"He's not *my* John." Taite frowned. "And why won't he come tonight?"

"For the same reason wounds that would ordinarily heal with Mr. Merrick's shift will not. Wounds inflicted by another werewolf take longer to heal." He made a vague gesture with one hand. "Something in their saliva, I suspect. Anyway, Mr. Merrick tore out much of John's throat, which will incapacitate him for tonight and possibly most of tomorrow." He looked at them and worry reflected in his gaze. "Although that part I am not certain of."

"Which part?" Declan asked. He held out his hands, palms up. "The incapacitated tonight part, or the most of tomorrow part?"

The worry in Cobb's gaze turned to irritation. "The most of tomorrow part," he enunciated slowly and clearly. As if he was talking to an idiot.

Or someone totally clueless.

Declan muttered a curse under his breath. He looked at Taite. Her face was pale, the freckles on her nose standing out against the ivory of her skin. She looked petrified at the idea of going near Ryder. Bastard.

"I'll go, sweetheart." And maybe the talking he'd planned on would be done with his fists.

She shook her head. Stubborn little cuss.

"No, Declan. I need to do this." One slender hand rubbed over her forehead. "I have to prove to myself I can."

"Facin' your fear, lass?" he asked. Going over to her, he pulled her back into his arms and rocked her gently. "You don't have to do this. No one will think any less of you."

"I will." She took a shaky breath. "Besides, I'd like to see for myself that he's chained up and not running loose. *That* I don't think I could handle." With a small smile, she pulled away from him and walked out of the room.

Declan clenched his jaw at her stubbornness but didn't try to stop her. He glanced at Cobb. Seeing the look of compassion on the other man's face didn't help anything. He wanted to smash something.

Someone.

If he couldn't take it out on Ryder, maybe . . .

He'd go hunting for Sumner. The werewolf was hurt, and

hurt badly if what Cobb said was true. Now would be the time to strike, before the bastard could heal and come after them again.

"I don't believe I like the look on your face, Mr. O'Connell." Cobb's voice held a wary note.

Declan glanced at him and raised one brow. "And what look would that be?"

"You are planning to do something dangerous. Foolhardy even, I dare say."

Declan checked his gun. "I'm going after Sumner and finish off the bloody bastard."

"No! You must not." Cobb started to swing his legs off the bed again, but stopped when Declan cleared his throat.

"You don't want Taite after me, do you, Cobb?" he asked, only half joking. Taite on a mission could be a scary thing.

"You're not telling me you're afraid of Miss Gibson," Cobb retorted. He clasped his hands over his belly. "I don't believe it."

Declan grinned. "She can be downright frightenin'."

Cobb tilted his head and with a sly smile said, "Then you certainly don't want to go off on your own after a werewolf, do you? Imagine what she would have to say about that."

A scowl replaced Declan's smile. "I didn't say I was afraid of her, Cobb. Just that she could be scary."

"Yes, of course, sir." Cobb settled back against the pillows with a small smile curving his lips.

Dammit. Declan wasn't scared of Taite. But as he thought more about it, going after Sumner was a pretty asinine idea. Regardless of what Cobb said about an injury caused by another werewolf taking longer to heal, Declan wasn't ready to face down a wounded animal on his own. But sitting here doing nothing was going to drive him crazy. He needed to do *something*. He glanced at Cobb. Perhaps now was the time to really talk about what had driven the wedge between the two of them. He took a deep breath and let it out. "Can we talk? About Pelicia."

Cobb's pleasant expression faded. "There's nothing to discuss. You made an assumption about my daughter that turned out to be false." His green eyes glittered with anger. "Because of you, she was arrested. Even though the charges were dropped, she lost her job and her reputation because you had to do your job and damn the consequences." The little man carefully slid down the mattress until he lay prone and rolled onto his side, presenting his back to Declan. "No, Mr. O'Connell. We have nothing to discuss."

Declan opened his mouth, then shut it. What was the use? Cobb was absolutely right. Declan had fucked things up, and royally.

But he wasn't ready to accept that there was no way to fix it.

Chapter 17

Long after Taite ran from him, Ryder stared down the empty hallway. His heart pounded a defeated beat behind his ribs, the dull thud echoing in his throat. Sighing, he closed his eyes.

He couldn't fault Taite for her reaction. It was what he'd expected, after all. She'd looked into his eyes and seen the beast he could no longer conceal.

He should never have tried. He should've given her the information she needed at the start, then she would have been on her way. But he was so tired of being alone, and she was so lovely. . . .

He'd grasped eagerly at an excuse to let her stay the evening she'd arrived. He'd gone on to pretend to himself that, by not giving her the necessary information, she'd find it on her own and leave, but the reality was he'd allowed his emotions to override his head. And now here he was, still alone.

Still unloved.

Whoever said it was better to have loved and lost than never to have loved at all was full of bullshit.

He'd never felt the weight of his curse more than he did at this moment. It was a physical ache deep inside his chest. That Miles and now Sumner had actively embraced this life confused the hell out of him. He could barely stand being around himself, let alone mingling with—or creating—other werewolves.

He growled at his whiny self-pity and yanked on a pair of jeans. He'd been working on an erection when Taite had come into the bathroom—shifting always did that to him—but it had quickly disappeared.

Ryder tucked his flaccid cock into his jeans and carefully pulled up the zipper. Grabbing a T-shirt, he stalked from the room and headed to the basement.

On his way past the wine rack, he grabbed the first bottle he came to and swiped one of the corkscrews sitting on the shelf above it. Once inside the smaller room, he tossed both the bottle and opener onto the bed and shoved the door closed with his foot.

Another night of the full moon.

Another plunge into the most animalistic part of his soul.

Grinding his jaw, he laid the T-shirt across the railing at the foot of the bed, then unfastened his jeans and draped them over the shirt. He got up on the mattress and settled his back against the wall, sucking in his breath as his skin touched the cold brick.

His gaze went to the largest of the manacles. Scowling, he reached out and took it in his hands. A little larger than a salad plate, but only about an inch wide, it had been fashioned to fit a neck slightly larger than his own.

The neck of his wolf.

Ryder stared at it until his eyes burned from not blinking. With a muttered oath, he fastened the manacle around his neck and snapped the locking mechanism into place. He pulled on the manacle, testing it, and closed his eyes. God, he hated this. He abhorred everything about it.

From the time he was twenty-five years old, he'd lived with his beast, had at times grudgingly accepted it. But now, with the recognition that he loved a woman who held him in fear and contempt . . . His gut twisted with despair. He'd never been as miserable as he was right now.

With a growl, Ryder opened his eyes and grabbed the wine bottle and corkscrew. After removing the cork, he brought the wine to his mouth and took a big gulp.

Cobb would be appalled at him chugging—he looked at the label—a fifteen hundred dollar bottle of Romane Conti like it was cheap ale, but what the hell. It was *his* damned wine cellar. If he wanted to treat expensive Burgundy as if it were part of a six-pack, he would. Anything that would help numb the pain, emotional and physical, of the shift to wolf was a good thing.

He didn't care how much it cost.

Lifting the bottle to his mouth again, he drank long and deep. Probably should've grabbed two bottles, since his metabolism would burn through the alcohol like nobody's business. Part of the curse, although his mother had always said it was a blessing in disguise. He wouldn't have to worry about getting thick around the middle, because his wolf used up calories at an accelerated rate.

Once he'd finished the wine, he dropped the bottle to the bed and leaned his head against the wall. His brain was starting to feel pleasantly fuzzy. He'd best get on with chaining himself up before he lost any more coherence.

Although getting drunk would certainly dull the pain of Taite's rejection. For a while, at least.

Ryder snapped a manacle around his left wrist. *Stop being such an ass,* he berated himself. Depression in a werewolf wasn't a pretty thing.

He snorted at that thought. It was good to see he hadn't lost his sense of humor. Everything else, maybe, but at least his funny bone seemed to be alive and kicking.

He slid his right wrist into the manacle and tried to close it. With his left wrist already restrained, he couldn't reach his other arm. He kept trying, wincing as the hard metal dug into his wrist.

"Fuck." He banged his head against the wall, then muttered another curse. Already he felt the temptation to reach up with his right hand to undo the manacle around his neck.

"Which is why I need both wrist restraints." He tried to reach the right manacle again, finally giving up with a sigh.

Ryder leaned his head against the wall and closed his eyes. Tucking his free hand under the opposite arm, he curled his fingers into a fist and tried to ignore the urge to unfasten the restraints.

His head spun from the wine. He was so focused on being frustrated he almost didn't catch the faint scent of flowers and warm, sultry woman.

Almost.

Mate.

His gut clenched. His cock started to harden.

Taite was coming down the stairs.

Coming to him.

Taite paused at the bottom of the basement steps. Her heart raced, her palms were cold and slick with sweat, and she could hardly breathe past her fear-tightened throat. On the other side of that door was a man about to turn into a werewolf. A man with whom, if she were honest with herself, she'd fallen in love.

And that was somehow as scary as everything else. She whirled around and started back up the steps. "I can't do this," she muttered.

At the top of the stairs, she paused. According to Cobb, if someone didn't go down and help Ryder with his manacles, there was a distinct possibility he would get free. And she'd meant it when she said she'd rather make sure he wasn't running loose.

She took a deep breath and held it a moment, then slowly exhaled. She had to do this. For her own sanity, if nothing else.

Turning around, Taite went back down the stairs. As she approached the door to the small room where she'd seen the manacles, she wiped her sweaty palms down the thighs of her jeans. She drew in another deep breath and pushed open the door.

And met Ryder's cobalt gaze.

His breath came fast from between slightly parted lips. He had the big manacle around his neck and a smaller restraint around one wrist.

"What are you doing here?"

She barely stopped herself from cringing at his harsh, low tone. She cleared her throat. "I, uh, I'm here to help with that," she said, pointing toward the empty manacle and trying very hard not to notice his nakedness.

With over six feet of tanned skin and rigid muscles—one in particular—it wasn't easy. When he spoke, though, there was such raw anger in his voice that her gaze shot to his face.

"Are you sure you're up for it?" His upper lip lifted in a snarl. "Even though you weren't adverse to shagging me before—we were both hungry enough to take what we could get. But from your reaction now I'm sure this is the last place on earth you want to be."

Surely it was her imagination that his canines looked longer than normal. Or maybe not. Her heart gave a hard thud, and she swallowed convulsively. God, she was thankful he'd already managed to fasten two of the manacles.

He must have read her fear, because he shook his head, a softer expression crossing his face. "I'm sorry, honey." He sighed and looked down. "You don't have to do this."

When he looked back up at her, she caught her breath. Blue eyes mixed with flecks of gold stared at her with such a mixture of emotions she was moved to tears in spite of her fright.

Love, shame, fear, self-hatred shone from his gaze. . . . But no malice toward her.

"Cobb offered," Taite told him and walked toward the bed. *Buck up, girl. You're not a coward, remember? You're strong. You can do this.* "But he needs to stay off that leg. Besides, this is something I wanted to do."

"Why?" His deep voice was soft. That incredible gaze searched her face. "I understand why you can't deal with this." Ryder rattled the chain attached to the manacle around his left wrist. "*I* have a hard time, and I've lived with it all my life."

She shook her head. How could she explain to him what she barely understood herself? That she had a driving need to prove her independence, her toughness, her ability to fend for herself.

"Just let me . . ." She moved forward, but paused at the edge of the bed. In order to reach the manacle, she'd have to kneel on the mattress. Close to him. Taking a deep breath, she got on the bed and grabbed the restraint.

Without a word, Ryder held out his right arm. She fitted the manacle around his wrist, then checked to make sure they were all fastened down tightly.

This close to him, Taite could smell his cologne, his skin, and she took a deep breath. *God, he smelled so good.*

For a werewolf.

She jerked away and saw Ryder's chest rise with his deep inhalation. His lashes fell over his eyes, and he held his breath.

"What are you doing?" she asked, perching nervously on the edge of the mattress. Not too close, but not that far away, either.

Far enough away, though, that she was out of his reach.

His eyes opened. "I want to remember how you smell," he whispered. His gaze roamed over her face. "How your eyes reflect what you're feeling, the way your nose tilts up at the end. So I have memories when you're gone."

Taite couldn't hold his gaze. She glanced down, looking past his brawny shoulders, down over his wide chest and muscled abdomen, eyes widening when they reached his groin.

His penis stood bold and thick, pointing toward his belly. She gulped, her gaze jerking back to his.

Ryder shrugged. "I'm a bit . . . mystified about this," he said, nodding toward his erection. "Usually during the full moon, all I can think about is changing, becoming the wolf. Hunting, feeding my hunger."

She blinked and edged away from him, getting to her feet slowly. "You, ah, don't usually . . ."

"Get a hard-on?" He shook his head. His eyes were dark with lust, the gold flecks becoming more and more prominent. "No. Not like this."

Taite couldn't seem to stop looking at his cock. It jerked as if responding to the touch of her gaze and hardened even more.

When he muttered a curse, she glanced up at him, her cheeks reddening. "Sorry." She chewed on her lower lip, then asked, "Is that why you wouldn't tell me about werewolves? Well, not that"—she pointed toward his erection—"but *this*." She gestured toward the manacles.

Ryder nodded. He inhaled through his nose and held it a moment. His breath gusted with his heavy exhalation. "I didn't want to take the chance that you would put the signs and symptoms together and come up with the only logical conclusion you could. That *I* was a werewolf."

"Why didn't you just send me home?" She remembered that first day—it wasn't all that long ago. Although she didn't know what it was, something had changed his mind.

She glanced back down at his groin and saw his erection had subsided somewhat. When she looked at his face, she saw a muscle in his jaw twitch.

His eyes closed briefly then he said, "Because I was stupid." Looking at her, he went on. "I should have done what I'd planned to do—send you home straight away. But, once I saw you, I couldn't. I . . . realize now that I didn't want to face the loneliness."

Taite looked down at her hands. She could tell from his

tautly held jaw it had been hard for him to admit that to her. He was opening up to her in ways he hadn't the first couple of days, in ways he hadn't even after they'd made love.

"I know this isn't something you want to hear from me, but I have to say it while I can." Ryder's voice was low, guttural. "I love you."

Her gaze darted to his face, and her breath hitched in her throat at the changes she saw there. She couldn't see past the alien appearance of his features. His brow was more prominent and—this time, she knew it wasn't her imagination—his teeth protruded over his lower lip.

"Taite, before you go . . ." He closed his eyes with a sigh and leaned his head against the wall. With one hand he pointed to a small wall safe. "Get my families' journals—my great-grandfather's as well as my father's. Maybe those will help you understand. The combination is two, four, one, one, seven." His voice became rougher, little more than a growl. "And have Cobb get you the gun loaded with silver bullets." His eyes opened. "Just in case."

Taite swallowed, but went to the safe like he'd indicated. Once she punched in the code on the keypad and opened the door, she removed the journals, holding them under one arm. Then, keeping a close eye on Ryder, she inched toward the door. She couldn't deal with this, not here. Not now. He was a werewolf, like John.

Evil.

She looked into eyes that were now completely tawny in color. Heart pounding so hard she thought it might burst from her chest, she shook her head. Her breath came short, hard, her mouth open with a cry she couldn't voice through her fear-tightened throat. She backed away from him until she reached the door. Slamming it shut, blocking her view of him, she pushed the heavy latch in place. Then she turned and fled.

A long, mournful howl, muffled by the door, nevertheless chased her up the stairs.

Fifteen minutes later, with Declan snoozing in the chair next to her and Cobb asleep in the bed, she opened to the first page of Ryder's great-grandfather's journal.

Phelan Mac Meiric's Personal Journal
4 August 1899

Exactly one year ago, on the day following my twenty-fifth birthday, I held my new bride in my arms and stared with bone-chilled horror at the dreadful cailleach—*witch—who stood before us.*

"I'll give you one more chance, little wolf." She always called me by the meaning of my name, which I didn't understand until it was too late. The cailleach *held out her hand to me. It was long-fingered and thick-knuckled, and somehow seemed the most horrifying thing about her.*

I drew away, holding my beloved wife closer still. "I gave you my answer three months ago, Isibéal MacDougal," I told her. "I cannot marry your daughter, for I love another. Moira is now my wife."

Anger filled the witch's eyes, making them appear to spark with rage. I held myself stiff against the fear that threatened to set my body to shuddering. This close, I could smell the acrid seaweed that wove through her stringy gray hair and the pungent fish scales that clung to her dingy white dress.

The cailleach *straightened. "Gods of the sea, attend to me," she screeched, with thin, nearly skeletal arms stretched above her head. Within seconds, clouds darkened the sky, and a strong wind carried the tang of the sea to those of us gathered outside the small church where my wedding had just taken place.*

Though the comforting, familiar, rolling green hills of my childhood surrounded us, I felt as though I were standing in the most dangerous place on earth. All of nature went completely still; birds stopped their cheery chirping, the village dogs ceased their cacophonous barking. And then the witch delivered the sentence that would follow me and my descendants throughout eternity.

Quick as lightning, she struck out with her athame and sliced deep into my jaw, scoring me from my left ear to the tip of my chin, giving me a scar I shall carry the rest of my life. I clapped my hand to my face, feeling the blood dripping through my fingers.

The assembled crowd gasped as one and backed away, many crossing themselves and calling on the Blessed Virgin.

Sprinkling my blood from the knife to the ground around her, the witch chanted these words:

"By the great gods of the sea are ye cursed,
And all your male bloodline to follow.
When the moon rises full and bright shall ye howl in the night,
Your pride bringing naught but sorrow.
Your accursed life extended unnaturally
So that the folly of your pride you see.
I set this curse three times three;
By my will, so mote it be."

She disappeared in a spray of water. I stood there, dumb as an addlepated half-wit, until my father walked up to me. His florid face held the familiar look of disapproval and disgust.

"I told you to marry her daughter, buyo," he said, his brogue thick on his tongue. "Would it hae been so hard for you to do? Marry her daughter an' we'd be rich beyond our ken. Now, look at you." He pulled my hand away from my face and threw it from him with great

anger. "You've got a cut on your jaw that will leave an unsightly scar, absolutely no prospects for wealth of any sort, an' now a curse."

Aye. And there's the rub.

The Curse.

I didn't fully understand it until the first night of the full moon. Moira and I had gone to bed as usual. I came awake from a sound sleep, the most horrendous pain, such as I'd never felt before in my gut. I truly thought I would die of it.

The pain doubled me over, growing in intensity. I could feel my bones shifting, sliding, changing. And then the pain was gone. I looked toward my wife to see her sitting upright in bed, both hands over her mouth, her beautiful face pale and eyes wide with fright. Stretching out my hand to her, I was horrified to see not my hand, but the great shaggy paw of a wolf.

Seemingly with the realization that I was no longer human, an overwhelming lust for blood overtook me. Lest I hurt my sweet Moira, I threw myself through our bedroom window and ran out into the night. That was the last I saw of my gentle wife until eight months later, when she deposited my newborn son on my doorstep with a note stating her great fear of her own child.

I left the village that very same day with my boy. We went to America, among so many others looking for a second chance. At Ellis Island, our name was Anglicized to Merrick, which suited me down to my toes. The farther away I could get from those I knew, from those I loved but who now feared me, was best for all.

My son, Marcus Alexander, was all I needed. All I would ever need.

Taite drew in a deep breath and held it. She could feel the anguish of the husband and father as he realized how com-

pletely his life had changed. But she could also sense the love
and devotion he'd felt for his family.

And the fear he'd had that he would harm them.

Yet he obviously had not hurt his son, who'd grown up
and married and had at least one child to carry on the Merrick line. And now, three generations later, another Merrick
suffered from the same curse wrought so long ago.

She skimmed the next few pages until something of particular interest caught her eye.

>   *We've lived on a small farm in the wilderness of the
>   Kansas Territory for three months. The babe is now six
>   months old. With the rise of each full moon, I have had
>   a woman from the nearby town of Arkansas City come
>   care for the boy while I chain myself up in the barn. She
>   has no notion of what's really going on—I have told her
>   I have business that will take me away from the farm
>   for several days. Once the full moon has passed, I re-
>   turn home to my son.*
>
>   *With these precautions, my fear that I would hurt
>   young Marcus has alleviated. Although, surprisingly, I
>   have never felt the urge to injure him—or worse—not
>   even in the moments of greatest stress when the beast
>   inside becomes stronger and howls for release.*
>
>   *I have begun to think that the only difference in me
>   between that fateful day and now is that I cannot con-
>   trol my shift during the full moon. Otherwise, I eat, I
>   sleep, I live each day as I did before.*

Taite stopped reading. This sounded very much like what
some of the books she'd read were saying—that if a man was
good before he was bitten or, in this case, cursed, then he'd
be good afterward.

She sighed and glanced toward Cobb. He slept on, undis-
turbed. She placed the burgundy journal on top of the other

one and flipped it open. This was Ryder's father's journal, started in 1967. Skimming along, she read of his own initial experience of the curse taking effect on his twenty-fifth birthday—he'd been the same age his grandfather had been when the curse was meted out.

This journal had a much less hopeful tone than the other. Ryder's father wrote of his despair, his hatred of that part of him that was the wolf. The writing became more and more slanted until the last entry, which was almost impossible to read.

But one thing stood out starkly. He wrote of his son, and the words brought tears to her eyes at the unfairness of it all.

I hope he will never find himself in the same dark despair as I.

Chapter 18

The next morning, Ryder sat on the bed and rested his head wearily on the cold brick behind him. The manacles from his wrists hung nearby on the wall, where they'd fallen free once he'd shifted to his wolf form last night. With an oath, he reached up and unfastened the larger manacle.

As usual when he changed from werewolf back to human, his cock was a rigid demand against his abdomen. With a grimace, he grabbed one of the pillows.

He pulled the case off and laid it over his thigh. Clasping his erection in one hand, he absently stroked while he waited for someone to come downstairs and unlock the door.

He had a feeling it would *not* be Taite and, with the way his cock was standing at attention, that probably was a good thing.

As long as he lived, he'd remember the look in her eyes when he'd told her he loved her. She'd glanced at his face, her eyes widening in horror, mouth opening in fear as her breath came in quick puffs.

His timing sucked. But he didn't think he'd get another chance. Once Sumner was taken care of, she'd be back to her life as an investigator, and he'd be back to his life as a recluse.

If he could really call it a life.

God, here he went again, feeling sorry for himself. He

growled low in his throat, clenching his jaw. He was what he was. There was no changing it. No cure.

Taite would go on with her life, and he'd go on with his. It was that simple.

Ryder closed his eyes and started pumping his erection more vigorously. With each stroke of his hand, he remembered how Taite felt beneath him, her snug, wet cunt grasping his cock. He moaned as his sac tightened and white-hot need feathered out from the base of his spine.

His hips rocked up, pushing his prick through the tight circle of his fingers. He swiped his thumb over the crown of his shaft, pushed into the opening. Hissing at the small pain, he moved his hand faster and faster until finally his release roiled through him.

Grabbing up the pillow case, Ryder wrapped it around his cock, spilling himself into its softness. Finally, he sat still, catching his breath. His softened cock subsided against his thigh.

Frowning, he wondered briefly what to do with the soiled pillow case, and finally settled on just stuffing it under the pillow.

Leaning toward the foot of the bed, he picked up his jeans where they still lay over the footboard. He shoved his legs into them, then lifted his hips and pulled the denim up over his ass. He tabbed up the zipper carefully over his cock and fastened the button. With a sigh, he stretched his legs out in front of him and settled down to wait.

He hoped his freedom would come soon, because he was ready to eat—an entire cow, by the way his stomach gurgled and moaned. Yet another "side-effect" of the Change. He always shifted back to his human form with hunger of more than one kind.

He smelled Declan before he heard his footsteps clomping down the stairs. His friend's annoyance and anger preceded him on a wave of sharp, vinegary odor.

The latch on the door slid back with a grating rasp. The

door swung open and the other man paused in the doorway. His dark eyes snapped fire, and a muscle flexed in his taut jaw. When he spoke, his voice was low and rasped with fury.

"Twenty years we've known each other," he ground out. "Twenty goddamned years, since we were at university together. And in all that time, you never thought to tell me you were a soddin' werewolf?"

"It's not exactly something I'm proud of, Declan." Ryder tamped down his own rising anger. He'd had a rough night—as all his chained-up werewolf nights were—and he wasn't in the mood to be taken to task as if he were still in knee pants. "And it's not something you casually bring up over a pint at the pub."

"Fine." Declan took a couple of steps into the room. His big hands were fisted, and Ryder could tell the other man wanted to take a swing at him. Declan stalked closer. "Then why in the name of all that's holy didn't you tell us when we first arrived? For God's sake, man, we needed your help on werewolves, and you stonewalled us. You, the goddamned werewolf expert. *Expert*." He snorted. "You could've told us from the first why you're so knowledgeable."

"And would you have believed me?" Ryder shifted on the bed. He understood Declan's anger, even accepted it, but the emotions roused in him were calling to his wolf. "I don't think you would have."

"Sure, an' all you would've had to do is give us a wee demonstration," Declan shot back, his accent thick. "How could we no' believe our own eyes when you shifted into a great furry beast?"

"It's not that simple," Ryder muttered.

"How hard can it be?" Declan grunted and took the few steps that brought him to the edge of the bed. Raising the pitch of his voice, he sing-songed, "'Hello, Declan, long time no see. Oh, by the way, I'm a werewolf.'"

As Declan stepped back, Ryder climbed off the bed and

glared at Declan, not appreciating the other man's humor. There was nothing funny about what he was. "I didn't want you to know."

"Aye. I figured that out on my own, boyo. What I want to know is why."

"I told you." Ryder picked up his T-shirt, yanking it over his head. He started to leave the room, only to be hauled back by Declan's hand on his arm.

"Don't you walk away from me, Ry." When Ryder turned and stared at him, he tightened his grip. "An' don' you be lookin' at me like that."

"Like what?"

"Like I'm about to be your next meal." Declan dropped his hand away and narrowed his eyes. "I don' like it."

Ryder sighed. "Declan, what do you want from me? I've been a werewolf since I was twenty-five, and I've always had to hide it. Keeping my . . . condition a secret isn't even something I think about anymore—I just do it."

"Self-preservation?"

"Something like that."

Declan crossed his arms and gave a short nod. "That I can understand. With anyone else but me. Christ, Ry. I've been your best mate since university. Doesn't that count for anythin'?"

He had a point. But Ryder had been too ashamed and too afraid of losing the one good friend he had to let Declan in on the family secret. But, knowing Declan . . . "You really wouldn't have minded being friends with Eddie Munster, would you?"

"You're not Eddie Munster, my friend." Declan grinned and clapped one hand on Ryder's shoulder. "But, no, I wouldn't have minded."

They started walking toward the basement stairs. Declan asked, "Anythin' else I should know about? Like . . . Cobb's really a vampire? God knows he acts like he wants *my* blood."

Ryder gave a bark of laughter. "Hell, no. Cobb is . . . Cobb.

And it's not your blood he wants, my friend. It's your balls. On a platter." He sighed. "I'm the only weird one here."

"Not weird," Declan defended from behind him as they started up the stairs. "Just different. And different can be good."

Ryder opened his mouth to respond, but a sharp scent of sage and ammonia wafted to his nostrils. He stopped at the top of the stairs so suddenly that Declan bumped into him.

"Christ, give a fella warning, would you?" When Ryder didn't respond, Declan asked in a hushed tone, "What is it?"

Ryder walked quietly into the hall and pressed against the paneling of the staircase. He took another sniff and snarled, "*Fuck*. He's here."

"Sumner?"

Ryder nodded. "He was after you, by the way. Miles set him on your trail to get to me. But once Sumner saw Taite, his priorities changed."

"Fuck." Declan slid into place beside him, his right hand wrapped around a gun.

A muscle flexed in Ryder's jaw. "How'd you get that?" he asked, recognizing the gun he kept for emergency purposes. It was the one loaded with silver bullets, the one Cobb refused to touch.

It would provide Declan with some sort of protection against the other werewolf. He hoped.

"Taite gave it to me. Said you'd told her to get it last night."

Ryder nodded, his mind focused on the scent of werewolf in the house. He and Declan had to get upstairs, now. Ryder could get there quicker in his wolf form. He glanced back at his friend. "You wanted a demonstration. . . . Here it is. Follow me."

Ryder had an impression of Declan's eyes widening and his uttering a low-voiced epithet as he suffered through the Change. Within seconds Ryder was a wolf. Growling low in his throat, he ran down the hallway, his paws sliding on the hardwood floor as he reached the staircase.

As he vaulted up the steps, Ryder vaguely heard Declan's pounding footsteps behind him. All his attention was focused on the second floor.

Just as he reached the landing, he heard Taite scream. The smell of fear was strong and pungent and mixed with Sumner's odor of lust. Cobb yelled. A gunshot reverberated through the house, then there was a loud crash.

Ryder burst into the room and took in the scene in half a second. Cobb was on the floor at the side of the bed, his hands wrapped around his calf, which had started bleeding again. Taite held a chair, jabbing the legs toward Sumner, who was in his wolf-man form. Her eyes, when she saw Ryder, widened even further.

"Holy shit," she muttered, her eyes going from Ryder to Sumner and back again.

Sumner whirled around.

Ryder saw the still-healing patch on his throat and realized he'd miscalculated. Badly. The other werewolf was stronger than he'd given him credit for, and now they were all in danger.

Ryder growled a warning, wishing he had the ability to shift into a form somewhere between man and animal. It would even the field.

Sumner's lips drew back in a snarl. "Usurper! This time you. Will. Die."

He charged, and they slammed into the hallway. Declan grunted as they crashed into him. They went down in a tangle of arms and legs. Ryder was aware that Declan rolled away from them, then sharp teeth bit down into Ryder's shoulder. He snarled, trying to twist away from the other werewolf's hold. Ryder heard the snick of a hammer being cocked on a gun and suddenly was free, as Sumner turned to face the new danger.

A silver bullet placed just right could do as much—if not more—damage than Ryder. Certainly it would do it faster.

Sumner barreled toward Declan. Declan pulled the trigger but, with the preternatural speed common to lycans, Sumner dodged the bullet. He rammed into Declan at waist level.

Scrabbling on the area rug that kept bunching under his paws, sliding along the high-wax wood floor, Ryder started after Sumner. He bit down on the back of Sumner's thigh just as the wolf-man clamped down on Declan.

Declan gave a shout of pain and started to bring the gun around toward Sumner. One furry, clawed hand reached out and wrapped around his wrist. Ryder heard bones crunch and Declan groaned, the gun dropping from his hand to be pushed away by Sumner.

Ryder bit down harder. Sumner yelped and let go of Declan.

With a surge, Sumner fit his shoulder under Ryder's belly and started pushing him toward the landing. Declan rolled to one side, and the gun was kicked even farther away.

Ryder's paws scrambled for purchase. He managed to push Sumner back a few steps but, with a grunt, Sumner picked Ryder up and threw him over the railing.

Ryder landed in the foyer with the crunch of breaking bones. He yelped and groaned, and tried to get up. Panting through the pain, he rolled from his side to his belly. Excruciating spasms streaked down his spine, and he lolled back to his side, the cool wood a welcome relief.

Hearing the sounds of continued fighting on the floor above him, he tried again, rolling back onto his stomach. He pulled himself toward the staircase. Every drag forward was agony, every breath brought sharp pain to his rib cage.

He had to get to Taite.

If he shifted to his human form and then back to wolf, the metamorphosis would help speed up the healing of the bones that were broken, the ligaments that were torn. The bite wouldn't heal as fast, since it had been caused by another werewolf.

Regardless, it was going to hurt like hell.

A loud gunshot and another scream from Taite propelled him into action. He took a shuddering breath and pictured himself in his human form. Fur slid into skin, muscles contracted and shortened. In jarring agony, bones shifted and remolded themselves.

He groaned, writhing against the bottom steps. Taite yelled again, and he heard Cobb shout out.

Then . . . nothing.

Ryder closed his eyes and focused on returning to his wolf form. Fur began to sprout as his bones and muscles realigned themselves. When the transformation was complete, he pushed back the remaining pain from the fall and started the arduous climb up the flight of stairs.

Taite backed away from the wolf-man and stumbled over the trailing edge of the bed's coverlet. She fell on her behind with a low cry and scrambled back in a crab walk.

Declan had held off the creature as long as he could, but even a strong man like him was no match for the supernatural strength Sumner possessed.

The werewolf—John!—now stalked forward, his massive claws curled into fists. His lips were drawn back from his teeth in a snarl.

She glanced around him. Declan lay on the floor just inside the doorway, his face turned away from her. He was so still. . . . She saw his chest rise, and she breathed a shaky sigh of relief. But she could see he was bloodied, and her heart raced at the implications.

If he lived, he'd be a werewolf. Like John.

And Ryder. From inside the bedroom she'd only heard the sounds of the fight. She hadn't seen any of the action, other than watching John and Ryder fighting as they went past the open doorway. She'd heard a few yelps and then . . . nothing.

Her gut churned. Had John killed Ryder? Had she, in her fear and ignorance, brought death to the man she loved?

The man who also was a werewolf.

Her eyes flicked back to John, and she realized she'd never make it past him. She also knew she had to try. She couldn't just sit here and wait for the big, furry bad to snatch her up.

With a small grunt, she launched herself to her feet and headed for the bed, thinking to crawl over it and get to the door that way.

She'd only made it a few steps when she felt John's hand—paw!—wrap around one wrist and jerk her to a halt. Taite struggled against him, twisting to her back and kicking out with her sock covered feet, and having no real effect.

Except to amuse the hell out of him, if his deep chuckles were any indication.

Only when her foot came perilously close to his groin did he seem to lose his patience. She saw one fist come toward her and tried to duck. With the impact of his knuckles against her jaw, pain exploded, and her vision began to darken. One last thought fluttered through her mind.

Ryder!

Taite awoke with a jerk and a sharp yell. She was sitting upright, propped against a hard surface. She started to put one hand out to steady herself and realized her hands were tied in front of her. Briefly, she closed her eyes against the feeling of dizziness assailing her.

As her head cleared, she opened her eyes and squinted in the darkness. A single battery-operated lantern sat on the ground in front of her and, from the dim light it provided, she saw she was in a cave.

A cold, damp and—beyond the small radius of the lantern's light—very *dark* cave.

Her breathing came fast at the realization of just how dark it would be without the lantern. As long as she had at least that dim light, she could, she hoped, hold her fear of the dark at bay.

With a very nasty, naked wolf-man sitting on the other side of the lantern, she had much bigger problems than a lack of light.

She swallowed and looked down at herself, searching for bite marks.

"Oh, I haven't bitten you." John leaned forward, balancing his weight with one hand against the wooden crate he was sitting on, a hairy hulk casting ominous shadows on the cave walls. "Not yet."

The opening to the small cavern was narrow and curved so that she couldn't see beyond the bend in the tunnel behind him. Once again he blocked her path to freedom.

He put one huge clawed hand against his throat and fingered the still-healing wound. In the light from the lantern, his eyes glinted. "I do owe you for this and for taking up with Ryder. You should have waited for me. First things first, though."

As Taite watched, he transformed to his human form, his face twisted in a pained grimace.

She gasped, horrified, as his muscles bunched and rolled over bones that shifted with a loud crunch. The flicker of light from the lantern cast eerie shadows over him, adding a macabre look to his Change.

When the transformation was complete, he moved the crate closer to the lantern. As he bent forward, his head closer to the light, she saw he'd tucked his hair behind his ears. The white-blond streak at his part was secured behind . . . Her eyes widened. There was a chunk of his right ear missing.

Just like the wolf's.

He sat down, stretching his legs out in front of him, and brought one hand down to wrap around his erection. His fingers slid up to cup over the head of his cock.

She drew in a strangled breath and looked away, away from the obscene sight of his thick, veined shaft.

"Look at me, Taite." John's voice held a note of arrogant demand. When she didn't immediately comply, he surged to his feet and crouched in front of her.

His bulk blocked the light from the lantern. The darkness started to close in on her, and her skin grew as clammy as the cave wall behind her.

Long fingers dug painfully into her jaw as he grabbed her face and turned it toward him. "You better get used to this," he growled, gesturing to his erection. "Once you've recuperated from your wounds, you'll be taking it as often as I want."

Taite jerked away from him, falling to her side. "What wounds?" she asked, trying not to gag at the image of being at his carnal mercy.

"The wounds you'll soon bear, after I punish you for your continued defiance." He yanked her upright, pulling her toward him, and took her hands in his. He tipped his hips forward and wrapped her fingers around his cock, holding them in place with one big hand.

Taite grimaced and tried to pull away, but his grip tightened. Leaning forward, he pressed his open mouth to hers, grinding down with brutal strength, lips moving, forcing her to open. His tongue, thick and wet, snaked into her mouth, stroking over her teeth.

His breath tasted foul, like something had crawled in his mouth and rotted. When she gagged and struggled against him, he released her mouth and laughed, his hot, fetid breath brushing against her cheek.

"You fucked someone else." John spoke close to her ear. "You belong to me. I showed myself to you in my wolf form so you would see my power, but you ignored me. You called O'Connell for protection, as I knew you would. But it still hurt."

She frowned. "What are you talking about? You *wanted* me to call Declan?"

He gave a short nod. "As payment for turning me, I promised to help Merrick's cousin. He wants to strike out at Merrick through O'Connell."

"But . . ." Taite shook her head. "Why?"

John shrugged. "Don't know. Don't care." His breath wafted hot against her skin, sending cold shivers through her body. "I wanted you and O'Connell here, on this island, so Merrick would witness the death of his friend the way his cousin wanted, and *you* would see me for what I really am—strong and powerful and *worthy*. But you weren't supposed to let him fuck you."

He licked beneath her ear. His voice, when it came again, was a silky whisper. "No one knows I came after you, sweet thing. I covered my tracks well. I could make you disappear, and no one would know where to even begin to look."

Taite drew in a shaky breath. If he'd covered his tracks, that meant she could make *him* disappear, too. There might be an investigation, but it would peter out when the trail grew cold.

First chance she got, she'd *disappear* him. Or die trying.

John pulled back far enough to stare into her eyes. His tongue swept over his lips and left them shiny with spit. "Even if you have been unfaithful, having you come here wasn't a total waste. I got to taste my first Brit. The young woman I killed in Cornwall was quite tasty. In more ways than one." He tightened his grip on her hands, forcing her fingers to curl around his cock with a firmer grasp. "She acted like you, like she didn't want me, but I knew better. Her cunt was hot and tight, just like I know yours will be." He grinned. It was an evil, twisted expression of glee. "I hurt her, and she *loved* it. You will, too."

Forcing her hand to slide up and down his length, he made her masturbate him. "But," he went on, "you hurt *me,* you know. First by breaking up with me, then here, letting *him* rut between your thighs. I could have made your transition somewhat pain-free, but no longer. I'm going to make sure you suffer."

His mouth came down over hers again in an act of pure dominance. He slid his mouth in a wet trail over her cheek to her ear. "I don't care what Miles wants anymore. As soon as your lover-boy comes to rescue you, I'm going to kill him. Then I'm going to fuck you until you beg me to kill *you*." His hand left her face and went to her breast. John squeezed it in a kneading motion. "But I won't, not until I get you pregnant. When my seed takes root, and you give me my heir . . . Whether I keep you after you deliver my first son will be up to you. You can be my queen, or you can be dead."

Taite fought the urge to spit in his face. Her heart raced. Sweat rolled down her back, beaded on her forehead. God, he was so close she could smell the strong odor of his body. And to increase her fear, her childhood terror of the dark churned through her, tightening her gut, nauseating her.

Not to mention having her fingers wrapped around a turgid length of werewolf meat. Reflexively, she tightened her grip with only one thought.

Cause him pain.

He snarled, and the back of his hand slammed into her cheek. Her head snapped sideways with the force of the blow. Sharp pain exploded across her face, and she fell to the ground.

John hauled her upright with one big hand around her throat. His eyes blazed down at her. "Don't do that again."

It had been instinctive, but stupid. Her lids fluttered. Her cold face grew hot. Her head began to feel fuzzy. The last thing she wanted was to faint. "Please," she whispered. "Could I have some water?"

Rocking back on his heels, he studied her for a moment. He reached for a half-full bottle on the ground beside her. Taite kept her eyes downcast, not meeting his gaze—trying to appear docile to his domination—and watched as he unscrewed the cap. He held the bottle to her lips, and she tilted her head back to drink.

As much as she didn't want to drink after him, she needed the water. After she took a few gulps, he pulled the bottle away and put the cap back on.

"That's enough." He pulled the lantern to one side. He studied her in the weak light and didn't look entirely pleased with what he saw. "It's not like you've got some place to go pee. Although," he said, his face curved into a leer, "I wouldn't mind watching you squat."

Oh, God. Taite didn't respond. Outwardly, at least. Inside she was screaming and desperately trying to think of a way out of this horrible nightmare.

He flexed one hand. The fingers lengthened and thickened, growing claws and sprouting with fur.

Her eyes widened as she watched the process reverse itself until his hand was once again human-looking.

"I've been working on controlling my ability to shift," John boasted with a laugh.

Taite inched sideways.

"Where do you think you're going?"

She stilled, feeling like a tiny mouse under the paw of a playful—though deadly—cat. "Nowhere." She bent her arms so that her hands were in front of her for protection.

Such as it was.

He tipped his head down to look at her. "Nowhere is right. Not until I say so, anyway." A wide grin creased his face.

Taite leaned back against the wall, shivering as the damp cold seeped through her thin blouse, and hunched down to look as small as possible. She closed her eyes. Desperation clawed at her throat.

"What's the matter, baby?" he asked. "This too much for you?"

Glancing up, she saw him swing his hips in a parody of a male stripper move, making his cock loop in a circle. She grimaced and looked back down.

"That's all right. You'll get used to it." He laughed again and moved toward her. Bending, he grabbed her by the hair at her nape and tilted her head back. His other hand wrapped around her throat and started to squeeze.

Taite gasped and choked, and brought her hands up. Fingers scrabbling at his, she dug her nails into his flesh. His response was to tighten his grip with a low growl.

Pressure built behind her eyes, and she started seeing tiny floating dots of light. Her mouth gaped. She bucked against him, desperate for oxygen. With a final, brutal squeeze, he released her.

Taite massaged her throat and coughed, wheezing as she drew badly needed air into her lungs. She reached up and wiped her watering eyes. Staring at him, she wondered what had set him off. She hadn't said anything.

"Perhaps now you'll show me a little more respect," John muttered and went to the other side of the cave. Sitting back down on the crate, he idly kicked one bare foot back and forth, scuffing his heel against the clumped sand of the cave floor. "And if you don't want a repeat of that, you'd better keep your eyes on me from now on."

She swallowed, wincing at the pain in her throat.

He wrapped his hand around his erection and started stroking it, sliding the foreskin up over the slick red tip. Unwilling to watch but afraid to look away because of his threat, Taite stared with unfocused eyes as he continued to jack off. At least he was doing it with his hand instead of having her do it.

It wasn't long before his hand was jerking faster and faster. He stiffened and threw his head back as his cock erupted, spurting thick gobs of semen over his fingers and onto the floor of the cave. Finally spent, he relaxed, keeping his hand on his softened shaft.

Taite glanced up at his face. His eyes blazed, holding hers with fiery intent. Even though he remained in his human form, there was such a look of wildness in his eyes that she knew the wolf wasn't far below the surface.

He rose to his feet slowly, never breaking eye contact, and walked toward her. He gave his hand a flick, sending drops of semen flying from his fingers.

She stiffened as he bent toward her. God, he was going to make good on his threat to rape her. She braced herself, prepared to go out kicking and screaming, even if it meant he would kill her.

John swiped his fingers down her cheek, and her hands came up instinctively to wipe off the semen he'd left behind. "Don't," he warned, his eyes narrowing. "Until I mark you with my bite, you'll wear the sight and scent of my seed."

He picked up the bottle of water and twisted off the cap. Tipping the bottle, he splashed water over his hand. One corner of his mouth tilted up. "Don't worry, sweet thing. I'm not going to fuck you just yet. I want my first time with you to be while you're still a human. I just have to take care of your lover first."

He reached past her and picked up a dark backpack she hadn't seen. He pulled out a cloth. Dropping the pack, he wiped off his hands then tossed the cloth at Taite.

She batted at it with her hands, scowling when it dropped on her foot. She kicked the cloth away and tried not to gag at the wet spot on her sock. God, she should've kept her shoes on, but no one had thought John would get such an early start. It had been barely past dawn when Declan had gone downstairs to set Ryder loose, and that'd been when John had struck.

Her fingers itched to wipe away the wetness on her cheek, and she barely restrained herself.

"One day soon, Taite, you'll be covered in my spunk," he said now, thrusting his hips at her in an obscene parody of the sex act. "It will be second nature to you. Every morning you'll suck me off—or you won't get breakfast." He cupped his balls in one hand. "And every night you won't go to sleep until after I've had my fill of you."

She nearly gagged. Her eyes burned with tears, but she wouldn't give him that satisfaction. She wouldn't cry. She wouldn't beg. No matter what he did to her, she would remain strong.

It was the only way she knew.

To give up was to fail, and failure wasn't an option.

She really didn't want to be a werewolf. Not if she'd end up like John.

He looked toward the opposite end of the cave. One big hand went back to his throat, fingering the raw-looking wound. "I had thought about going after your lover-boy, after I'd secured you here. But, with this . . ." He gestured toward his neck. "Well, I decided to wait and heal as much as I could and let him come after me. That way I'll have home court advantage. Plus Miles has mentioned Merrick's irrational fear of caves. That should play in my favor, too."

After glancing at her, he walked away, leaving the circle of light provided by the lantern. She waited until his shuffling footsteps faded, then she pushed to her feet and went to work on the ropes binding her wrists.

Bringing her hands up to her mouth, she started by gnawing on the ropes with her teeth, trying to loosen the first knot. She inserted her eyetooth between two tight loops and wiggled her jaw, trying to work the tooth farther down. Then she began tugging, wincing at the pressure the action put on the tooth.

Her teeth slipped from the rope, and she accidentally bit down on the inside of her lower lip. "Ouch," she muttered. "Well, that's not gonna work."

Taite picked up the lantern and peered more closely at the rocks around her, looking for one that was sharp enough to saw through the rope. She'd just knelt by a jagged piece sticking out from the cave wall when the rattle of stones signaled John's return.

With a gasp, she replaced the lantern and moved back to where she'd been sitting. Putting her hands in her lap, she licked over the small wound on her lip. Hopefully it wasn't bleeding and wouldn't give away what she'd been up to. She glanced down at the ropes, didn't see any blood, and breathed a sigh of relief.

John stepped into the lantern light and squatted down beside her. His nostrils flared. "You're bleeding." His eyes narrowed as he looked her over. "What've you been up to, Taite?"

She shook her head. "Nothing. I, uh, bit my lip by accident."

"Must've been one hell of a bite to bring blood." He stared at her a moment longer, then shrugged. "It makes no difference to me. You'll be bleeding for real soon enough."

Trying to distract him, Taite motioned toward the direction from which he'd just come, which she assumed was the entrance to the cave. "What's going on out there?"

"Not a thing." He tilted his head to one side. "Guess I hurt lover-boy worse than I thought, throwing him off the landing." His expression was full of prideful glee, and Taite barely resisted the urge to kick him in the balls.

She'd known Declan was hurt. She'd seen the blood, knew John had bitten him. Now he was condemned to live his life as a werewolf, and it was all her fault.

But now she also knew what he'd done to Ryder. Could he have survived that fall?

Her heart cramped. It didn't seem to matter to her as much anymore that he was a werewolf. She loved him, and coming here had been a mistake. One that might have cost him his life.

God, she should've tried something else in Tucson. There had to have been another way to discourage John rather than involving Ryder. But if there had been, it hadn't been evident to her at the time.

Movement from John brought her attention back to him.

He brought one hand down and clasped his cock. A couple of strokes gave him another erection. "I'm tired of waiting. I think I'll just go ahead and take advantage of the injuries in the enemy camp," he mused and reached for her.

Taite yelled and tried to dodge out of his way. He grabbed her by one foot and dragged her squirming body between his legs, blocking her knee with one thick thigh.

"Uh-uh, darling." He pressed her arms above her head, and slipped her bound wrists over a natural protrusion in the rock wall of the cave. His knees spread her legs apart. "That wasn't very nice. You'll regret trying it."

Chapter 19

Ryder reached the landing of the second floor and limped down the hallway. Already he could feel his bones healing, becoming stronger. There was still some residual muscle soreness, but it would fade within a matter of minutes.

He paused in the hallway before the bedroom door and focused on shifting back to human. If there were injuries inside that room, he would be of little use in his wolf form.

With a deep groan, he shifted, bones crunching back into place, muscles and tendons following with a painful slide.

When he walked in, the first thing he saw was a shirtless Declan, lying on his back with Cobb pressing a bath towel to his right side. Declan had his right wrist cradled on his chest. From the swelling and redness of his hand, Ryder knew the wrist was broken. He knelt beside the pair, and Declan's eyes flickered open.

"Where's Taite?" Ryder asked urgently.

"Son of a bitch took her and jumped out the fuckin' window, after he got me," Declan muttered. "Just busted through the wood and jumped."

Cobb lifted the towel and then pressed down again, and Declan hissed in a breath through his teeth. "Fuckin-A! That hurts." His gaze flicked to Ryder's groin, then he closed his eyes. "I see you lost your clothes again."

"It happens when I shift." Ryder put one hand out and touched Declan's shoulder. "As you'll find out soon enough." He looked at Cobb "Take care of him. I have to go get Taite."

Declan stirred restlessly, grimacing with pain. His expression was stoic, though Ryder had a good idea of the anguish his friend must be feeling. He'd felt it often enough himself.

"Aye," Declan muttered. "I'd figured out already I was gonna have a furry ass once a month. And I'm comin' with you."

As Cobb pressed down harder with the towel, Declan's eyes shot open, and he grabbed the little man around one wrist. "Goddammit, boyo. Ease up, would ya?"

Cobb pulled his hand out of Declan's hold. "We must stop the bleeding, Mr. O'Connell."

"Let's take a look, Cobb." Ryder leaned forward as Cobb drew the towel away. Though it looked bruised and angry, the wound had closed, the bleeding stopped.

"I hadn't realized . . ." Cobb trailed off and looked at Ryder. "I thought there would be a . . . gestation period, if you will pardon the expression."

Ryder shook his head. "There's something in a werewolf's saliva that acts as a catalyst for the infection, and the reaction is instantaneous. Though he won't go through the transformation until the next full moon, his metabolism is already changing."

As Declan struggled to sit up, Ryder put one hand under his back then slid one shoulder under his friend's arm to help him to his feet. "I'm sorry, mate. I'd never wish this on another person, least of all my friend."

Declan stood hunched over for a minute and nodded. He straightened, his jaw white with pain. "Let's go." He took one step and tottered, then another, and would have fallen had Ryder not caught him.

"The only place you're going is to bed." Ryder strong-armed him to the bed and shoved him down. The fact that he was able to do so showed him very clearly that Declan was as hurt as he'd thought. "*I'll* go after Taite."

"I hope to God he hasn't hurt her." Declan's deep voice was raspy with fear and rage.

"If he has, there'll be hell to pay," Ryder muttered. He'd make better time if he went after Sumner in his wolf form, but he wanted to make sure the bastard died this time. Silver would do it. He looked at Cobb. "Where's the gun?"

While he could track Sumner more quickly in his wolf form, he couldn't easily carry the gun that way, and he wanted those silver bullets ready and available when he met up with the furry bastard again.

Cobb went to the bed and picked up the gun from where it lay on top of the covers. He made sure the safety was on and turned the weapon in his hand to give it to Ryder grip out.

Ryder checked the clip. Seven rounds. Then, to save time he jumped from the window, following Sumner's exit. Since he was in control this time, he was able to land on his feet, bending his knees to help absorb the impact. He glanced up at the window to see Cobb's pale face looking down at him.

"Sir!" his employee called. "Your shoes."

There was no time to put on shoes. He'd lost too much ground already. Ryder would gladly suffer the abuse of sharp rocks and rough ground to be able to get to Taite. Focusing on his sense of smell, he started tracking Sumner's foul scent.

The trail led him across the island, away from the ocean. The farther inland he went, the more desperate he became. If Sumner hurt Taite, Ryder would never be able to forgive himself. He should've been able to protect her.

She was his mate. It was his job to see to her safety.

He swallowed the bitter bile of defeat and realized with dread where Sumner's scent trail was taking him.

To the caves. The place where, as a boy, his cousin had left him trapped and helpless. Ryder had never been able to go more than a few meters inside since then, no matter how often he'd tried.

Pausing outside the entrance to the large cave, he took a deep breath through his nose to verify what his gut was telling him. Sumner and Taite were inside—and it couldn't be a coincidence. Miles had to have told Sumner about the cave-in and Ryder's ensuing fear of enclosed spaces.

What broke him out in a cold sweat wasn't so much the thought of being in the dark as it was the idea of being closed in without a way out.

As a boy, he'd tried his best, scrabbling at the rocks blocking the entrance until his fingers were torn and bloody. He'd finally had to sit back and wait.

And wait.

It had been a torturous couple of days, and he'd not been able to force himself into this cave—or *any* cave on his island—since then.

Now he had no choice.

Ryder drew another breath. He thumbed off the safety on the gun, and started into the cave.

Immediately, panic clawed at his throat. His heart began pounding against his ribs like a misfiring engine. He tightened his grip on the pistol and kept his left hand on the clammy wall, feeling his way as he went deeper and deeper into the cave.

He had to hold himself together, for Taite's sake. Stopping, he closed his eyes and focused on his breathing, trying to ignore the clamminess of his skin that had nothing to do with the coldness of the cave and everything to do with his memories.

In. Out. A long breath in. Slowly out. A muscle ticked in his jaw as he opened his eyes and continued on. He ignored the painful jabs of the odd sharp stones he trod upon and made his way into the black as sin depths.

He narrowed his eyes. There was light up ahead. He heard the murmur of voices, then Sumner called out, "Come out, come out, wherever you are."

Ryder clenched his jaw and put his gun hand behind his back. If Sumner didn't know he had a weapon, Ryder might just have an advantage.

He walked forward until he rounded a bend in the tunnel and came to a dead end. A small battery-operated lantern was set on the floor in the center, and Taite and Sumner were on the other side of it.

Ryder's jaw clenched tighter at seeing Taite. Her hands were tied in front of her, her blouse in tatters at her feet. Sumner had sliced through the front of her bra, and it hung loosely off her shoulders. In human form, he had a hand on one of her breasts, slowly kneading it, while the other hand was at her throat, fingers wrapped under her jaw, tilting her head back.

Miles had set this maniac onto Taite. Perhaps not deliberately, but by sending him after Declan, he'd put him right in Taite's path. Now she was being terrorized, and as far as Ryder was concerned, it was all Miles's fault.

"I figured you'd be here sooner or later," Sumner said. He moved his hand to her other breast. "These are mine." He slid his hand between her legs and cupped her sex through her jeans. "This is mine."

Ryder took a step forward, stopping when Sumner tilted Taite's head back even farther. It wouldn't take much for the bastard to snap her neck. Ryder had never felt so helpless.

Or so furious.

"If you hurt her, I will rip you apart." His skin was icy; his heart settled into a slow, steady rhythm as he prepared for battle. He eased his finger onto the trigger, but kept the pistol behind his back.

Taite's eyes were huge dark pools in her pale face, filled with a mixture of fear and anger. Anger!

God, he loved her.

Sumner snorted. "You can try."

Ryder needed to get the other man off-balance, to get him acting emotionally instead of thinking. Picturing his father in his mind, recalling every time he'd gotten a dressing down from the old man, he mimicked the well-remembered and always dreaded tone of disdain. "It seems to me, old boy, I've already come very close."

Sumner let loose a low growl and started to transform.

Taite gasped, her eyes widening as the hand at her throat and the one still buried between her legs thickened and grew claws and fur.

His voice garbled by the distortion of his half-transformed face, the werewolf muttered, "You son of a bitch. Killing you will be a joy." His eyes glowed. "And even if I fail—and I won't—there are others out there like me."

What the hell did that mean? That Miles had turned more men into werewolves to do his bidding? Ryder narrowed his eyes. It didn't matter. He wouldn't worry about something he had no control over. But as far as he was concerned, Sumner's life would end here. Now.

Although standing here starkers wasn't the way he'd wanted to face down the other werewolf. But until he could use the gun to put a silver bullet through Sumner's heart, changing to his wolf form wasn't an option.

Sumner stood, pulling Taite up with him, never taking his hand from her throat. "Why don't you show me what you've got behind your back?"

Filling Sumner full of silver might be the only thing to save Taite. Ryder wouldn't keep his weapon and jeopardize her life, but if he could distract the other werewolf and get him to stop using Taite as a shield, he might have a chance to use the gun.

"Why don't you stop hiding behind a woman?" Ryder taunted. "Afraid you don't have the stones?"

Sumner bristled and let out a low snarl. "You got lucky before. You won't this time." He lowered his head and rested his chin on Taite's shoulder. "And I don't mean to give you an advantage by letting you keep whatever it is you've got in your right hand." He slid one clawed finger over Taite's jugular and pressed the clawed tip against her skin.

Ryder got the message.

He looked at Taite. Her eyes were round. He could smell the sharp odor of her fear, saw a tiny muscle twitching at the corner of one eye.

Without another word, he brought his hand from behind his back. Holding the gun's grip with his forefinger and thumb, slowly and with great care he placed the gun on the ground then straightened.

Sumner's nostrils quivered. "Kick it over here."

Taite shook her head and pleaded, "Don't. Ryder, don't." Her words ended on a rasp as Sumner tightened his hand around her throat.

"Kick. It. Over."

Ryder gave the gun a little shove with his foot, deliberately not putting much force behind the kick. If he could get Sumner to come closer, he might be able to charge him while his attention was on the gun.

Sumner scowled. Pushing Taite in front of him, he shuffled forward, keeping his claw at her throat. When they reached the gun, he forced Taite to bend over to pick it up.

As her fingers closed around the grip, Taite began to struggle against him, twisting under his hand to the point that she drove her neck deeper into his clawed fingers. It didn't feel like he'd punctured her skin yet, but she refused to put her own safety ahead of Ryder's. She couldn't let John shoot Ryder.

She couldn't let him make *her* shoot Ryder.

Regardless that she was still mixed up about how she felt, she wouldn't be the one to take his life.

Behind her, she heard John growl low in his throat. "Every time you fight me," he muttered, his breath hot against her skin, "is one additional bite I give you. Think about that."

Barely able to draw in a breath through the constriction of her throat, she fought on. She'd take the bites if it meant Ryder didn't get shot. With a short grunt, she brought the heel of her left foot down on John's instep while she plunged her elbow into his midsection as hard as she could.

He roared with fury and threw her away from him by the grip around her neck. She flew through the air to land with a hard thud against the cave wall. Her head smacked the unforgiving stone, and she cried out at the sharp shaft of pain that reverberated through her skull. She fell to her side on the cave floor and lay there, trying to shake off the pain.

The gun fell from her grip and bounced a few feet away. Her eyes closed as she fought for breath and tried not to vomit.

The sound of snarling animals brought her eyes open with a jerk. Both men were now in their wolf forms. Their paws scrabbled for a foothold in the damp, sandy floor of the cave as their jaws snapped at each other.

Lips drawn back over gleaming white teeth, noses wrinkled with their ferocious barks and growls, they circled each other, looking for an opening to attack.

The tip of a long tail brushed her hip. Drawing her knees up to her chest, she pressed back against the wall. Angry growls and sharp yips echoed in the cave, sounding loud even over the pounding of the pulse in her ears.

She licked dry lips. This wasn't good. Two alpha werewolves squaring off, looking for the quickest, most deadly opening they could find.

Because of her.

Her eyes darted from one big wolf to the other. Which one was Ryder? They appeared to be the same size. One was a rich, dark brown, the other black.

She looked again at the brown one. The fur seemed like that of John when he was in his wolf-man form. Reaching out with trembling fingers, she snatched up the gun and pushed to a sitting position, her back against the wall, the pistol clutched in both shaking hands.

A sharp yelp brought her gaze to the black wolf. John had Ryder by the ruff of his neck, his jaw clamped tight. He gave Ryder a hard shake, jerking the other wolf back and forth like a rag toy while blood streamed down his fur.

Taite screamed and aimed the gun. She pulled the trigger.

The bullet hit John high on his left flank. He yelped and let go of Ryder. Turning his gaze on her, he flattened his ears against his head and drew his lips back in a snarl. She could almost hear him saying, *That's another bite for you.*

He started to turn back to Ryder, but taking his attention off his opponent for just that one second had been a mistake—one she hoped would be fatal.

Ryder fastened his jaws around John's throat and bore the other wolf to the ground. He shook his head like a dog playing tug-of-war. As blood and spittle sprayed over her face, Taite closed her eyes to keep the spatter out of them and fought against a scream.

She heard a deep groan and opened her eyes to see John on his side, his large chest heaving, his paws pushing at Ryder, trying to shove him off. Ryder grimly held on, keeping his jaws tightly around John's throat.

Taite thought about firing her weapon again, but Ryder blocked a clear shot, and it seemed as if he had things well under control. Still, she kept the gun aimed, ready to fire if things turned bad.

The brown wolf gave a long shudder and a loud sigh. John's paws slowly dropped to the ground, and he lay still.

Ryder remained where he was for several more minutes. Then, as he drew back, he took most of John's throat out with his razor-sharp teeth. He turned his blood-soaked face toward Taite.

His gaze was dark and fierce, and she didn't see any sign of Ryder behind the tawny wildness of the wolf's eyes.

Chapter 20

Ryder slowly slid his tongue over his muzzle, relishing the taste of the enemy's blood. His heart raced from the heat of battle, his lungs labored for breath.

He felt alive. Primal.

King of his territory and everything in it.

He looked at Taite with one thought.

She was his. He had fought for her and won.

He took a step toward her, then another. Her loud gasp echoed in the cavern. She brought her hands up and pointed the gun at him. He stopped.

She thought he would hurt her. He couldn't blame her—he'd always thought he would hurt someone when he was in this state. But right now, all he could think about was getting back to his human form so he could fuck her, mate with her.

Make her his.

But not at the risk of taking a silver bullet between the eyes.

He took a shuddering breath, trying to push back the beast that still roared with bloodlust. With adrenaline pulsing through his veins, he was unable to shift just yet.

He didn't want her scared of him so, instead of moving any closer, he sat back on his haunches and whined softly, trying to tell her he wasn't going to hurt her. The gun didn't waver. So he went down on his belly in a show of non-aggression.

Only with his mate would he prostrate himself in such a way. He hoped she appreciated the gesture.

Tilting his head, he realized the gun still hadn't moved. He chuffed lightly and wagged his tail.

Taite's eyes narrowed. "I can't tell if that's an 'I'm happy to see you' wag or a 'You look like you'd taste good' wag." She balanced the gun on her knee, still pointing it at him. "Either way, I don't want you to come any closer. Do you understand me?"

He swished his tail twice and whined.

"Oh, God. Don't look at me with those sad doggy eyes." She sighed and rubbed her forehead with the fingers of her left hand. He noticed she kept her right hand—her dominant hand—firmly wrapped around the gun, forefinger on the trigger.

"You're not a sad dog," she muttered. "You're a frickin' werewolf."

He was more than a werewolf. He was a man, too. Maybe it was time to reveal himself as both.

His heart rate had calmed enough that he believed he'd be able to complete his shift. With a deep sigh, he focused on changing back to his human form and rode through the agony of muscles and bones sliding into another shape.

When the shift was finished, he was on his hands and knees, still shuddering from the pain.

But there was more to it than just the physical ache. Now that the rush from the fight was fading, his old phobia of enclosed spaces was trying to surface. He fought it back. He had to stay strong, in control. For Taite.

"Ryder?" Her voice was soft and shaking.

He rolled back to his heels and started to reassure her, only to find his throat was raspy. Once he'd cleared it, he tried again. "I won't hurt you, honey."

Taite glanced over his shoulder to where Sumner's body lay still and silent. She didn't look like she believed him. Her gaze came back to him and lingered on his neck. "You're hurt."

Ryder reached up and touched his nape. He could feel warm stickiness on his back and, though his hand came away wet and slick with blood, he could tell the wound wasn't serious. The thick ruff at the back of his neck had protected him, and Sumner hadn't been able to dig in as deeply as Ryder had when the tables were turned.

"I'll be all right," he murmured. "How about you? Did he . . . hurt you?"

A sob broke from her throat before she stubbornly suppressed it. She shook her head.

He slowly stood, and his gaze traveled over her, taking in bruises and scrapes, but nothing that looked like bite marks. Thank God he was hurt and feeling the clammy fear of his phobia. Otherwise, he'd have an erection that would drill through stone. That would hardly engender trust from her. "Are you sure you're all right?"

Taite gave a short nod. "He kept threatening to . . . to . . ." She broke off and, leaning one elbow on her knee, she rested her head on her fist. Rolling her head back and forth, she whispered, "He wanted to take care of you first, so he . . . he'd be able to take his time with me."

Ryder pushed back the surge of rage that came at the reminder of what Sumner had been about to do. Too bad the bastard could only die once.

"But he didn't bite you?" His heart lodged in his throat. The last thing he'd wish on her was to be like him.

"No." She looked at him. Tears streamed down her cheeks, and she made a vague gesture with the gun. It was almost as if she'd forgotten she held it, but he didn't want to push his luck just yet. She sniffed and scrubbed at her cheeks with her free hand.

Ryder moved closer until he was only an arm's length away.

Taite seemed to realize how near he was, because the gun came up and pointed at him. He went almost cross-eyed, looking down the barrel aimed between his eyes.

"Please . . ." Her voice was raspy, and she cleared her throat. Her left hand came up to steady the gun. "Please back up."

He held up one hand and obediently moved back. "I'm not going to hurt you, love," he repeated. "Have I ever? Even before you knew what I was . . . what I *am*, did I ever give you a reason to be afraid of me?"

She bit her lip. Tears welled in her eyes again as she shook her head.

Ryder heaved a sigh. Here he was, trying to convince her he was no danger to her, yet the beast still clawed away at him, demanding to be set free. And he knew, come nightfall when the moon rose full and bright, he wouldn't be able to control it.

It would take over, and the man would be lost to the beast. But for now, he—not his wolf—was in control.

"Listen," he said. "I'm not really a big fan of caves. Can we go back to the house?"

She gave a short nod, and a small smile flitted across her lips. "You know, you should probably keep clothes in different places all over the island. That way, in these types of"— she gestured in the general vicinity of his groin—"situations, you'd have something to put on."

Ryder grinned in response. She must be feeling a bit more at ease, or she wouldn't be able to joke. He held one hand out to her, which she ignored.

Hmm. So much for her being at ease.

Bracing her left palm against the rock wall behind her, she folded her right arm over her breasts, hiding her nudity from him, and pushed to her feet. She tottered for a minute, and he reached for her.

Her eyes widened. With a soft curse, she brought the gun up.

Ryder stopped, his hand frozen in midair. "Taite—"

"Behind you!"

As he whirled, he heard the retort of the gun. Heat from the bullet seared his cheek. Sumner, still in his wolf form, had risen groggily to his feet and now fell back to the ground with an abbreviated groan.

Ryder walked a few steps closer and looked down. Sumner's wolf eyes were wide open and already glazing over in death. A small, round hole sat neatly in the middle of his forehead. Ryder looked over at Taite. His gaze flicked down to the gun in her hand. "Remind me not to get you mad at me while you're holding a gun."

She laughed. The laughter turned to heaving sobs that shuddered through her entire body. The gun dropped from her fingers as she sagged against the wall. "I'm sorry," she sobbed, her hands coming up to cover her face. "I never lose it like this."

Ryder went to her and pulled her into his arms. "God, baby, don't. It's all right."

"It's just . . . everything that's happened to me." She took a shuddering breath, trying to get herself under control, and he knew she had a need to show him she was strong.

He wished she realized she didn't need to always be strong with him. He liked seeing the cracks in her armor, because it meant she let him in, let him get closer.

"First I find out that John is a werewolf, then you . . ."

He pressed her face into his shoulder and rocked her back and forth, rubbing his hands up and down her back in a comforting gesture. Her skin was cool against his, her nipples hard little points against his chest. His cock perked up, but quickly subsided as Ryder swallowed down his persistent fear of enclosed spaces. Besides, there was still enough of the gentleman in him to not take advantage of her misery.

The fact that Taite didn't fight to get out of his arms told him more than words just how vulnerable she was feeling. "I won't let anything hurt you, love," he murmured. "Ever."

When she sagged against him, he swept her up and carried her out of the cave as fast as he could. Once outside, he paused and breathed the first deep breath he'd taken since he walked into that damned cave.

Taite stirred in his arms. "What about John?" she asked.

"I'll come back later to take care of his corpse," Ryder murmured. "He died in his wolf form, so he'll stay in his wolf form." He pressed a kiss to her forehead and, when she didn't flinch from him, said a silent prayer of thanksgiving.

The first he'd said in a very long time.

"He told me no one knew he was here," she whispered. She brought up one hand and swiped at her eyes. Ryder knew she once again battled against tears. "We should be safe from the authorities. But I'm sure I'll be questioned—when he comes up missing, they'll probably talk to everyone who knew him."

Ryder started walking. "You can tell them that Declan brought you here, trying to get you away from your stalker, and you've no idea what happened to Sumner. As far as you know, he could be anywhere."

"As far as I know, he could be anywhere," she parroted. "But he's a wolf buried on Phelan's Keep."

"Now, love, you don't need to add that part." Ryder shifted her slightly, his muscles beginning to feel the burn of her weight in his arms.

"I can walk," she said, though her hands remained clasped around his neck.

"And I can carry you," he responded.

"But . . . you're wounded."

The muscles in the back of his neck burned with strain, though he wouldn't admit it to her. He wasn't giving her any excuses to leave his arms. "I don't need to use my neck to carry you, sweetheart." When she would have continued arguing, he set his lips gently on hers. Her mouth opened for him, and his heart raced at this sign of trust, no matter how small it might be. "Let me carry you."

She settled into his arms without another word, her sigh heavy against his throat.

By the time he reached the house, she was almost asleep, and he was ready to drop with fatigue. He kicked the front door with the pad of his foot.

Taite roused, lifting her head from his shoulder. "Whazzit?"

Ryder grinned and thumped on the door again. "I'm trying to get Cobb to come open the door."

"Is it locked?"

He looked down at her with one brow raised. "Well, Miss Gibson, I don't know. But I seem to have my hands full at the moment and can't really check."

It didn't matter to him that the muscles in his back and arms were burning with fatigue. He'd carry her to forever and back if he had to.

"Smartass," she muttered and put her head back on his shoulder. She brought one arm from around his neck and folded it over her bare breasts. "You could just put me down."

He noticed she wasn't trying to get down, and he grinned again. While he didn't think she was ready to profess her undying love, it did give him hope she would at least give him another chance.

He was just getting ready to kick the door again when it swung open. Cobb stood there with a shotgun to his shoulder, aimed straight at Ryder. The little man's eyes widened, and he immediately dropped the shotgun to his side. "Sir! Are you all right? Ms. Gibson?"

"We're all right," Ryder said as he walked through the door. "Just tired."

"And naked. Again," came the dry response.

As they started down the hallway toward his room, Ryder asked, "Declan?"

Cobb sighed. "He's resting, sir. But he was a little restless, with the full moon. Next month he'll . . ."

"He'll become a werewolf," Ryder finished as Cobb trailed off. "During the next full moon."

Taite stiffened in his arms and turned her face into the crook of his neck.

"It's not your fault, honey," he murmured.

"It *is*." She rubbed her face against his skin, wetting his neck with her tears. "If I hadn't called him—"

"Then you and I might never have met." He walked into the master bathroom and set her gently on the bench by the sunken tub. He straightened slowly and flexed his arms and shoulders, working some of the strain out of his sore muscles.

"Sir."

Ryder glanced at Cobb. The little man was holding a towel and nodding toward Taite, who sat with her arms crossed over her breasts. Ryder took the towel and handed it to her. She promptly covered up with it and smiled a watery thanks at Cobb.

When Cobb cleared his throat, Ryder looked at him again. Pursing his lips, he took the robe the other man held out to him and shrugged into it. He tied the sash and sat beside Taite. Realizing she hadn't responded to his earlier statement, he said in a low voice, "At least tell me you don't regret that we met."

She looked at him, then down at her hands, twisting in her lap. "I don't regret meeting you, Ryder."

He heard the hesitation in her voice, and his heart dropped to his stomach. He really couldn't blame her. She'd come all the way to the Isles of Scilly looking for a werewolf expert and she'd found a werewolf instead.

Not for the first time, he cursed the witch who had started all this so many years ago. Why she'd focused her attention on his great-grandfather was anyone's guess. But she had.

And the transgressions of the father had been visited upon each generation that followed.

"Why don't you take a bath, get cleaned up," he murmured, getting to his feet. "I'm just going to check on Declan."

Taite stood as well. "I want to see him, too."

Ryder started to protest, but she talked over him.

"I'll take a bath later." She walked out of the bathroom, clutching the towel to her chest, and Ryder and Cobb trailed after her.

"Fine," Ryder muttered, a little irritated at her stubbornness but impressed by her fierce loyalty to her friend. If only she could feel that way toward *him*. "Let me get you a shirt."

She took the T-shirt he found for her. Turning her back to them, she dragged it over her head, thrusting her arms through the sleeves and smoothing the material over her hips. "I want to make sure he's all right. Well, as all right as can be expected."

Ryder sighed at the wry note in her voice.

Taite sat beside Declan and gently brushed hair away from his forehead. He was so still, his chest barely moving. His skin was pale and clammy with cold sweat.

From behind her, Ryder took Declan's uninjured wrist and checked his pulse. "His pulse is strong."

"But he looks so . . ." She couldn't finish. If Declan died because of her, she'd never be able to forgive herself.

Hell. If he lived, he'd be a werewolf the rest of his life. She'd never be able to forgive herself regardless of what happened next.

"He's a fighter, honey." Ryder squeezed her shoulder. He motioned toward Declan's broken wrist, where the skin rippled. "Even now his bones are healing. That wrist will be fine by morning. But right now he needs sleep. His body is being changed on a genetic level. He'll most likely sleep twelve to fourteen hours a day for the next week."

She took a shuddering breath. He'd sleep, and then what?

"Go take care of yourself, Taite," Ryder said. She let him

pull her to her feet and turn her toward the door. He went on, "There's nothing you can do for him."

"But he shouldn't be alone," she protested, looking over her shoulder. "In case he wakes up."

"Cobb will sit with him." He pressed a kiss to her forehead, his lips soft and warm against her skin. "Go on. Take your bath."

Taite nodded. There was one problem solved. But if Cobb was going to sit with Declan, what was Ryder going to do? "What about you?"

He grimaced. "I'm going to grab one of the swords from the foyer and take care of Sumner."

She looked at him in alarm. "What do you mean?" she demanded. "He was dead. Wasn't he?"

"He has a silver bullet in his skull. I just want to be sure."

Decapitation was one way to make sure a werewolf stayed down. She frowned at the thought that he was about to go chop off someone's head but, really, better John than any of them. Who knew she could be so bloodthirsty?

"You shouldn't go alone," she told him.

"I'll be fine." He put his hand at the small of her back, and she allowed him to lead her to the stairs. With a gesture at his robe, he said, "I'll just put on some clothes and go."

He continued heading toward the stairs.

"I think we've done enough walking for one night. Can't we take the elevator?"

"I can't believe I'm hearing this from pedometer-woman." Ryder flashed a grin, but he shook his head in answer to her question. "I've had about all of the enclosed spaces I care to, especially since I'm heading back into that fucking cave." His voice was deep and dry with self-effacing humor. "But you feel free to ride down."

He started down the steps. Taite just didn't think she had it in her to take the stairs, so she pushed the button on the control panel. By the time the elevator reached her and she'd ridden it down to the ground floor, Ryder was in a pair of jeans and a T-shirt, and had a sturdy pair of hiking boots on his feet. He was just reaching for one of the swords on the wall when she stepped off the elevator.

"I'll grab a shovel from the garden shed and bury the bastard. I should be back in about an hour," Ryder murmured, and made to step around her.

She put one hand on his chest. "Wait." She stared up into his deep blue eyes and wished she could sort through the confusion gripping her heart. "I'm sorry. Your cousin did this . . ." She sighed. "I'm sorry."

Ryder shook his head. "Our mothers were sisters, that's true, but he was never really family. I never wanted to believe it, but I think he did deliberately cause the cave-in when we were kids. And I think he drove my father to suicide." He shrugged. "Now he's trying to get to my friends. There was no other way for this to end. At least now I know." His eyes glittered. "I can be prepared to protect what's mine."

He looked straight at her when he said that. It sent a thrill through her even as she emotionally backed away from what he was saying. "Still, I'm sorry." She wanted to say more, *needed* to say more, but there was too much to make sense of. Finally, all she said was, "Please be careful."

When he reached for her hand, she quickly withdrew it, fisting it at her side. She wasn't sure she could take his touching her again, not with her emotions in such turmoil.

His lips tightened, and he gave her a nod. He walked away, the long sword in one broad hand.

She watched him until he closed the door behind him, then she turned and went back into his master bath. She could take a bath upstairs, but she wasn't about to pass up an opportunity to be decadent in Ryder's sunken tub.

When she finally settled into the warm water, she closed her eyes and leaned her head back onto a rolled up towel. God, this felt good. Perhaps now that she had some time to herself, she could figure out how she felt—about the direction her life had taken, and about Ryder.

She knew one thing. She was in love with him. The question was, what now? He was a werewolf.

He certainly hadn't threatened her at any time. Back in the cave, fresh from the fight with John, with blood still lingering in his mouth, on his muzzle, he'd seen her fear and reacted to it. Compassionately, the way a human would.

Not as an animal.

Not a beast.

A man.

She replayed her time on the island, remembering her first moments with Ryder and the instant attraction she'd felt. Then, as she'd gotten to know him, as they became intimate, she'd discovered that attraction went deeper. For both of them.

And he was nothing like John. John Sumner had stalked her and threatened to kill her. And it had all been done with a twisted, sick perversity that Ryder just didn't possess.

Taite took a deep breath and settled deeper in the water, letting it slosh over her chin. Her original question came back to her.

What now?

Could she move past her fear and accept Ryder for everything he was? Or did she settle for a comfortable, safe life without him?

Chapter 21

Ryder closed the front door behind him. He was bone-tired and needed to rest. But he needed to clean the sword before he hung it up. He'd swiped it against the tall grass in the clearing before he reached the house, but it still needed a good cleaning.

He rubbed one hand over the back of his neck and walked down the hallway to his bedroom. He'd found the wolf exactly where they'd left him, his sightless eyes staring up at the ceiling of the cave.

Ryder had used the sword, ensuring Sumner wouldn't be coming back this time, then he'd buried the body. By the time he'd left the cave, he'd been wet with sweat from exertion and his lingering childhood fear.

Whoever heard of the big, bad wolf being afraid of small spaces?

He'd stayed out much longer than necessary, partly to give Taite time to take a long, much deserved bath, but mostly to give himself time to come to terms with losing her.

Going straight into the bathroom, he caught her lingering sweet scent in the damp, warm air. He closed his eyes. God, he loved her.

But she was out of reach. She'd made that pretty clear when she'd jerked her hand away from his chest earlier, before he could take it in his. That had cut deep. But he couldn't blame her.

He was, after all, a wolf in man's clothing. At least, three nights out of every month he was. And he had the wall manacles in his basement to prove it.

Ryder stared down at the sword in his hand. Fuck it. He'd take care of it in the morning. He placed the sword on the ledge by the tub.

He took a quick shower. After he dried off, he put on clean clothes and headed upstairs to check on Declan.

As Ryder entered the bedroom, Cobb looked up from his place by the bedside. Putting one finger to his lips, the little man got to his feet and walked over to the door.

"He just went back to sleep, sir. He was most relieved to hear that Sumner is dead." He looked up at Ryder. "How did it go?"

Ryder took a deep breath and let it out slowly. "Sumner won't be coming back." He scrubbed one hand across the back of his neck. "Where's Taite?"

Cobb nodded toward the bedroom across the hall. "She laid down about fifteen minutes ago, sir."

"Thanks." Ryder cupped Cobb's thin shoulder and gave it a grateful squeeze. Walking to the other bedroom door, he eased it open and entered the room.

Taite lay on her back on top of the coverlet, her arms flung out to her sides. Her breathing was deep and heavy. He sat down in the brocade chair next to the bed.

Poor baby. She was exhausted. As was he. He was tempted, so tempted, to curl up beside her. But he didn't. He sat there, watching her, for a long time. Then, with a sigh, he got up quietly and left the room.

Hours later, Ryder stalked into the small bedroom in the basement and stopped, staring at the damned manacles on the wall. His fists were clenched so tightly his fingers hurt.

The rest of his life, chained here three nights every month, loomed in front of him.

Footsteps padded down the stairs, and Taite's scent wafted to him. A mixture of stubborn determination, bravery in the face of great uncertainty, and the soft florals of her perfume jumbled together in one intoxicating aroma.

His cock immediately jumped to attention as his beast yowled with carnal hunger. He clenched his jaw and fought for control. "Taite, go back upstairs."

"No." She ventured closer, coming into the small room. Soft blue knit pants and a matching T-shirt hugged her slim curves. Her slender feet were encased in thick white socks.

She nodded toward the manacles. "You'll need help with those, if you really think they're still necessary." A vein pulsed in her throat, drawing his attention.

Ryder stalked closer, part of him wanting to frighten her so she'd run back upstairs, away from him, where it was safe. The other part of him howled to claim her again and again, to slake at least one kind of hunger with her soft, giving body. "What makes you think help is what I want from you?"

She swallowed, her creamy skin moving over the muscles of her throat.

A growl of hungry desire worked its way up from his chest, and he barely caught it. She heard enough of it to make her eyes widen.

"Whether you want my help or not," she said, her voice firm, "you're going to get it." She motioned toward the bed. "Get on the bed."

His heart lifted. Maybe, just maybe, things weren't as dark as he'd feared. "I usually strip," he told her. She blinked at him, and he shrugged. "It saves on clothes. They get ripped when I change," he elaborated when she still appeared confused.

"Oh." Taite stood there, and looked from him to the bed, then back at him.

"All right." Ryder toed off his shoes, then pulled his T-shirt

off and kicked off his jeans. He sat on the edge of the mattress and yanked off his socks. Scooting back, he rested his
back against the wall. He lifted his left arm toward the manacle. "I'm ready."

And he was, in more ways than one. His erection was at
full mast, stiff and jutting toward his navel.

"Stop that," she muttered. Leaning over the bed, she
grabbed his wrist and fastened a restraint around it. She
moved down and did the same with the other wrist.

Her gaze darted to the larger manacle that hung by his
shoulder.

"That goes around my neck," he reminded her.

She blinked a few times. "Is that really necessary?"

"Yes." Now, more than ever, he had to make sure those in
his house were safe from him. They'd been terrorized enough
already.

With trembling hands, Taite fitted the manacle around his
neck and fastened it. Her fingers lingered at the metal strip,
touching his skin just above it. "It's not too tight?"

Ryder shook his head. "It's fine, honey." He cleared his
suddenly full throat. "You need to go upstairs now."

She glanced at her watch. "But it's only five o'clock." She
looked at him, her eyes soft. "It won't be dark for another
hour or more. Can't I stay here and keep you company?"

Her gaze strayed down his body to his groin. She lifted an
eyebrow and looked back up at his face. "*He* seems to want
me to stay."

Ryder snorted. "Yes, well, he doesn't always know what's
best. You should go upstairs."

She didn't move.

He scowled in confusion. "Aren't you afraid of me?" He'd
been sure she was, but she wasn't acting afraid, just a little
nervous.

"Yes." Now she was the one to frown. "No. Yes." A heavy,
quick sigh left her. "Maybe." She stared at him. "Should I
be?"

"I'd like to say no, honey." He started to reach for her and was brought up short by his restraints. "But I can't always control the wolf. Especially this close to the full moon."

"But you did earlier, in the cave." She sat on the bed. "I don't understand this at all."

"I wasn't acting under the impulse of the full moon then," he explained. His heart drummed a fast rhythm against his ribs, hope warring with disbelief that she actually might be willing to stay with him.

"All right," Taite said slowly. "But you're all tied up now." An imp of mischief sparkled in her eyes, as well as something hotter. Her gaze traveled down his body again and lingered on his stiff cock. "I've never had a manacled man at my mercy before."

The manacles made her feel safe. He got that. *Him* in manacles made her horny. He got that, too.

He just wasn't sure this was the best idea. . . . Soft hands drifting up the insides of his thighs drove all thought out of his head, and all the blood, too. As her fingers brushed over his groin and started a slow glide up his abdomen, a trail of fire followed in their wake.

"Taite, honey, I don't think—"

"Sshh. Don't think. Just feel." She swung one leg over him, straddling his thighs, both hands bracing herself on his shoulders. Leaning down, she took his mouth with hers, lips moving slowly, warmly, tongue dipping teasingly inside the seam of his mouth.

She drew back and stared down at him. "I've fallen in love with you, Ryder. It's not something I was looking for, and I can't tell you that it doesn't still scare me, you being a werewolf and all. But I can't walk away from you. Not now. Probably not ever."

"Taite—"

"No, don't say anything. Just feel," she said again. She slid down his legs, kissing her way over his abdomen, her soft breasts pressing against his erection for a too-brief moment.

"You'll be down here all night by yourself. I want to give you something to keep you warm."

Her tongue slid into his navel, and his breath hissed out of him. Stomach muscles clenched. Her mouth moved farther down. When she nuzzled his sac and raked her nails lightly over his belly, he grunted and bucked against her.

Her tongue flicked out, licking around his balls, then started a slow path up his engorged shaft. One slender hand wrapped around him while the other stroked his scrotum. She licked around the bulbous crown of his cock, dipped briefly in the slit at the tip, making him groan and harden even more.

Ryder tensed under her, his breathing deepening as she made her way around and around his cock head. He shifted his thighs farther apart, giving her more room. His balls drew up tight against the base of his cock.

Taite went back to his sac and gave the tightly drawn skin delicate little licks, chuckling when he arched against her. Her hand swept up and down his shaft in light strokes, taking the pre-come at his tip and spreading it over his hard length.

"God, honey, you're killing me here," he groaned, his head going back against the wall. He wanted to hold her, guide her movements, make her do what he wanted her to. But with his wrists in restraints, it wasn't up to him.

"I can stop if you want." Her smile was sly and sultry, full of feminine secrets. Brown eyes were dark with sensual heat.

"No." His hands fisted, and he pushed his hips upward. "Suck!" he commanded, unable to do anything but follow her lead and succumb to the passionate demand of his body.

She gave him a saucy salute. "Yessir." Shifting her weight, she grasped the base of his cock in one hand and took him in her mouth.

He growled, his body arching, his hands clenching and un-clenching, arms jerking in his restraints.

She kept up a steady rhythm, sucking strongly and stroking and swirling her tongue over the head of his cock with each pass. Before long, his hips pumped steadily, driving more and more of his stiff length into her mouth until he was hitting the back of her throat.

When Ryder realized how rough he was being, he slowed down. Her hands curled under him, digging into his buttocks, and she pulled him to her. She hummed around the thick stalk of flesh in her mouth, and he felt the vibration to his toes.

His thrusts became frantic and choppy. The base of his spine began to tingle, a feathery sensation that spread outward, signaling the onset of his climax. Taite seemed to sense it, for she withdrew suddenly, clasping his cock at the base.

He couldn't stop the growl that left his throat.

Instead of looking afraid, she narrowed her eyes and threw him a mock scowl. "Don't snarl at me, Wolfie."

Taite was amazed that the rough, animalistic sound didn't frighten her. What amazed her even more was how turned on she was by it. Knowing that it was her—her hands, her mouth—bringing the wildness to him ramped her arousal to a fever level.

She grinned in feminine triumph at Ryder's startled look. When she moved away from him, his look was replaced by one of disappointment. Her smile widened.

"Don't pout, either," she murmured. Placing her hands at the bottom of her knit top, she pulled the top up and over her head, and dropped it to the floor.

"I do *not* pout," he muttered with a scowl.

"Uh-huh." Looking at his full lower lip, she wasn't as convinced of that as he seemed to be. She saw his gaze was riveted to her bare breasts, so she brought her hands up to cup them and push them together.

His arms jerked in the manacles as he tried to reach for her. She tsked and wiggled her index finger at him. "Patience is its own reward, Ryder."

"That's what they say, love, but I don't believe it." He

stirred against the bed, his hips moving restlessly. "Are you just going to leave me like this?"

Her smile returned. With her heart beating fast and hard, she yanked off her socks and then pushed down her thin knit pants, giving a little shimmy to help them on their way before kicking them off. Standing naked before him, a situation that would otherwise make her feel vulnerable, Taite was high on the feeling of being a sexy, wanton beast. She brought her hands back to her breasts and plumped them together.

A growl sounded low in his throat and, instead of being scared, she once again reveled in the sound. While having Ryder in the manacles did give her a sense of security, it also engendered a thrill of power. He was at her mercy.

All of him. Her gaze darted to his erection, still bold and thick, pointing to his navel. With a rough snarl of her own, Taite started toward him. She wanted his hard length inside her, now.

As she got on the bed, straddling his thighs, his eyes blazed with passion. He leaned his head back against the wall and licked slowly over his lips.

"Let me taste you first," he said. "Bring that sweet pussy of yours up here to my mouth and let me taste you."

The heavy-lidded look on his face made her breath come faster. Without a word, she stood on the bed and edged closer, angling her hips toward his mouth.

"Spread yourself for me." His voice was dark and hot, raspy with desire. "Let me see that beautiful pink flesh."

Taite swallowed and did as he asked. When her fingers delved between her folds and separated them, he groaned and leaned forward.

"Come closer," he whispered, "so I can taste you."

As soon as her pussy pressed against his lips, his tongue darted out and wrapped around her clit, sucking it inside the heat of his mouth. She gasped and pushed against him, a soft mewl coming from her throat as he suckled with a hard, fast rhythm designed to drive her wild.

And it was working. Boy-howdy was it working.

His tongue left her pleasure bud and swiped down her slit. He speared inside her channel, fucking into her with hard, fast strokes.

Taite moaned and thrust against his mouth, her hands on the wall steadying her atop the bed. Her entire world spiraled down until it centered on his mouth, his tongue, and, as he gave her labia a light nip, his teeth. She was wound tight, her arousal at a fever pitch, so that she trembled with the building pressure.

It wasn't enough. She wanted him inside her, nothing separating them, his thickness stretching her to the point of pain.

She jerked away from his mouth, ignoring his growled demand to "Get back here." On her haunches, she grasped his erection and guided it to her opening, then slowly lowered herself, inch by exquisite inch, until her buttocks rested against his hard thighs.

He was so thick inside her, filled her so completely, it was hard to tell where she left off and he began. She lifted up, her gaze holding his, and dropped back down. They both gasped.

Ryder started thrusting up against her. Taite met each thrust eagerly, urging him on with her every movement. She leaned forward and licked a rivulet of sweat sliding down his neck. He tasted salty and smelled of masculine musk and sex. She wanted to hold his scent to her forever.

Using all her strength, she lifted and dropped onto his cock faster and faster until they both panted with pleasure. Her orgasm erupted with the force of a steamy geyser. Muscles seizing with pleasure, she threw back her head and screamed.

Ryder thrust up into her one last time and held himself still while his cock spurted his release. The muscles of her pussy clenched around him. When she leaned in, acting on instinct alone, he sank his teeth into the thick muscle where her shoulder joined her neck.

She was his and would wear his mark. It was his way.

The way of the beast.

Reality slammed into him. He lifted his head and stared down at her. Sweet God in heaven. He'd just bitten her.

But he'd not broken the skin. A rough groan left him. He leaned his head against the wall, eyes closed so he wouldn't have to look at her face. A face he was sure held such a look of shocked horror it would break his heart.

"Ryder?" Taite's voice was soft, uncertain. "What's wrong?"

His eyes shot open, and he looked at her in disbelief. "What's wrong?" he parroted. His gaze dropped to her shoulder, where his teeth marks still showed against her silky skin. "How can you ask that?"

She followed his gaze, her head tilting and a slight grimace crossing her face. Looking back up at him, she frowned. "You mean because you bit me?"

At his nod, she shrugged. "It didn't hurt. Well," she clarified, "not much. And . . . it won't make me a werewolf, right? Because you didn't draw blood."

He shook his head, the only response he could manage. His heart was in his throat, pounding like a jackhammer.

Taite took his face in her hands. "I love you, Ryder. All of you." She pressed a light kiss against one corner of his mouth. "It took me a while to get to this point, but I know you're nothing like John. You won't hurt me."

He shook his head. "How can you be so sure? *I'm* not sure."

"I am." She stroked his cheek, brushed the hair from his brow. "You were ferocious in the cave, with John. You fatally wounded him, Ryder. And when you started toward me . . ."

Her eyes searched his, and in them he saw only honesty and such a deep tenderness it touched him in ways he'd never known before. "I was scared, I'll admit it. But when you saw my fear, you stopped. You. Stopped."

She was right. Even in his wildness, he'd still retained something of his humanity. But he didn't trust the beast completely. Not yet.

"You're more than just an animal, sweetie. You're the man I love." Her lips came down over his, soft and tender, and he groaned. Against his mouth, she whispered, "Doesn't that count for something?"

It counted for everything. It seemed she, at least, could see beyond the beast.

For him, that was all he needed.

Her fingers went to the manacles around his wrists. Even as he protested, she unfastened them, then the one around his neck.

"Taite—"

"If you won't trust yourself, trust me. Trust Cobb, who's been with you his entire life." She leaned in and kissed him. "We both love you and trust *you*. You won't hurt us."

She jangled his manacles. "And you won't need these anymore." One slender eyebrow arched. "Of course, that doesn't mean we might not still use 'em from time to time. It's kinda sexy, having you in chains."

Ryder's smile turned to a laugh. With Taite by his side, for the first time in his life he felt like he could conquer anything.

Even the beast.

Epilogue

Declan peered at the full moon with bleary eyes. From behind him, Cobb snored in the bedside chair, unaware that Declan had risen and now stood at the window.

He could feel the pull of the moon, like an ocean tide ebbing and flowing in his veins. Though he didn't have the strength to go through the Change now, he knew it wouldn't be this way a month from now.

Dammit.

He didn't blame Taite. He loved her like a sister and, if he had to do it all over again, he would.

No, he blamed Sumner. And, by extension, Miles Hampston, Ryder's cousin, who'd set everything in motion. He'd get his, just like Sumner had.

But it was too damn bad that slimy son of a bitch Sumner couldn't die again. Declan would give his right arm for the opportunity to be the one to put the bastard in his grave.

He'd barely gotten out of this one by the hair on his chinny chin chin. Declan rubbed his hand over his wound, which had already closed over. The muscles remained sore to the touch, but he knew by morning they would be completely healed.

He was a werewolf now.

And the overriding thought in his mind. Find Pelicia.

She was his, and he *would* claim her.

If you liked this book, you'll love Karen Kelley's
MY FAVORITE PHANTOM,
in stores now from Brava. . . .

Hell, he knew the real reason he didn't want her in the house: He had a weakness for women. Always had. His siblings had teased him unmercifully, calling him Don Juan—more so now that he was teaching that other class.

Kaci hadn't looked like she would be that hard to resist, though. Not when she wore baggy clothes and that cap. He snorted. It hadn't been that long since he'd gone on a date. Okay, he was safe. No worries.

"I just wanted to let you know I'll be coming in and out of the house as I bring my equipment in," a voice spoke behind him, softer than before but still with a slight edge.

"Good. The sooner you can rid me of my problem, the better." He set his soda can on the table and stood, turning around to face her.

His mouth dropped open. No, no, no! What happened to the baggy clothes and the baseball cap pulled down low and she hadn't looked like this and . . . Damn it!

He waved his arm in front of him. "You changed." Where were her other clothes? The ones that made her safe. Hell, the ones that made *him* safe.

She wore short-shorts that showed off long, wrap-around-his-waist-and-pull-him-in-closer legs, and a little blue tank top that stretched across her full breasts. And no more baseball cap. Now her long beautiful blond hair tumbled over her shoulders.

She glanced down, then shrugged. "I'm cold-natured in the mornings. By afternoon, I get hot. I'll start getting my equipment." She turned and left the patio.

His glance dropped to her sweet little ass. His mouth started to water.

By afternoon she got hot? Is that what she'd said? That was the understatement of the year. He wasn't sure what was going to be worse, the ghost or keeping his hands off the sexy exterminator.

Damn, he hadn't bargained for this. It seemed the hole he was getting precariously closer to falling inside just kept getting deeper and deeper.

Damn, she'd had a really nice twist in her walk, though.

No, he would not seduce Kaci. She was off limits—at least until she got rid of the ghost. But his mouth was already starting to water.

When his cell phone rang, he pulled it out of his pocket and flipped it open. He glanced at the number. His older brother. Great. He frowned. Things just got better and better.

"Hello."

"Hey, Peyton. How's it going? Has your ghost exterminator arrived?"

Peyton heard the unmistakable laughter in his brother's voice. Why had he even told Joe about his ghost? "Yeah, she's here."

"She?" The humor immediately vanished.

"Yeah."

"Get rid of her. You know how you are with women. It'll be the same as the last town."

He shook his head. "The last town, as you like to refer to it, was nothing more than a young woman who was infatuated with her professor. Nothing happened. I only left because I wanted to teach this other class as well as my history class and the dean offered me that opportunity. Have a little faith. Besides, I do have a ghost, and she can get rid of it."

"She stalked you." His sigh came over the phone lines. "A woman to you is like someone on a diet crashing into a candy store. You know you can't change. At least tell me she's ugly."

Okay, he could do that. "She's ugly." He wasn't lying or anything. Just telling Joe what he'd asked to be told. "I can't get rid of her until the ghost is gone."

"Please, just be careful."

"I'm always careful." Joe was acting as though he had a disease or something. Hell, maybe he did, but he really enjoyed a woman's company.

"If you need anything, I'm only a phone call away."

"Yeah, thanks, bro." He closed the phone, then slipped it into his pocket as he walked toward the front door.

Man, he should've told Joe not to tell his other brother or his sister. If they got wind there was a woman living with him, even if it was business, he'd never hear the last of it.

Could he help it if he loved women? It wouldn't matter if Kaci had been old or young. There was just something about women that he loved. All women.

The baggy sweats and cap had made her safer, though. Sort of.

But he would stay on guard around her. Just as soon as he helped her carry in the rest of her things. A slow grin curved his lips. She was damned sexy.

For just a moment, he closed his eyes and lost himself in the fantasy of her body pressed against his. Her naked body. His hands caressing her.

He quickly shook off the image.

Damn it, he was not going to sleep with her.

He wasn't.

And don't miss Lucy Monroe's latest,
THE SPY WHO WANTS ME, available now. . . .

"That is one sweet ride," Beau said as he got out of the passenger side of Elle's Spider.

"I like it."

"It's easy to see why."

They'd pulled up in front of a sprawling Mission-style home, an hour east of L.A. in the desert. The neighboring houses were far enough away to ensure real privacy. Used to the cramped and crowded conditions, even in their smaller community south of Los Angeles city proper, Beau took a deep breath, enjoying the sense of space. "Nice."

"It was a good place to grow up."

"It reminds me of home."

"Where is that?"

"East Texas."

"So, that's where that sexy drawl comes from."

"You think my drawl is sexy?" he asked, purposefully stretching his syllables with a Texan twang.

She grinned. "It's sexier when you aren't doing a Keith Urban impersonation."

"Bite your tongue. That good ol' boy is from Down Under. Not the sacred state of Texas. His drawl ain't anything like mine."

"I didn't know there was such a thing as a sacred state." She rolled her eyes for emphasis.

He leaned forward until he was whispering right next to her ear. "That's because you weren't raised in Texas."

"Oh," she whispered back. "So, it's some kind of secret, huh?"

He moved even closer until he was as close to her super-model body as he could get without actually touching. Then he leaned in so his lips actually did touch the shell of her ear. "I'll share my secrets with you if you share yours with me."

Her whole body shuddered, and if that didn't send him zero to sixty from one breath to the next. His cock ached and pressed insistently against the fly of his good jeans.

He flicked his tongue out and tasted the sensitive skin just under her earlobe. "What do you say? You ready to share your secrets with me?"

Damn if she didn't turn just so and lean her forehead against his shoulder. She didn't say anything, but he could feel tension emanating off of her.

He nuzzled into her neck, still whispering. "You got a lot of secrets, princess?"

"Who doesn't?" Her voice was quiet and muffled against his body.

He didn't know why he did it, but he rubbed her back in comfort. Just right then, the beautiful government agent who was lying to him and pretending to be nothing more than a security consultant seemed vulnerable. And he wanted to protect her. Take all her cares away.

What a sap.

Vulnerable. Right.

It was probably part of her act. Her cover. Only he felt like there was something growing between them. Something real and inescapable.

Dumb.

She was just doing her job and pretending to be something

she wasn't to get information her agency wanted about his company.

He *had* to remember that.

If only he could convince his body to listen. Never mind the heart he was smart enough not to risk for a woman who was living a lie.

Keep an eye out for
INSTANT ATTRACTION,
the first in a new series from Jill Shalvis,
on shelves next month from Brava. . . .

She'd been working for Wilder Adventures for a week now, the best week in recent memory. Up until right this second when a shadowy outline of a man appeared in her room. Like the newly brave woman she was, she threw the covers over her head and hoped he hadn't seen her.

"Hey," he said, blowing that hope all to hell.

His voice was low and husky, sounding just as surprised as she. With a deep breath, she lurched upright to a seated position on the bed and reached out for her handy-dandy baseball bat before remembering she hadn't brought it with her. Instead, her hands connected with her glasses and they went flying.

Which might just have been a blessing in disguise, because now she wouldn't be able to witness her own death.

But then the tall shadow bent and scooped up her glasses and . . .

Handed them to her.

A considerate bad guy?

She jammed the frames on her face and focused in the dim light coming from the living room lamp. He stood at the foot of the bed frowning right back at her, hands on his hips.

Huh.

He didn't look like an ax murderer, which was good, very good, but at more than six feet of impressive, rangy, solid-looking muscle, he didn't exactly look like a harmless tooth fairy, either.

"Why are you in my bed?" he asked warily, as if maybe he'd put her there but couldn't quite remember.

He had a black duffel bag slung over a shoulder. Light brown hair stuck out from the edges of his knit ski cap to curl around his neck. Sharp green eyes were leveled on hers, steady and calm but irritated as he opened his denim jacket.

If he was an ax murderer, he was quite possibly the most attractive one she'd ever seen, which didn't do a thing for her frustration level. She'd been finally sleeping.

Sleeping!

He could have no idea what a welcome miracle that had been, dammit.

"Earth to Goldilocks." He waved a gloved hand until she dragged her gaze back up to his face. "Yeah, hi. My bed. Want to tell me why you're in it?"

"I've been sleeping here for a week." Granted, she'd had a hard time of it lately, but she definitely would have noticed *him* in bed with her.

"Who told you to sleep here?"

"My boss, Stone Wilder. Well, technically, Annie the chef, but—" She broke off when he reached toward her, clutching the comforter to her chin as if the down feathers could protect her, really wishing for that handy-dandy bat.

But instead of killing her, he hit the switch to the lamp on the nightstand and more fully illuminated the room as he dropped his duffel bag.

While Katie tried to slow her heart rate, he pulled off his jacket and gloves, and tossed them territorially to the chest at the foot of the bed.

His clothes seemed normal enough. Beneath the jacket he wore a fleece-lined sweatshirt opened over a long-sleeved brown Henley, half untucked over faded Levi's. The jeans were loose and low on his hips, baggy over unlaced Sorrels, the entire ensemble revealing that he was in prime condition.

"My name is Katie Kramer," she told him, hoping he'd return the favor. "Wilder Adventures's new office temp." She paused, but he didn't even attempt to fill the awkward silence. "So that leaves you . . ."

"What happened to Riley?"

"Who?"

"The current office manager."

"I think she's on maternity leave."

"That must be news to his wife."

She met his cool gaze. "Okay, obviously I'm new. I don't know all the details since I've only been here a week."

"Here, being my cabin, of course."

"Stone told me that the person who used to live here had left."

"Ah." His eyes were the deepest, most solid green she'd ever seen as they regarded her. "I did leave. I also just came back."

She winced, clutching the covers a little tighter to her chest. "So this cabin . . . Does it belong to an ax murderer?"

That tugged a rusty-sounding laugh from him. "Haven't sunk that low. Yet." Pulling off his cap, he shoved his fingers through his hair. With those sleepy-lidded eyes, disheveled hair, and at least two days' growth on his jaw, he looked big and bad and edgy—and quite disturbingly sexy with it. "I need sleep." He dropped his long, tough self to the chair by the bed, as if so weary, he could no longer stand. He set first one and then the other booted foot on the mattress, grimacing as if he were hurting, though she didn't see any reason for that on his body as he settled back, lightly linking his hands together low on his flat abs. Then he let out a long, shuddering sigh.

She stared at more than six feet of raw power and testosterone in disbelief. "You still haven't said who you are."

"Too Exhausted To Go Away."

She did some more staring at him, but he didn't appear to care. "Hello?" she said after a full moment of stunned silence. "You can't just—"

"Can. And am." And with that, he closed his eyes. " 'Night, Goldilocks."